About Tania

MW00334810

Tania Joyce is an Australian author of contemporary and new adult romance novels. Her stories thread romance, drama and passion into beautiful locations ranging from the dazzling lights and glitter of New York, to the rural countryside of the Hunter Valley.

She's widely traveled, has a diverse background in the corporate world and has a love for sparkles, shoes and shiraz.

Tania draws on her real-life experiences and combines them with her *very* vivid imagination to form the foundation of her novels. She likes to write about strong-minded, career-oriented heroes and heroines that go through drama-filled hell, have steamy encounters and risk everything as they endeavor to find their happy-ever-after.

Tania shuffles the hours in her day between part-time work, family life and writing. One day she hopes to find balance!

Visit www.taniajoyce.com

Tempting Propositions

Strictly Business – Book 1
by
Tania Joyce

First published in 2015

Republished by Gatwick Enterprises in 2017

Brisbane, Australia.

Copyright © Tania Joyce 2017

The moral right of the author has been asserted.

All rights reserved. This publication (or any part of it) may not be reproduced or transmitted, copied, stored, distributed or otherwise made available by any person or entity (including Google, Amazon or similar organisations), in any form (electronic, digital, optical, mechanical) or by any means (photocopying, recording, scanning or otherwise) without prior written permission from the publisher.

Tempting Propositions - Strictly Business – Book 1

(Formerly known as: Propositions)

EPUB format: ISBN: 978-0-9945774-6-7

Mobi format: ISBN: 978-0-9945774-7-4

Paperback: ISBN: 978-0-9945774-8-1

Cover design by Danielle Maait

Edited by Dianne Blacklock

Tania Joyce: www.taniajoyce.com

To report a typographical error, please visit http://taniajoyce.com/contact-form Visit www.taniajoyce.com to read more about all our books and to buy books online. You will also find features, author interviews and news of any author events.

This is a work of fiction. Names, characters, businesses, places, events and incidents are either the products of the author's imagination or used in a fictitious manner. Any resemblance to actual persons, living or dead, or actual events is purely coincidental.

For lovers of a Happy Ever After.

Prologue

Two suitcases packed to the brim. One suit bag bulged at the seams. Nate Somers stood beside his bed and assessed the luggage lying before him. He rubbed the back of his neck with the palm of his hand as he surveyed his room yet again. *What else will I need?* He was unsure if he'd packed enough—he'd never stayed in one location for more than a few weeks at a time since his university days.

Living in Sydney for the next six months overseeing the opening of the new hotel for his family's business on one hand was exhilarating and exciting, while on the other it was making him apprehensive. Because this was his project. The first one he'd seen from the ground up. Location, designs and plans had all been his idea.

Out of the bay window of his Chelsea home he caught a glimpse of the dawn erasing away the night sky, and the glow from the streetlights shimmering upon the murky waters of the Thames River. He hesitated for a moment to take in the view before he crossed the room and drew the curtains closed. This time leaving London somehow felt different. He tried to shrug off the niggling sensation that had settled in the center of his shoulder blades. Surely it was nothing. Maybe it was because he had no idea when he'd be back here again.

He made one last round of his rooms to make sure he hadn't missed anything. In his office, his desk was all in order. Not a pen out of place. Just the way he liked it. Back in his bedroom, the metal runners on his drawers glided smoothly on their tracks when he opened them. They were nearly bare of all contents. A few neatly folded socks and jocks remained. His walk-in robe echoed with the sound of his movements as he skimmed his eyes over the railings where only a few suits and shirts hung, half still wrapped in their dry cleaning plastic. In the bathroom he checked his toiletry tote again before packing it into his luggage. He should've found the time to go shopping because he didn't like the toothpaste from Japan that tasted like strawberries, or the mouthwash from China that was too sickly and sweet. But yet again this had been a fleeting visit. He spent more time away from his home than he cared to think about.

As he started to zip up his bags, the picture of Lucy on his bedside table caught his eye. He picked up the silver frame and stared at the vision of his daughter before him. Her dimpled cheeks and long black hair always filled him with conflicting emotions because she reminded him so much of her mother. Heart heavy he opened his bag, tucked the frame carefully between his clothes and zipped up his case.

Nate lugged his bags down the stairs and stood them at the front door. He checked his watch. Yes, he had time for a quick cup of tea before his driver was scheduled to arrive.

As he savored the last mouthful, the doorbell buzzed loudly. Nate opened the door and greeted his driver.

"Hey Lawrence. There's all my things." He pointed to his luggage. "I'll just be a few minutes."

Nate scuttled over to the kitchen to clean up his dishes. As he picked up the cup, something caught him by surprise. For years the loose tea-leaf dregs in the bottom of his cup had never changed. They always fell the same way—in lines—

indicating travel. But today they fell in the shape of heart. *Love.* He let out a loud snicker as he quickly rinsed the pot and put everything away. Love was the furthest thing from his mind. Not an option. Not going to happen. Regardless how much he had tried to ignore his grandmother when he was a boy, her silly superstitions and tea-leaf reading antics had become embedded deep within his psyche—whether he liked it or not!

Nate put the nonsensical thoughts out of his mind as he slid into his jacket, picked up his laptop bag, headed out the door and into the waiting limousine.

Stuck in early morning peak hour traffic on the way to Heathrow airport, he double-checked his flight itinerary on his phone. Yet again, he was flying through Singapore. Yet again unable to see his daughter because of the short timeframe between his connecting flights. He hadn't played a major role in Lucy's life since she was born, so why was it starting to bother him now? He strummed his fingers against his thigh. Should he ring her or not? It wasn't time for his scheduled call, but he thought '*What the hell*' and dialed the number.

"Hey Luce. How are you sweetheart?" He let out a sigh of relief when it was her voice on the line.

"Daddy!" Her excitement warmed his heart.

"Lucy—who is it?" The sound of his ex-wife Rachael's voice in the background turned everything cold again.

"Daddy, Mommy's mad at me for not eating my dinner. I don't like sushi. It's yucky. Do I have to eat it?"

Nate didn't like sushi either, so he knew where Lucy was coming from. "I'll talk to your mom about it, okay?

"Daddy, when are you coming to see me again?"

"Soon, baby. Soon. In three months. For the September holidays."

"Nathan?"

He winced as Rachael's voice suddenly screeched in his ear.

What did she do, rip the handset out of Lucy's fingers?

"What are you doing calling now? Lucy has to finish her dinner and her homework. Call back on your designated day."

"Come on Rachael, it's just a phone call. I'm stuck in traffic on the way to the airport—"

"No, Nathan. Lucy doesn't need the interruption. We have a deal. If you don't like it, you'll be hearing from my lawyers."

Nate's back stiffened. He'd had enough of lawyers in business and in his personal life to last a lifetime. The thought of losing what little access he had to his daughter sent a chill through him. Rachael was pushing his buttons the wrong way. "*Should* we get the lawyers involved this time? I'm sure I could easily get partial or full custody of our daughter."

Rachael laughed down the line. "Your threats have no substance, Nathan. You know that. You're too tied to your business. What kind of life would Lucy have with you?"

He hated it when she dismissed him. She was the only person in the world who could get under his skin. He'd never suspected the innocent-looking Singaporean girl, who he became smitten with, would be the one to take him for a ride.

"Okay, Rachael. Enough is enough. I have to go. I'm nearly at the airport."

Infuriated, he hung up and put his phone back in his jacket pocket. He massaged the tension throbbing in his temples. He hated to admit it—but Rachael was right. The truth sent a shudder through his body. What kind of father could he ever be? He had no time to be a father. Not now. Not ever. Business always came first. Always would.

Chapter 1

Rain pelted against the window of Jessica Mason's office. She glanced out at the crowded Haymarket Street below where impatient drivers honked their horns and people hid beneath umbrellas as they darted along in the wet. She shivered, grateful to be indoors out of the cold June weather. She turned back to her desk to face the two large Mac screens that glared brightly in the dim room. Artwork for her Audi print advertisement was sprawled across one monitor's screen and the word processor was open on the other. She rubbed her hands together to warm them and returned to typing. Her fingers tinkered across the keyboard as she wrote the advertising copy for her next campaign.

"You got a sec?"

Jessica looked up from her work. Her business partner, Alex Chambers, crossed the room with quick steps and sat down in the chair opposite her desk.

"I've only got about ten minutes before my next meeting." Jessica noted the time on her watch. "What's up?"

He wriggled around on the seat. "Do you remember months ago when we put in a bid for the opening of Somers Hotel—the one being built as part of the north-eastern redevelopment of Darling Harbour?"

"Yes. Of course." She recalled countless late nights working with Alex on the creative elements for their proposal—advertising and promotions, social media, press and entertainment.

"Well, I've been to-ing and fro-ing with them for months ..." He waved his hand about, rambling on about shortlists, amendments and costings, antagonizing Jessica to the point where she wanted to throw something hard at him. "And you know these things take time—"

"Are you going to get to the point or not?"

"Okay. Okay. Well, we won the job."

"Really?" Her eyes widened with excitement. "That job was such a long shot. This is incredible news. We'll have to celebrate tonight over a bottle of champagne!"

"Abso-freaking-lutely. But here's the thing." Stress crept into Alex's usually happy face, making the creases around his eyes deepen. "I've just rechecked the figures and the margins on this job are low, leaving little room for error."

The depth of his words hit Jessica hard. This would be the biggest project that they'd ever taken on. She wasn't naïve to think everything would be smooth sailing, but ... "We'll be fine. If all goes well, this'll put our name up in lights and we'll attract a whole heap of new clients. You just wait and see." She sucked in a deep breath. "Wow, we really beat EyeOn Marketing and Meredith Bowen?"

That did surprise Jessica and thrilled her endlessly. Meredith was ruthless competition with power and money behind her. Years ago when EyeOn, the American giant, entered the Australian marketplace, they'd approached Kick to buy them out. Alex had dollar signs dancing in his eyes, but Jessica had managed to keep his head out of the clouds. The very thought of selling Kick Marketing and Events Management was unbearable. She never wanted to be swallowed up in a company acquisition and lose everything that she and Alex had spent so long building. This was her life and the very essence of her soul.

"Yep, but here's the deal," Alex continued. "Somers have requested that only the best people work on their campaign and we both know you're better at events management than I am. This is a huge multi-million dollar project and you're the only one capable of pulling it off. So ... the job's yours."

"What? But you did the tender." Jessica looked at the overwhelming pile of work already mounted on her desk. She wasn't going to deny that the thought of managing another big international client thrilled her to the bone. "What about one of the Account Managers? How about Mel? She's good with hospitality."

"No, Jess. Not Mel. She's good, but we both know she can be a bit of a vamp in her outside-of-work behavior. I don't need that around this client." Alex sat up tall and straightened his tie. "It's Mr Henry Somers coming here to personally oversee the final touches for the opening in November. And with his reputation, we don't need the two of them together."

Jessica smiled. "Henry Somers? The head honcho himself? You think Mel will throw herself at the old guy just because he's rich?" *Wouldn't put it past her, given the opportunity.*

"Yep. Come on, Jess. This is a huge client. We can't afford to fuck this up."

Jessica sighed and tapped one of her fingernails against the glass top of her desk. A vision flashed in her mind. She saw Meredith Bowen, the owner of EyeOn Marketing, raucously laughing if gossip hit the headlines or if they were unable to deliver the opening for whatever reason. That was *not* going to happen. Jessica's bulldog determination kicked in. She wasn't going to ever give Meredith the satisfaction. Reshuffling of accounts and the team she'd want to work on the project was already brewing inside her head. "When do we have to start?"

"Oh, you're going to love this. The Somers team are flying in from the UK and will be here first thing on Friday morning to meet with us."

* * *

Jessica pulled up outside the security roller door at the office underground carpark just after nine o'clock on Friday morning. She pressed the button on her garage door opener. Nothing happened.

"Oh, you've got to be kidding me," she cursed as she pressed the button frantically. Was the battery dead? As if sitting in a traffic jam all the way into the city wasn't stressful enough, today's weather forecast had been spot on accurate with its prediction of more rain. It fell in blinding sheets against her windscreen, hindering her vision. She was already running late.

After parking in the alley, Jessica made the dash up to the street entrance without an umbrella. Hers was still in her office, left propped up by the door so she wouldn't forget to take it home. Fat lot of good that did her now. The wind whipped around her body from all directions; the icy rain bit into her skin and soaked her through.

"Oh, my new Jimmy Choos," she whimpered at the sight of her saturated shoes as she leapt over a puddle. But she didn't stop running, not until she reached her office on the first floor.

"Oh my God! Look what the tide washed in." Zoe Peterson, her personal assistant, giggled.

"Funny." With her teeth chattering and water dripping off her hair and suit, Jessica was not amused. Her cheeks felt flushed from a combination of running and the chilly weather.

Why did this have to happen when she was about to meet her new client? But she was determined not to let being wet through to the core stop things from proceeding.

"Alex is already with the Somers Hotel team in the boardroom. But you might want to quickly go sort yourself out in the bathroom first." Zoe waved a finger at her. "I'll let Alex know you're here, then I'll make you your tea and bring it in to you. Okay?"

Jessica dumped her folders in her office and fled into the restroom. She kicked off her shoes and peeled the soggy stockings away from her legs. Then she looked in the mirror, horrified by the reflection before her. Wet was an understatement. She tousled out her shoulder-length blonde hair with her fingers. "So much for straightening it this morning. What the hell do I do with it now?" Rummaging in her bag, she dug out a hair tie and comb. A slicked-back ponytail would have to do.

Her shivering fingers were reluctant to cooperate as she buttoned up her black suit jacket to hide the lace of her bra showing through her white shirt. She looked like she'd been through a carwash with the windows down. Usually she kept a change of clothes in the office but today, of all days, they were at the drycleaners.

After a quick blow dry under the hand dryer to warm up, she reapplied her favourite lipstick—oriental red. She smoothed her hands over the front of her jacket and let out a sigh. She'd done her best under the circumstances not to look like a drenched cat.

With haste in her step, Jessica dropped her bag off in her office and rushed for the boardroom. Just outside she stopped. She closed her eyes, took a long, deep breath and gathered her wits. *It's just another client. Just another event. Clear the head. That's it. Let's go.* She opened the door and entered the room.

* * *

The overhead projector buzzed and a presentation lit the screen as Jessica made her way to the head of the large, black glass table. Alex looked relieved that she'd arrived, but she could see he was struggling to withhold a laugh at the sight of her soggy attire.

"Good morning," Jessica said to everyone. "Sorry I'm late. Nothing like Sydney traffic and broken garage doors in wet weather." She was lucky it was only twenty minutes. It could have been much longer.

"All is fine, Jess," Alex chirped.

As she walked to her place at the table, she glanced over the assembled group. A young man with thick black hair typed on his notebook computer, a middle-aged man sipped his hot steaming drink, a young woman scrolled through emails on her tablet. Then her eyes met those of the fourth person sitting at the end of the table across from Alex. Jessica did her best to hide her surprise because this was not Henry Somers—this was Nathan, his son. She instantly recognized him after having spent hours searching for information on the net about the British hotelier and his empire. It had been an effort to find anything useful among all the gossip surrounding Henry Somers and his affairs. Here, in person, there was something about his son that the photos just hadn't captured. *Wow!*

She smiled warmly as Nathan stood up to shake her hand. His wide shoulders and broad chest filled out his suit in all the right places. She couldn't help but admire the fine lines of his athletic physique. His vivid blue-gray eyes locked onto hers for that moment too long, making her pulse quicken unexpectedly. The man exuded confidence.

Jessica's mouth went dry, but she did manage to speak. "I'm Jessica Mason, Sales and Creative Director. Nice to meet you." She pulled her shoulders back, hoping to regain her professional composure.

"Good morning. I'm Nathan Somers, President of Global Business Development and Operations. But please, call me Nate." He spoke with a velvety-smooth, rounded English accent that made her knees weaken.

As they broke their connection physically, something still had a hold on her. She couldn't put her finger on it. He wasn't that good-looking. Was he? Actually, yes, he was.

A soft knock at the door saw Zoe enter the room with Jessica's tea in hand. Relieved by the interruption, Jessica managed to draw herself away from Nate's captivating gaze.

Nate cleared his throat. "I'd like to introduce my team. Brooke Read, my personal assistant." The strawberry-blonde Kate Winslet look-alike smiled brightly at Jessica. "William Grangeville, our food and beverage manager." The youthful man looked up from his laptop and nodded. "And Martin Windsor, the hotel's general manager." Martin raised his cup to Jessica.

"Nice to meet you all. Has Alex introduced you to everyone who will be working on your opening?" They all nodded as she looked around the table at her team: Lin, the entertainment manager, Gabby, her media specialist, and graphic designers Matt and Darren.

"I was expecting to meet with Henry Somers," said Jessica.

"Sorry, there must have been some miscommunication," Nate replied. "I look after all business development and project ventures such as this."

"Well, we look forward to working with you and your team."

Savoring the first long sip of hot tea, and with her heartbeat back to normal, Jessica finally felt like she was firing on all cylinders for the meeting.

As the hours ticked over, she led the team through the agenda. Her brain was in overdrive as she went through all the plans and preliminary schedules of the campaign for the November opening of the twin Somers Hotel and Residential

Towers. Social marketing had to start right away. The first magazine advertisements had to be done by next Friday. A PR trip had been scheduled for Melbourne for Monday week. Videos had to be made for web promotions. And then there was the grand opening itself. It certainly didn't give her very long to pull together a no-expenses-spared launch for the new venue, but she could do it. Twelve months would have been nice, not a tight six.

"There's just one thing I'd like to add to the plan," Nate interjected, making Jessica balk. "I'd like to hold a night to entertain industry representatives—travel agents, flight operators and the like. We open up to reservation bookings in August and I want to be at the forefront of their minds."

"According to your information," Jessica flipped back through her paperwork, "the hotel opens to guests in early October, is that correct?"

"Yes, but we won't be able to hold any functions at the hotel until after the official opening. We need to open to guests and make sure we can operate without any glitches in the weeks before the grand opening celebrations in mid-November. So on that note, I look forward to hearing what creative ideas you can come up with."

Jessica clenched her teeth together for a moment and took a calming breath. One major event was hard enough given the timeframe, but two was pushing the limit. Was this the start of this client causing her nothing but grief? But she had to take it on the chin and do everything in her power to make the client happy. "Sure, we can do that. I will come up with some concepts and costings for your review."

"Thank you. I'm sorry it wasn't included in the original documentation."

She forced a smile and returned to the agenda.

As the meeting continued, Nate's intense gaze kept

catching Jessica off guard. It threatened to derail her train of thought. When he spoke his deep voice resonated throughout her entire body. His cologne lingered in the air. It was subtle and alluring, spicy with a hint of sandalwood and cinnamon. So warm and inviting. She found herself daydreaming of sipping champagne in a hot bubble bath with his arms tightly wrapped around her while he ran kisses along her shoulder and nuzzled her neck. Jessica shook her head and blinked to clear away her outrageous thoughts.

Don't be stupid. He's your client. Don't even go there. Stay focused on the job.

How could this man affect her so? At lunch last Friday her best friend, Maxine, had suggested that she should start dating again. Did that have Jessica suddenly looking at men in a different light? *Oh, Max, look what you've done.*

She rattled some numbers in her head. Had it really been six months since her last date and two years since her divorce? Where did time go? The thought didn't really bother her though. She didn't feel the need to date. Men only caused problems ... and then they left. Graeme, her ex-husband, had left her for another woman, a much younger woman, ten years his junior. Her divorce had been a blessing in disguise. At thirty-six, Jessica had never felt so free, empowered and content. No one to answer to, no one complaining about her endless hours at the office or her doing the things she loved doing. Why on earth would she want a man back in her life?

"Right," said Jessica, wrapping up. "I'll write up the minutes of the meeting, adjust the project plan, and email the new version and notes out to everyone. We'll start with a photo shoot and video interviews at the hotel on Monday for the social media campaign, then meet here every Tuesday morning at ten."

"Excellent," Nate said as he closed his leather-bound

compendium. "We certainly have an exciting launch ahead of us."

Alex and Jessica stood at the door and shook hands with the Somers team as they shuffled out into the foyer. Jessica felt an overpowering warming of her blood as Nate firmly took her hand and looked deep into her eyes.

"I look forward to seeing you on Monday, Ms Mason."

Jessica felt a catch in her throat as he flashed a breathtaking smile at her.

* * *

Nate pinched the bridge of his nose as he tried to concentrate on the job at hand. It had been all of seventy-two hours since he'd met Jessica Mason and he found himself thinking about her every few minutes. It was the first time in nearly five years he'd felt so distracted from his work, and he struggled to refocus.

"When will the hotel kitchen installation be complete?" Nate asked the construction manager.

"Two more weeks," he said.

"We can't have any more hold-ups. We have our safety inspection and testing for our fire certificate in four weeks. If there are any more problems, come and see me and I'll deal with these suppliers personally."

"Yes, Mr Somers."

Nate fought to clear his mind as he looked over the plans scattered across the work desk set up in the lobby area. He reached for his now-cold cup of tea and drained the contents in one long gulp. Staring at the dregs in the bottom, the leaves clearly formed the shape of a kite. *Think before acting.* Great! That was all he needed on the top of everything else, his grandmother's superstitions screwing with his head. He thumped the cup back down on the desk. What was wrong with him? Everything with the hotel was right on track. So why did he feel so flustered?

The clicking of heels on tiles caught his attention. Jessica walked into the lobby from the retail corridor that connected the hotel to the residential tower. Another woman walked by her side—what was her name? Ah yes, Gabby. But it was Jessica who seized his attention. She was tall and slender, her long legs accentuated by killer high heels. Her shoulder-length blonde hair shimmered and her olive skin shone golden in the soft lighting.

"Excuse me," he said to the manager. "I have some other business to attend to."

He walked toward Jessica and Gabby. Warmth flooded through his veins as he shook her hand—a strange sensation he had honestly never experienced before. He smiled when he saw her cheeks flush as she glanced up at him from under her long eyelashes. There was no denying she was a beautiful woman. But why should she affect him in such a manner? He worked around stunning women all the time, why should Jessica be any different? He was without a doubt impressed by her conduct and competence in refining the final plans for the launch. Her knowledge of event management and her creative flair had astounded him. But there was something about her dark chocolate-colored eyes. The way she looked at him ...

Oh bollocks! Nate cursed himself when he realized he'd forgotten to let her hand go. Releasing his hold, he overcame his momentary lapse in concentration by offering to take her heavy equipment bag. He turned and directed them to follow him to the suite of offices hidden behind the wall of the reception area.

"Are you ready for a productive afternoon, ladies?"

Walking beside him, Jessica relayed their agenda for the afternoon. As she tucked her hair behind her ear, the sweet scent of her perfume brought his whole body to attention. Heat rushed to his groin.

I'm going absolutely barmy!

This nonsense had to stop! Sydney was too important. He was determined to prove to his retiring father and the board that he had the savvy to grow and run the Somers empire. This venture had to put their hotels back into a positive light. He didn't need to deal with any more scandal or drama. Somers had had enough of that in recent times, with the exposure of his father's affairs tarnishing their good name.

Nate's clarity of purpose returned as they reached his office at the end of the hallway. He opened the door and made way for the women to enter.

"Let's leave your gear here and I'll give you a quick tour of the function areas before we get underway."

"Sounds great. Let's go."

* * *

"So what do you think of the hotel?" Nate asked as he followed them back into his office after showing the women around. "As you can see it's still a bit of a construction zone in some areas. All the internals will be complete in four weeks, and then clean-up commences along with staff training and operational simulations. We're on schedule to receive our first guests in October."

"It's stunning. I can't wait to see the place finished," Jessica replied, as she picked up her case. "After seeing the size of the ballroom and outdoor pool area, I've a few more ideas that you might want to consider for the opening."

"Such as?" Nate arched his eyebrow.

"A few years ago we did a champagne launch where we built a clear platform over the top of a pool. Maybe we could do something similar for the fashion parade?" she suggested. "I've also come up with some ideas for your industry rep night. How does a massive boat docked in front of the hotel sound?"

Jessica barely took a breath as she prattled on with new suggestions and highlighted some of the innovative events that Kick had done for other clients. As she talked, Nate noticed she was trying to unknot a cable, and her fingers fumbled. She glanced up at him and managed a smile. Was she nervous? Surely someone of her experience wouldn't be anxious in this setting. He should have been interested in what she was saying, but he was entranced by the movement of her lips. They were full and red, and the thought of tasting them was ... *absurd.*

"So what do you think?"

Nate didn't have a clue what Jessica had suggested because he'd been focused on her mouth rather than her words. He rubbed at his forehead, he didn't have time for this nonsense. Work was his one and only priority. "Let's discuss everything in more detail at our next meeting."

Nate reluctantly grabbed his phone that started ringing in his jacket pocket. He looked at the caller ID. It was Rachael. *Blast! Why now?* She only called if it was urgent ... or she wanted money.

"Excuse me, but I need to take this quickly." He stepped out into the hall and put the phone to his ear. "Rachael, what's up?" He couldn't hide the sting in his voice.

"I've just received the account for Lucy's school fees. They've gone up. You have to send me more money."

"Hi Rachael, how's Lucy?" He blatantly ignored her question. He knew perfectly well Lucy's fees had been paid at the beginning of the year.

"No time for chitchat, Nathan. I need more money."

He shook his head in disbelief. With his flustered thoughts still on Jessica, he was not in the mood for Rachael's games. "Remember we had a thing called a divorce settlement, and you received a ludicrous amount of money? You have full custody and your monthly allowance is way beyond the means of normal living to cover Lucy's expenses. So how did you come to the conclusion that I need to give you more money?"

"You don't understand. Everything is more expensive now!"

"Then move to a more affordable area."

"Ergh!" Rachael sounded like she was suppressing a scream through clenched teeth. She had tried every tactic in the book since their divorce to get more and more money from him. He'd had enough of her games and was ready for an all-out battle.

"I need more money, Nathan," she insisted, no doubt stomping her foot on the ground and throwing a tantrum like a three year old when she didn't get her way.

Nate's shoulders filled with tension and his blood started to boil. "How many times did you go shopping this past month? How many designer shoes and fancy dresses did you purchase? Where and how often did you catch up with your girlfriends for lunch? If you make some lifestyle adjustments you might be surprised at how much money you do have. I pay you more than enough to support Lucy. So I'm afraid this is something you're going to have to sort out on your own."

He hung up and paced the floor back and forth. Every muscle in his body bristled with tension as he took deep breaths to calm down.

Every time he spoke to Rachael Nate cursed himself for being so blind and foolish, for falling in love with her. Well, what he thought was love. He'd been impressed by her confidence in pursuing him. Stunned at her suggestion that they marry. Crushed by her lies and reneging on the plans that they had made together.

A bitter taste rose in his mouth thinking about how he used to enjoy flying Rachael all around the world. Things changed literally the day after they married. The sweet girl had gone and replaced by her evil twin. She suddenly refused to move to England, insisting on staying in Singapore. A few short months later she fell pregnant, and six months after Lucy was born, she served him with divorce papers.

She blamed his excessive travel and inability to settle down. Maybe that was true. But he couldn't erase the nagging feeling that she was only after his coin. The years since had proven him right.

He was no longer that young, naive man. He was never going to get close to anyone like that again. His heart was now enclosed by an icy barrier. His ability to trust or love anyone again long gone.

As visions of Rachael concocting her next plan to swindle more money from his bank account flickered though his mind, it was just another firm reminder why he didn't do relationships.

Chapter 2

"Jess, do you mind if I take off?" Gabby asked as they packed up the last of the video equipment. Lights, cameras, tripod stands and cables galore. "I'm catching up with friends for dinner and I'm already late."

"Sure. I'll get one of Nate's staff members to help me load all this into my car. Off you go. Have fun."

As Gabby disappeared out the door, Jessica went to close down her laptop but knocked her folder of papers off the table and onto the floor. With a heavy sigh, she dropped down onto her hands and knees and started to gather them up when an impeccably polished pair of black leather lace-up shoes appeared before her. *Size ten, if I had to guess.* Her pulse went up a notch. She slid her gaze up the legs of the tailored trousers, up the front of the black jacket, before meeting Nate's blue-gray eyes. She felt a little shock to her solar plexus and clambered to her feet, refusing his offered hand. She shoved her folder into her bag and hastily straightened her skirt. Even after spending all afternoon in the same room as him, something in the air changed when he stood this close.

"It's been a long day. Would you like to join me for a drink on the boardwalk?" Nate asked as he handed her a piece of paper she'd missed off the floor.

Jessica dropped her eyes to the desk and swallowed hard. A drink? Surely no harm would come from having a friendly drink.

All afternoon Nate had been attentive to Gabby and her, every request he seemed only too happy to please. He ensured they had enough food and water. Mid-afternoon, he personally made them cups of tea for their break. He was well-mannered; the consummate English gentleman, never faulting in his professionalism, even when Gabby made him repeat a section of interview questions several times to capture his detailed responses correctly.

Would he be different outside the office environment? Maybe finding out more about Nate would put her somersaulting stomach to rest. But would she find anything negative about him that would turn off the attraction? She tried not to judge books by their covers—but *my oh my*—Nate was eye-catching, glossy and had '*Get your hands on me now*' written all over him. "Sure. Sounds wonderful."

"After you." Nate gestured toward the door.

* * *

Once they were seated at a restaurant on the rim of Cockle Bay, nestled under the amber warmth of an outdoor heater, Nate ordered a bottle of red wine. The winter evening was cool and the harbor waters rippled with dark blue and rosy pink hues as the sun disappeared in the western sky.

"So have you been to Australia before?" Jessica asked as the waiter poured wine into her glass. She needed a drink to take the edge off. Nate's presence made her nerves spark.

"Yes, twice. I came here on a holiday to Cairns when I was about ten years old, and four years ago when our scouts found the location for the hotel."

"Well you certainly have a winner on your hands. Darling Harbour was in desperate need of a new waterfront hotel."

"We like to think it adds to the glamor of the city and will become an iconic landmark of the Sydney skyline."

"Are you staying here until the launch or is it just a visit to see that everything gets underway?"

"I should be here the whole time. Maybe a week in Singapore to see my daughter."

"You're married?" No one had mentioned that little detail to her before.

"Oh, dear lord, no. Not anymore." Jessica heard a certain amount of disdain in his tone. "I was married at the ripe old age of twenty-four and it lasted a whole eighteen months."

Shocked by the news and without thinking, Jessica blurted back, "I have a son, too. He's nineteen though; all grown up now and out of home."

"Are you serious?" Nate looked startled as he placed his glass on the table. "You don't look old enough to have a grown child?"

"Not one of my finer moments in life, but yes, I had Conner when I was sixteen." She shouldn't have brought it up. Was she really so flustered? *Calm down, Jess.* To avoid further questions, she turned the conversation back to Nate. "It must be hard for you not seeing your daughter."

Nate let out a deep breath and sank back into his chair. "Rachael makes it very difficult. We had an ugly, bitter divorce. With my demanding job I had to think of what was best for Lucy, so I granted Rachael full custody. The least I could do was offer financial stability for them both, and Rachael ensures that I'll be paying the price for the rest of my days."

Bad end to his marriage, Jessica could relate to that. "Well my ex-husband, Graeme, left me for someone ten years younger. Now he's shacked up in a new house that *I* paid for."

Nate grinned as he ran his hand over his five o'clock shadow. "I can relate to the house thing. My ex-wife took notes off Zsa Zsa Gabor. You know that saying about being a *housekeeper*. We divorced—she kept the house."

Jessica chuckled, nearly choking on a mouthful of wine. "Yes, you never understand the value of money until you get divorced."

"There was no *value* in my marriage, only cost." He smirked. "The only time I knew I made Rachael happy was when I signed our divorce papers."

His sarcastic sense of humor made her laugh. As they tried to outdo each other on whose ex was the worse, Jessica's belly hurt from giggling so much. Her marriage had always loomed in the back of her mind as one of the biggest failures of her life, but joking about it with someone who'd had a rough ending as well, it didn't feel so bad after all.

Nate's eyes locked on hers in all seriousness. "I don't mean to pry too much, but is Alex your partner now?"

"Partner? Definitely not." She struggled to keep a straight face. "You've met Alex, right? He's gay as Elton John."

Nate nodded as if the pieces of the puzzle clicked together. "That explains a lot."

"We met during our first job out of university at a small advertising firm in North Sydney, and hit it off. He handles all the operations, business processes and bid management, whereas I manage sales, the creative team and events." She was baffled that anyone could think she and Alex were together. "I'm very content being single. No ... wait, I'm married to my business." She threw her head back with a laugh, and then peered into his eyes. "You? Which supermodel are you dating at present?"

Snideness crept into her voice as she remembered seeing him photographed with various women on the internet.

He leaned toward her, took a long, slow breath and looked straight at her with a very stern expression. "Are you sure you're not thinking of my father?" Noting his reaction, this was definitely a sour subject. "Just for your information, I don't think I've ever dated a supermodel. Not even an actress. And recently, no one at all. Work consumes all my time."

Her breath faltered as a smile returned to his face. She didn't know if it was the wine affecting her, but his English accent seemed to coil itself around her body and warm her deep inside. She wondered what it would be like to have his naked body ... *What the...?*Jessica blinked and turned her eyes away. Her hands were trembling so she slipped them into her lap. She glanced across the table at his fingers. He was stroking the stem of the wine glass absentmindedly. Why did she wish for those hands to be on her instead? How was she going to work with him if her temperature rose like the mercury on a hot summer's day whenever he was near?

The more he said, the more she wanted to taste his lips that were now slightly stained with red wine. So much for trying to find out his bad points. Other than an ex-wife and a daughter he hardly saw, Nate Somers had too many ticks in all the right boxes: easy to talk to, funny, work was his life, and they had many things in common, including the love of red wine, tropical island holidays and attending Spring Racing Carnivals.

After their meal, they strolled along the boardwalk toward the Somers Residential Tower. Nate stopped and leaned on the railing overlooking the water. The breeze danced through his short brown hair. "Would you believe that this stay in Australia will be one of my longest anywhere? I'm usually never in one place for more than a month."

"Well, Sydney is a beautiful city. I'm sure you'll find things to do to keep you entertained." Jessica settled back against the railing next to him and enjoyed the cool evening air upon her face.

"I don't have a lot of spare time, but I already like what I see." Nate turned. He stood barely a body-width in front of her. "But I wasn't anticipating anything like you. You're impossible to ignore." Nate hesitated, his eyes searching her face.

His close proximity caught her off guard. Jessica felt her cheeks color. She wanted to blame the alcohol, but the presence of this man before her had her unraveling. Where had all her years of professional conduct gone? As if the ground turned to quicksand, she felt herself sinking further and further under the spell of Nate Somers. His alluring voice pulled her along like the Pied Piper.

She had to resist, but was unable to look away. "I think you're suffering from delusion."

He lowered his head toward hers. The scent of his spicy cologne filled her senses and Jessica felt her body temperature rise as he closed the gap between them. She closed her eyes and held her breath. Her body tensed and waited for his lips to press against hers.

But they never came.

She opened her eyes to see Nate's darkened with desire, just inches from hers.

"Am I?" His lip curled at the corners.

Why had he stopped? *No, that's a good thing.* Jessica blinked several times to regain her composure. Flushed with embarrassment, she stepped away. "Yes. I think we should head back. It's been a long day."

Chapter 3

Thanks to strict advertising deadlines and conflicting meetings, Jessica and her team had a late night of work ahead of them as they arrived at Somers Residential Tower on Thursday evening. Their first run of promotions and advertisements was due tomorrow and the whole crew was full of energy.

Nate met them in the lobby. "Come, we're going up to my apartment. There's more room for us all to work, and the view is spectacular."

Jessica's jaw strained and her palms went clammy at the thought. His apartment? Even though she was going to have others around her, the prospect of spending an evening working in his private dwelling made her break out in a cold sweat. She needed space, distance and formal settings to avoid intimate situations with Nate. Since Monday evening, she'd failed dismally to not think about his lips and what they would taste like. The chemistry between them was impossible to ignore. Regardless, the flame needed to be extinguished. She sucked in a long hard breath to calm herself down as Nate led them into the elevators and headed on up to his floor.

Nate's apartment was sleek and luxurious like the rest of the residential complex. In the dimly lit room, white furniture stood out against the plush, charcoal-colored carpet. A leather modular couch surrounded a glossy coffee table scattered with newspapers and magazines. Full-length glass windows framed spectacular views over Darling Harbour, Sydney Wharf Apartments and the casino, all of which looked peaceful from thirty-two stories up.

Jessica noted the empty suitcase left standing by the far wall, a sole photo frame on top of the sideboard; laptop and work folders piled high upon the desk.

"I've ordered pizzas. They should be here any minute. So, what can I get everyone to drink? Beer? Wine? Soft drink?" Nate asked, as he grabbed glasses from the kitchen cupboard and waited on everyone's requests.

The doorbell rang and Nate disappeared down the hallway, returning with pizzas in hand. The smell of garlic and pepperoni filled the air, making Jessica's mouth water. She had to laugh as she saw Nate roll up his business shirtsleeves and hook into pizza, just like one of the boys.

"Jess, you want the last piece?" Martin asked her. She put up her hand and shook her head. No, definitely not. Her belly was full. "Dibs, it's mine then." Martin reached across the table and started to gobble down the last slice.

"Can I get you something else, Jessica?" Nate asked as he wiped his fingertips with a napkin. "I don't have much as I've only been shopping once. But I have more alcohol, tea and crisps. Or I could order up something from the restaurant."

"No, thank you. I'm fine."

After the team finished dinner, they buckled down to work. Martin sat at the table with Matt and Darren in front of their Macs, modifying artwork designs. Jessica sat on the couch with Nate and Gabby, sifting through dozens of photo proofs and watching video edits.

"You'll have to point out my imperfections, Ms Mason," said Nate. "I hope your team will Photoshop out any irregularities they find in the images." He spoke softly as he handed her a second glass of wine. When she closed her hand around the glass, he didn't let go. His slight hesitation made her look up at his face.

"There don't seem to be any—none that I can find." Jessica held his gaze until she became conscious of the others in the room. She didn't need her staff making speculations, so, with a subtle shimmy of her hips, she edged across the couch, putting more distance between her body and his.

The work that should have taken an hour or two ended up taking four. As everyone readied to leave, Nate turned to Jessica. "Do you mind waiting for a moment while the approvals print off, and I'll sign them for you?"

"Sure." She prayed that the laser printer in the far corner produced the documents at lightning speed so everyone could head for home.

"Jess, we have to go or we'll miss the train," Matt pleaded.

"Okay. Go on ahead, guys. Brilliant work as always. I'll see you tomorrow." More than anything, Jessica wanted to depart with them, but everyone, including Martin, disappeared out the door. She gulped loudly when Nate closed the door behind them and she heard the soft click of the latch.

Jessica closed her eyes and bit hard into her lip. She was very aware that she was now alone with Nate in his apartment. *Not good.*

The air prickled with electricity as he walked back down the hallway toward her. Every nerve in her body felt on edge. After sculling the last of her wine, she placed the glass on the coffee table. She couldn't deny Nate's allure, but there was a line not to be crossed.

Quick. Get these documents. Clean up and get out of here.

Jessica gathered up empty pizza boxes and took them to the kitchen. She was stacking them on the counter when she felt him come up and stand behind her. She didn't even need to turn around. His body radiated heat, just inches from pressing into hers. *Too close.* Slowly she turned to face him. Her heart thundered in her chest. His vivid blue-gray eyes took possession of her. *This is not good.*

With his eyes fixed on her, Nate slowly drank the last of his wine. Then he reached around her, placed his glass on the bench and seductively licked his lips. Jessica's breath deepened. She struggled to swallow.

"I have a solution," he said softly.

"What's the problem?" She could feel her pulse tapping in her throat.

Nate edged closer, his eyes not leaving hers. "You ... and making the most out of my stay in Sydney."

"Nate!" Jessica gasped as she leaned back, trapped up against the bench.

"Hmm?"

"I have to go." Her voice quivered, threatening to break in spite of her resolve.

"Okay," he whispered, but didn't move aside. His face angled toward hers. She placed her hand on his chest to stop his advances, but the feel of his hard body beneath his cotton shirt ignited a fire within her that had been dormant for too long.

His warm breath gently brushed across her face.

"This ... is wrong," she whispered.

His lips were an inch from hers. "Very." His voice was soft as silk.

"We shouldn't." She wanted to run, but her feet felt glued to the ground.

"I know." Distance evaporated into nothingness as his lips pressed against hers.

Her mind screamed so loudly she was sure Nate could hear her thoughts. *Stop. He's your client!*But his lips were warm and soft. The wine lingered on his mouth and she couldn't help but want to taste a little bit more. With her pulse racing and her head spinning, all sense went out the door.

Jessica's hands shot up and latched around Nate's neck. She laced her fingers into his thick soft hair. With a gentle moan, she parted her lips and kissed him deeply.

Nate's breath against hers was hot and fiery as her tongue found his. The scorching touch of his hands as they ran around her hips sent shivers to every part of her being. Her breasts nestled firmly against his muscular torso and she could feel his heart throbbing. Never in her life had she wanted to kiss a man or to touch and feel his skin so badly. She was shocked at the desperate want burning inside her. Nate's hands slipped to the lapels of her jacket and slid it from her shoulders onto the floor. She wanted more. More to taste. More to touch. More of him.

"Jess." The sound of him whispering her name into her ear made her knees feel weak.

In a heated frenzy, zips, buttons and belts went flying in all directions. They tore each other's clothes off, down to their underwear, leaving a scattered trail between the kitchen and the bedroom. Falling on the bed, he hovered over her, grinding his hips into hers. Jessica groaned as she felt his erection swollen and hard against her belly. His demanding, hungry kisses made their way down the arch of her neck and across the line of her shoulder as his fingers slid her bra strap away from her skin.

The fabric of his trunks felt smooth against her hand as Jessica glided her fingers over his buttocks. So firm. So hot. She playfully rolled Nate over onto his back and straddled his hips. Just looking at his hot body and handsome face nestled amongst the throw of pillows turned her on.

This was so out of character. Her calm, cool facade disappeared with his kisses.

His stomach flexed beneath her fingertips as she ran her hands over every groove. Her mouth watered at the taste of his skin as she snaked kisses down his chest. As she wriggled her body downward she admired the smooth skin across the arch of his hips before she peeled his trunks away. The sight of his nakedness sent a shock of pleasure to her very core. She took him in her hand and firmly stroked up and down his length and rubbed across his head. His hard, warm skin in the palm of her hand made the muscles between her legs clench in eager anticipation.

He sat upright and pulled her back up onto his lap before their lips and tongues continued to entwine in a frenzy. Jessica's skin felt on fire from the touch of his hands. He reached around her back and freed the clasp on her bra, pulling it away and throwing it somewhere onto the floor. His hands returned to cup and play with her breasts.

Nate groaned with sounds of deep pleasure as she writhed against him, feeling his erection grow harder beneath her and pressing into her wet spot. Lifting her off his lap, he lay her down gently on her back onto the bed. Her chest heaved in time with his as they continued with frantic kisses and his hands wandered all over her body. Her skin quivered as his fingertips edged beneath the lace of her panties. Unable to control herself she moaned as he rubbed firmly against her hot arousal. He teased her, stroking her gently up and down the length of her slit and slowly circling her clitoris. His touch sent ripples of heat to every nerve ending within her body and her eyelids flutter closed.

With a wicked grin, he whisked off her knickers and tossed them aside. He trailed kisses up her body until he reached one of her nipples and suckled it into his mouth. As his tongue circled around her hardened peak, her back arched toward his sensual taunt. *God!* In spite of the urgency and the desperation to have each other, Nate seemed to be relishing her body. Making her feel so sensual. Sexy. Desirable.

"Don't move," he said as he reached into his bedside table and dug a foil packet from the drawer. Ripping the condom open with his teeth, he rolled it onto his shaft.

Her eyes widened as she watched him roll the condom on.

"Like what you see?" He grinned at her.

She shrugged. "I mean. It looks okay. But you better show me what you can do with it."

She was on fire and needed him inside of her. As he nestled back between her legs, he prodded the tip of his firmness against her opening.

"Oh, I will. Don't you worry about that."

Her giggles were silenced as he kissed her. His breath cascaded across her skin as their tongues danced, her heart pounded and her flesh flooded with goosebumps. She curled her legs around his, feeling the hairs on the backs of his limbs brush against her skin. Her hands rode over the defined muscles on his back, feeling them flex with his every move.

With their bodies melded together, Jessica drew her knees further apart and invited him in. His erection pulsed as he slid into her. She gasped at the pleasurable sensation.

Nate groaned as he pulled back and then rocked his hips into her again. His deep penetration was intense as Jessica succumbed to and met his every move. Faster. Harder. Nate plunged into her, making her body burn with sheer ecstasy.

Her stomach muscles and thighs strained and begged for release as he drove into her. Her fingers dug into Nate's skin as sweat started to lick their bodies.

With his entire length deeply embedded within her, he

rubbed against her, over and over again.

Her toes curled into the bedding. Her muscles quaked. Her jaw clenched.

She pulsed her hips rhythmically against his.

"Yes!" Jessica gasped as she orgasmed beneath his expert maneuvers and felt his body convulse and climax with her.

Panting breaths filled the air as Jessica tried to lower her racing heartbeat. With eyes blazing with satisfaction, Nate slumped next to her on the pillows. Feeling sated, she lay beside him and stared at the ceiling.

For a brief moment Jessica felt delirious. *That was fantastic!* Then she froze in horror. She remembered Alex's face as he'd ask her to take the Somers account. We *can'tafford to fuck this up!*he'd said. Like a guided missile hitting its target and leaving a quake of destruction in its path—guilt, shame and self-loathing hit her all at once. *Oh God, what have I done?* Jumping out of bed, she stumbled around trying to find her underwear.

Panic hit. *How could I be so stupid?You fool.*

Jessica slipped on her panties and fastened her bra.

"Jess, what are you doing? Please don't go."

"I have to. I have work tomorrow." She followed the scattering of clothes, picking hers up along the way as she fled out into the living room.

Nate followed her. He'd pulled on a pair of loose sweatpants that hung low upon his hips. His naked stomach was a blazing reminder that she'd just been sitting astride him in his bed. She turned away to avoid looking at such temptation as she struggled into her pants.

"Why are you leaving?"

"We shouldn't have done this." She pulled the zip up, and then slid her arms into the sleeves of her blouse. "Nate, I can't stay."

"Why?"

"You're my client, for Christ's sake. I'll see you Tuesday. At the meeting." Scanning around the room she spotted her bag, crossed the room and grabbed it. Her hands shook as she stuffed her papers and laptop into it and headed for the door. She couldn't get out of there fast enough.

"I have to go. Goodnight." She slipped out the door, cursing herself and feeling ashamed of her lack of professional conduct. Temporary insanity had been amazing, but now she had to deal with the consequences.

Chapter 4

Outside Jessica's bedroom window the wind was moaning softly. The trees in the garden swayed, casting shadows on the ceiling. Jessica lay staring up at them, hoping to be distracted. One second her body hummed all over, blissed at the mind-blowing sex she'd had with Nate. It was hot! Crazy! But, in the next instant she curled into a ball, shuddering at what she'd done. Like indulging in too much chocolate cake, then feeling guilty, she was riddled with shame. If anyone found out that she'd slept with Nate, especially Alex, they'd be furious. She knew the golden rule not to mix business with pleasure. It always caused problems. How could she work with Nate now?

Watching the hours tick by, Jessica wrestled the night away until the alarm buzzed at six o'clock. A run on the treadmill, a shower, breakfast and a cup of tea did little to settle her mind. The lack of sleep and her inability to stop thinking about the great, thigh-numbing sex she'd had with Nate had her riding a roller-coaster of emotions as she headed into her office after a client meeting.

Zoe grinned from ear to ear and her emerald green eyes shone vividly as Jessica walked up to her desk. "Morning, Jess."

"Morning." Jessica was puzzled by Zoe's overzealous behavior. Did Zoe know her mannerisms so well that she could tell something was different this morning? Was she walking funny? Jessica felt like she had *'I've just had sex'* written in bold black pen on her forehead. "Can you grab me my tea please, Zo? And make it extra strong."

"Sure can. Here's your mail, and Nate Somers has called twice this morning," Zoe said as she sprang off her chair.

"Do you know what he wants? Is it about changes to artwork?" Jessica tried to seem aloof and calm, but knots tightened inside her stomach at the mention of his name.

"He wouldn't tell me anything."

"Okay, I'll call him." Jessica shrugged and headed into her office to seek some sanctuary.

It took no more than two steps through her door for the fragrance to hit her. She looked up from sifting through her letters. There on her desk was a huge bouquet of bright yellow and pink gerberas.

Oh crap!

She apprehensively walked over to the desk, and grabbed the card from among the stems.

' Thanks for a memorable night. N.S.'

Memorable night! Jessica wished she didn't remember. But as images of Nate's naked body filled her head, she couldn't keep the smile at bay.

But last night shouldn't have happened.

Jessica placed her hand on her hip and tapped her fingers against her side. How was she going to rectify the situation? Maybe Nate was a real playboy and it was simply a one-night stand already forgotten. He probably had his personal assistant send the flowers. She grabbed her phone and texted Nate.

'*Thanks for flowers. Nice. See you Tuesday.*'

She turned with a gasp as Zoe breezed into her office, tea in hand. "So, tell me. Who are they from?"

"Um. Nate."

"Guys don't send flowers for no reason. What happened?"

Zoe's eagerness for gossip made Jessica's nausea return as she sat down at her desk. She didn't want to be the source of the latest office scandal. She was the boss, for God's sake, and needed to be a figure for her staff to look up to and respect.

"Nothing. He just likes the work we're doing."

Zoe's interrogation was thankfully interrupted as Alex knocked on the office door. "You got a sec, Jess?"

"Yeah, sure," Jessica said.

Zoe huffed and crossed her arms, clearly not satisfied with Jessica's explanation. She spun on her red stiletto heels and strode out the door, her long dark hair swishing behind her.

"Nice flowers. Since when do you have an admirer?" Alex raised his eyebrows and strutted over to her desk.

"I don't. They're from Somers thanking us for kicking off the launch campaign." The lie made her skin crawl with guilt.

He looked up in surprise. "I wish Nathan Somers was sending *me* flowers." He purred as he smelled the arrangement. "Before I forget why I came in here, I urgently have to go to Melbourne for a few days to see a client, and then to Canberra for that Business Management conference. I know we're super busy, but are you all right to hold down the fort?"

"Most definitely." Jessica covered a yawn with her hand.

"You look tired, sweetie. You're not ill, are you?" She saw concern flicker in his eyes.

No, just tired from being up all night having wild sex.

"Matt told me you guys had a late night working. It's Friday. Why don't you take off for the weekend and go out to that winery retreat you like to visit?"

Maybe a weekend away was what she needed. Some fresh, country air might help her clear her head and sort out how to deal with Nate Somers next week and beyond. She wasn't one to run away from her mistakes. Never. But a little space might do her a world of good. "Gumtrees. I might just do that. I'll call them and head up tomorrow morning because I'm having dinner tonight with Max."

* * *

Jessica was at her usual spot at the Verve Bar, downstairs from her office, drinking bourbon and dry when Max arrived.

"Hey, how are you?" Max kissed her on the cheek in greeting. "I can't stay late tonight, I gotta get home to take the kids to the nine o'clock movies. I promised them ages ago." Max sat on the bar stool next to her. For the end of the work day she looked amazing as always with her not-a-hair-out-of-place, tailored-suit appearance. She glanced at Jessica's drink. "O-Oh! Hard liquor. What's up?"

Jessica raised her hand to get the bartender's attention. She turned to Max. "What are you drinking? I'm buying."

When two bourbons arrived, Max took a long sip and then proceeded to tap her flaming red fingernails against the glass. "Come on, out with it."

"Okay, here goes." Jessica shuffled around on the bar stool. "You know how I'm looking after the Somers Hotel account? Well, Nate Somers is out here overseeing everything."

"Yeah. The British hotelier guy."

"Anyway, last night things went late, we were working in his apartment ... we had a few drinks ... I stayed on after everyone left ... and—" Jessica felt the color rise in her cheeks as she struggled to get the words out.

"Oh!" Max gasped, as she smacked the glass down hard on the bar. "What happened?" Her eyes widened as she wriggled to the edge of her seat.

"Well ... *it* happened. I broke the cardinal rule."

Max's eyes widened. "You mean ...?" she whispered.

Jessica winced. "What have I done? I'm a mess." She threw her face into her hands. "My life was so perfectly normal and in control until we took on this account."

"You slept with *Nate Somers*?" Max squealed excitedly.

"Shh ... keep your voice down." Jessica looked around anxiously, horrified that someone might overhear. "Yes, but I shouldn't have."

"Why not? You're single. He's single. Isn't he?"

"Yes. But he's my client."

"Yeah." Max frowned, taking in the seriousness of it all. "Okay, that's a problem. But was he good?" Her eyes glowed and she couldn't sit still, just itching to know more detail.

Jessica nodded her head. Her cheeks felt like they were on fire. Oh yes, Nate was good. But then she sighed heavily. "What am I going to do? I have to face this guy every week for the next few months."

"Have you talked to him?"

"I texted him. Is that wrong?"

"Ouch!" Max smiled cheekily. "Why don't you have a fling with him for the next couple of months while he's here? Have some fun. Some great sex. Then he leaves."

"No, Max. It's bad enough I did it once. I've never had a fling in my life."

"Hell, I would. Keep it purely as sex. No intimacy and no emotions so no one gets hurt at the end."

"Max, stop. It's not going to happen." Jessica giggled at Max's crazy proposal. "Can you come with me out to the winery this weekend? I wanna get out of here for a while, drink a couple of bottles of good wine and clear my head." Jessica was hoping to put all this mess behind her. Then she'd apologize to Nate and focus on her business as always.

"I can't." Max pouted her lips and genuinely looked disappointed. "Billy has his soccer game on tomorrow. Maybe next time."

* * *

The drive northwest out to Gumtrees Winery and Ranch Retreat in Pokolbin took Jessica just over two hours from the city. Nestled at the foothills of the mountains, the cozy Hunter Valley getaway backed onto a flowing creek lined with towering silver-gray eucalypts and sweet scented wattles. The sandstone homestead, stables, boutique restaurant, cellar door and several timber cabins sat on the crest of a small hill. Vineyards covered the rolling hills in all other directions. Winter had turned everything to shades of earthy brown. Crisp, dry grass blanketed the ground and leafless vines hung precariously on their trestles. Even in the harsh, cold conditions, it was picture perfect, and felt like a million miles away from the hustle and bustle of city life.

Jessica loved coming out to Gumtrees once a month or so to relax, do some work in the peace and quiet, and ride horses. She'd grown up in the nearby town of Cessnock and had been coming here on and off for over ten years. It made her appreciate all she had achieved at such a young age. She'd been very lucky her hard work and sacrifices had paid off.

After driving up the long gravel driveway, past rows and rows of grapevines that seemed to long for the return of the warm summer sun, she parked outside her usual cabin next to the homestead. Stepping outside, she sucked the fresh country air deep into her lungs and instantly felt better.

As she unlocked the back of her car to unload her gear, she caught sight of Nick Hill, the owner, coming out of the reception office. Rugged up in an oversized brown parka and blue woolen beanie, he strolled down the pathway to greet her.

"Good to see you as always. Here's your key," Nick offered politely. "Are you okay? You were only out here three weeks ago."

Jessica slipped her sunglasses back on in an effort to hide the dark, tired circles under her eyes. "Yeah, I'm fine. I just need a break."

"Don't we all," Nick said as he gathered her luggage and food basket out of the back of her car. He led her up the steps and placed her belongings at the door.

Jessica slid the key into the lock. "I think I'll go for a ride and get some fresh air into my system. I'll take Stirling out, if that's okay? I'll ride up along the top ridge paddock and back down the vineyard trail."

"Sounds good. I'll be in the office. Let me know if you need anything."

After changing into her riding gear, Jessica made her way to the horse yards. Stirling, her favorite chestnut quarterhorse, hung his head over the rail and whinnied softly at seeing her.

"Hey boy, how are you? Miss me?" she said as she rubbed the white star on his forehead. As she entered the yard through the gate, he stuck his nose out and nuzzled into her as she put his halter on. "You ready for a ride? Come on, let's go and get you saddled up."

Jessica rode all afternoon, and hit the same trails on Stirling the following morning. The scent of eucalyptus in the air cleansed her soul. The cascading sound of the rocky creek calmed her mind. After much reflection, cursing herself and analyzing everything, Jessica put the incidents from the past few days to rest. She would just apologize to Nate and then they could go on as if nothing had happened. But why did Max's comment, 'Just have a fling', keep humming in her mind?

She couldn't, could she? *No, that's ridiculous!* She flicked the thought away. Somers was a big account for her agency. She couldn't afford to screw this up.

After her ride, Jessica was about to pick up her saddle and bridle off the ground when a shadow passed across her face.

"Well, well. Fancy seeing you grace these pastures, Jessica Mason. What's it been? Twenty years?" Without looking up, somewhere in the back of her mind she knew that voice. She struggled to sift through her memories. That voice. Where did she know it from? It was a little deeper. Mature. Yet somehow so familiar.

Jessica glanced up. The bright midday sun silhouetted the figure before her eyes adjusted. The air shot out of her lungs. Her heart lurched. Her body trembled all over with shock. She dropped her riding gear and took a step backward. Was she seeing a ghost? What cruel trick was her mind playing?

Not overly tall, with a stocky frame, his skin was leathered by the sun. But the Akubra hat couldn't hide those eyes. Those stunning sapphire eyes were as blue as a cloudless summer's day. No one in the world had eyes like this. No one else but her son. Not even Nate's could compare. These had haunted her every day of her life.

"Troy?" The whispered name managed to slip past her lips, her throat too dry to make more of an audible sound. "Troy Smith?"

"Yes. It's me." He smiled. "What on earth are you doing here?"

"I come out here all the time for some R and R. But what are you doing here?" Jessica took another step back from him. Her heartbeat pounded and her head rattled like a roller-coaster.

"I started working here a few weeks ago."

"What?" Jessica gasped. She tried to move but her body was not responding. Troy, of all people, stood before her. Why him? Why?

"I've gotta go." Jessica dug down deep inside, pulling on all her inner strength to move. She grabbed her gear, pushed past him and headed to the barn.

"Wait. Do you want to catch up for a beer? For old time's sake?"

"Old times. Old times. You've got to be kidding, right?" Jessica tried to breathe normally. In. Out. In. Out. But her head was wheeling out of control.

"Jess?"

She could feel him watching her storm off. It made her quicken her pace.

The wind was picking up and storm clouds were starting to build in the west. She raced back to her cabin, packed her bags, threw them in her car and sped off, leaving a trail of dust behind her.

Halfway home, Jessica's hands shook as she searched on her phone for Max's number and hit the call button. "Max, code red, code red. Please don't ask any questions right now. Just please meet me at my house in an hour. I need to talk to you now more than ever. Shit. Shit. Shit," Jessica hollered down the Bluetooth phone connection. She raced toward the city, trying to beat the storm that looked like it was about to unleash its force upon the earth. Her body was still trembling. Her brain still trying to process who she'd just seen.

"Jess? What's happened? Is it Nate?"

"Worse than Nate. Please come over?"

"Jessica?" Max's voice was full of worry. "You're freaking me out. I'm on my way. See you soon."

* * *

At her house, Jessica's shaky hands managed to pour a full-bodied red wine into an oversized glass. With her fingers wrapped firmly around the glass, she nestled down onto the couch and watched the unsettled harbor waters in the distance. Wind rattled the windows and tossed trees viciously about as the late afternoon turned dark and gloomy. Rain began to splash down. She stared out the window at the drops as they picked up intensity and covered the ground.

So many questions bombarded her mind. Why? How? Troy was working at Gumtrees. What the …?

How could a few days unravel her perfect world? First Nate. Now Troy. Jessica never cried—not in years. Not even when her loveless marriage to Graeme ended. She excelled in her professional life because she kept her feelings under control. She was always so organized and meticulous in detail, but right now she felt like everything was falling apart.

Sex screwed up everything.

She was on her second glass when Max arrived.

Max threw her handbag and car keys on the granite benchtop in the kitchen. "What's happened?"

"You'd better grab a drink and sit down for this one. It's a real doozy."

"You betcha. I need it after a weekend of playing soccer mom and chauffeur." She poured a red, placed the bottle on the coffee table in front of them and, tucking her feet beneath her, joined Jessica on the couch. "Now, this has nothing to do with Nate?"

"No." Jessica drew the scent of the wine into every cell of her body in an attempt to find an inner calm. "Max, I have something to tell you that only a few people on the face of this planet know."

"Okay, now I'm intrigued." Max wriggled and sank further into the soft leather.

"I was out at Gumtrees and ran into someone from my past." She shook her head, still in disbelief. "It's like he's back from the dead. My old high school boyfriend … Troy Smith."

"Yeah, so?" Max's eyes looked vacant, then she gasped. "Oh, did you sleep with him too?"

"No." Jessica shot Maxine a horrified look. "Well yes—a very long time ago. Max, why did he have to come back after all this time? Why?" She snuffled and wiped a tear away from her cheek with the back of her hand.

"What's so wrong about running into an old ex? Are you still crazy about him after all this time?"

"No. It's so much more than that, Max. Troy ... Troy is Conner's father."

Chapter 5

"What the fuck?" Max spluttered, choking on a mouthful of her drink.

"Oh, I wish I was joking, but I'm not." Jessica looked vacantly off into the distance as she sipped on her drink. "Troy *is* Conner's father. I haven't seen him since high school in Cessnock. When he finished school, he wanted to travel overseas for a few months before going to university. The night before he left we didn't have a condom. I fell pregnant with Conner."

Jessica remembered the evening all too well, as though it were only yesterday. It was November, humid and still. Everyone had been complaining throughout the day, begging it to storm to relieve the heat that hung in the air. She'd been at Troy's for dinner and he was driving her home when they stopped at the park on the edge of town. Their favorite spot to make out had been underneath the protective curtain of the branches of a weeping willow tree that overlooked the old rusty playground. Of all nights not to have protection.

Max gasped in shock. It seemed her friend was lost for

words for the first time in her life.

Jessica's jaw tensed as she fought back tears. She'd been repressing this information for so long, she was finding it hard put the words right. "My parents were mortified. Being strict Catholics, abortion wasn't an option. They were so ashamed of me that they shipped me off to my aunt's in Melbourne so no one would know that their bright-eyed little girl had got knocked up."

Her mother cried for hours and her father wanted to hunt Troy down, castrate him, toss him in jail and throw away the key. Jessica wished he had—at least then she would've known where he was for the past twenty years.

"Dad transferred to Melbourne with the police force. I know they moved to avoid humiliation around town. Mom refused to let me be a teenage dropout and waste my life. She helped look after Conner while I finished high school and university. I'll be forever grateful to her as it got me to where I am today. Plus they love Conner to bits," Jessica said in their defense.

"Does Troy know?" Max asked.

Jessica hand trembled as she took a sip of her wine. "Yes. Though, it took me nearly three years to find him. When he left, he was supposed to only go on a holiday, but I got a postcard from him saying he was staying in the US and our relationship was over. Dumped by postcard. Who does that? That's like breaking up with someone via text message these days, isn't it? When I tried to contact his mom to get his details, she'd moved to God only knows where.

"Conner was three by the time I tracked Troy down through an old school friend. When I rang the ranch where Troy was working, a woman answered. She was rude. 'She didn't want me to call anymore. She was his new girlfriend, they were engaged and he wanted nothing to do with me. I didn't believe it at first, so I tried several more times and left message after message.

I sent him letters, photos and details of Conner. When I heard nothing in return, eventually I had to give up." Jessica felt the hurt wash over her as if the words were fresh in her ears. She had locked all this pain away for so long. One sighting of Troy had opened up old wounds.

Jessica shuddered as a loud bolt of lightning and thunder rumbled across the darkened sky. It added to the somber mood in the air.

"Geez, Jess, I never suspected that Graeme wasn't Conner's dad." Max shook her head. Disbelief written all over her face.

"Graeme loved Conner from day one." Jessica smiled, remembering back to university and what seemed a lifetime ago. Those first few years with Conner were tough. Her life was filled with nothing but him and study. She rarely went to parties or out with friends. Seeing Graeme on the bus and studying together was her only form of social life.

Conner needed a father and Graeme was kind, loving and had a decent family. "He was all I could ever want for Conner—a father who was going to be there for him. We married after university and moved back here for work when Conner was five. I made new friends and a new life. No one needed to know the finer details."

"How dare you keep a secret like this from me?" Max playfully punched Jessica in the arm.

"I'm so sorry I've never told you." Jessica let out a huge sigh of relief. Finally her best friend knew. "It's been one of the biggest hurdles to overcome and my motivation in establishing my career. I wanted to ensure people saw me as the best in my field—not the silly teenage girl who got pregnant.

"For years I have been heading out to Gumtrees. Troy's the last person I would have expected to turn up. And now he's working there?"

"What?" Max's eyes nearly popped out of her head. "Oh!

This just gets better. Your past has more twists in it than a French braid. What did you say to him?"

"Nothing. I flipped out. I ran off. Literally." Jessica had played out so many scenarios in her head on what she'd do and say if she ever saw him again. None of them came to fruition.

"I've never known you to walk away from anything." Max's eyes were full of concern as she looked at Jessica. "I think you need to talk to Troy. You've finally found him after all these years."

Jessica closed her eyes and bit down hard upon her lip. "I know. The thought of talking to him after all this time is just scaring the hell out of me. What do I say to someone who abandoned not only me but his son as well? I need to sort this mess out in my head, and then I suppose I'll have to arrange to go and see him."

Jessica looked down at her hands in her lap and twisted the throw rug that lay across her legs into knots. "Conner has his eyes, Max. Every day of his life I looked into them and saw Troy. And now he's back."

"Maybe he has a good explanation or excuse. I've heard a lot of them in my court cases." Max's eyes widened with intrigue and she jovially hit one of Jessica's throw cushions. "He might have come up with something new."

Jessica tried not to roll her eyes at Max's optimistic outlook on everything.

Max leaned over to the coffee table, grabbed the bottle of wine and refilled their glasses as the setting sun broke through the clearing storm clouds. Mist swirled across the icy harbor waters in the distance as the cold winter's night started to set in. Max finally knowing her secret felt like the weight of the world had been lifted from Jessica's shoulders. She inhaled deeply and took a long, soothing sip of her wine. Her phone vibrated on the coffee table. She picked it up and read the text message. It was from Nate.

When can I see you again? Dinner?

"Crap." Jessica's shoulders sank and she rubbed her forehead with her hand. She couldn't deal with him as well right now.

"What is it?" Max reached out and touched Jessica's leg.

Just when Jessica got her head above the water, something dragged her back down under. She'd never been like this ... all emotional, not knowing what to do.

"It's Nate. He wants to see me again."

"And?" Max grinned widely.

"I can't see him again. He's my client."

"Mr ComeFuckMe just sent you a text to see him and you're turning him down?"

"Don't call him that." Jessica couldn't help but smile at the vision of Nate in her mind. "But yes. I have to."

Max looked disappointed. "Well then, what are you going to do about Troy?"

"I don't know. Conner knows Graeme isn't his dad. We've always been honest with him. Conner's strong-willed and has never suffered any identity issues. Well, not that I know of."

Max took Jessica's hand and squeezed it tightly. "Conner is a grown man. He might want to meet Troy, knowing he's around. Plus, after all this time, Jess, don't you want to know where Troy's been and what happened?"

Chapter 6

Breathing deeply, Jessica tried to calm the uneasiness brewing in the pit of her stomach as she headed in to meet with Nate and his team. Surely she'd be able to find a quiet moment during a break or something to apologize to him. Then she'd be able to carry on with business as if nothing had happened. Holding her shoulders back, she said hello to everyone present and took her seat at the head of the table. Nate slid into the chair next to her. Jessica tried with all her might to refrain from looking at him and focus her attention on the other people in the room. Lin with news on sourcing international artists to perform as part of the entertainment; Matt with his round of new designs. And then there were her promotional schedules to present. But all the while she could feel the magnetic pull of Nate's eyes. She needed more distance away from him—feet, not inches. His smell and his presence made it hard not to fantasize. And even harder not to think about how good he looked in his charcoal suit, or how his sky-colored shirt made his eyes look even bluer. Oh, how she would like to tear off every layer of his clothing ...

"Jessica?" The sound of her name pulled her from her inappropriate thoughts.

"I'm sorry, what was the question?" She dropped her pen and looked around.

"I'd like to hear those new ideas of yours you mentioned last week," Nate said as he flipped through his documentation. "But first, can we take a quick ten-minute tea break? Those pastries Zoe brought in look delicious."

"Sure. That sounds good." Yes, tea was what she needed. Strong tea.

She finished writing down some notes from the meeting while the staff made drinks, grabbed some food and drifted to the far end of the room to stretch their legs.

Jessica stood to make her way over to the bench. "Would you like anything, Nate?"

"Tea, would be lovely. The stronger the better."

That'd be right! Yet another thing they had in common.

Jessica grabbed two bright orange Kick-logoed cups and searched through the tea box for her favorite flavor. She placed the bags in the mugs, poured in boiling water and waited for them to brew.

"I like mine white, one sugar," Nate whispered in her ear as he came up and stood behind her. Jessica jumped at his close proximity. His warm breath made the hairs on the back of her neck stand on end and goosebumps shoot down her arm. He was so close—barely an inch away from brushing up against her hip. She found it difficult to concentrate and her hands trembled as she scooped in the sugar and stirred in some milk.

"I apologize for not having any loose leaf tea today, but we've unfortunately run out. I'll send Zoe to the shops later."

"I'll forgive you just this once." He winked.

"Oh no, the tag fell off," she fretted as she fished around in his cup with a spoon trying to dish out the tea bag.

She looked up at Nate and saw concern drawn across his face.

"Is there something wrong?" she asked.

"No. It's nothing. Just a silly old superstition." He shrugged. "When the tag falls off, it's supposed to mean that you will lose something major within the next week."

"Well, as long it's not your business, I have nothing to fear." She tried to make light of his comment, but damn it, he'd planted a seed. Now she was going to worry endlessly about what could possibly happen over the next seven days.

"Well, you can rest easy. I'm not going anywhere," said Nate.

"Good." She took a sip of her tea. "Are you generally superstitious?"

"My grandmother was. She was convinced one's whole life could be determined by making a pot of tea and by tasseography, the reading of the leaves in the bottom of the cup."

He sounded so genuine that Jessica wondered whether the man before her was sane or not, as she placed her empty cup on the tray. Everyone had their own quirks, well, this was obviously Nate's.

"So do you believe in them?" she asked.

"I'm trying not to." He smiled as he drained his cup.

"Here, let me take that for you."

As she reached for his cup, her fingers softly swept over his, sending a sizzling sensation up her arm and down her spine. Her eyes turned sharply toward his. She tried to open her mouth to speak, but words failed her. His stance straightened as he quickly pulled his hand away, turned and went back to the table.

Jessica faced the bench to make herself another drink. Her head was reeling. Nate was making her lose her mind. *I can't work like this. I can't think straight around him.* So much for pretending nothing had happened. It was clearly not working.

She would have to talk to Alex about swapping accounts before she did something else she'd regret. Surely Alex would understand.

* * *

"Jess, are you up for lunch?" Nate asked as the meeting concluded. He needed the chance to apologize for his behavior the other night. Was she just going to ignore what happened?

"Sorry, I have a client meeting with Audi."

"No we don't," Darren interjected. "It's not until tomorrow."

Nate hid his smile as he saw Jessica flare her eyes in Darren's direction. "Lunch it is then."

"Right." She hesitated, looking anxious. "Well then, I'll just be a moment and grab my handbag."

Nate stood with his hands in his pockets while he waited for her in the reception area. What was taking her so long?

Sleeping with Jessica had been at the forefront of his mind ever since it happened. In a moment of madness, he'd thought his simple plan to sleep with her would make all these crazy feelings disappear. But he hadn't been prepared for her to respond to him the way she did. It was like nothing he had ever experienced before. It made his mind spin like a roulette wheel. Bet on black—he'd put the incident out of his mind and act like the consummate gentleman. Bet on red—he'd strip her down and do it again. He jumped between the two every split second, unable to decide where to place his bet.

But the right thing to do was apologize for his unprofessional behavior. No more flirting. No more meetings in his apartment. Go on as if it didn't happen. Too much wine was surely the cause behind their undoing the other night. It was best that this all be put behind them so they could continue working together.

That's what the guardian angel sitting on one shoulder said. But the devil on the other was hard to ignore.

The very thought of not having Jessica in his bed again made him restless. He had been seduced from her very first touch. He hated this sensation of being preoccupied by a woman. But she had his blood swirling like a cauldron on fire. No other woman he'd ever been with held a candle to the way she'd turned him on. The mere thought of her naked skin beneath him made his body react. His dick started to bulge in his trousers from just thinking about her. *Jesus.* Embarrassed, he spun away from the girl sitting at the reception desk as he tried to deal with his predicament.

Then Jessica entered the foyer. Her golden hair was striking against her black suit. He admired her sexy legs that he knew were long enough to tie themselves in knots around his waist. And in those four-inch high heels she was equal to his height— he liked that. Arousing images of her naked body filled his mind again as she walked toward him. He watched her gaze drop to his feet and slowly run up over his body. Her lips parted just a fraction as she momentarily paused at his groin. That only made his body respond even more. He clenched his teeth as subtly as he could. He had to get his body under control. Somehow.

"Shall we?" Nate pointed to the elevator.

* * *

They made their way down to the cafe restaurant on the ground floor of the building, taking a booth toward the back. Jessica ordered a light salad and Nate the creamy beef and asparagus risotto. Their meals arrived quickly and Jessica toyed with the lettuce leaves on her plate.

"Jess, I think we need to clear the air about what happened the other night." Nate wiped his hands on his napkin.

"About that ... I haven't had time to call. I sent you a text because I was busy. Did you have Brooke send the flowers?"

"No. I sent them." Oh—she could be harsh. She'd driven a

knife right through the center of his ego.

Her eyebrows rose. Was she questioning his sincerity? He'd never get Brooke to send flowers on his behalf.

"Look, what happened the other night was a mistake," she said. "It shouldn't have happened. It was very unprofessional of me. I swear I've never done anything like that before, and it won't happen again."

The tension in Nate's shoulders disappeared. Relief washed over him knowing that she felt the same way. This was just a moment of craziness they could both put behind them. "I also want to apologize for being so bold. While we were both consenting on the night, I agree with you entirely about the unethical behavior on both our parts." He paused. "But I certainly don't apologize for the phenomenal sex."

Jessica stared down at the table and fumbled with her water glass. "Believe me, I didn't know I had it in me," she said. "I think it's best if I talk to Alex and see if he can take over your account so we don't have any further issues." Her eyes looked full of disappointment.

"No. That won't be necessary. I'm sure we'll be able to control ourselves." He would do anything to avoid gossip and scandal; his father had caused enough of that for the business. Nate couldn't risk losing suppliers, or the financial backing of sponsors for the launch.

As he watched Jessica across the table, however, all his rational thought started to trickle down the drain. Her smile captivated him; her deep brown eyes hypnotized him. He sighed as the blood rushed from his brain to his groin again. So much for wanting to forget about having had sex with her. So much for not wanting more of it.

"Well you can be assured, it won't happen again," Jessica replied in all seriousness. "My work is my life. I will not jeopardize your launch, so let's keep our relationship strictly above the table—not on it. If you want me on the account, that's the way it has to be. There will be no more escapades."

He had to agree. While she'd been the first woman to grab his undivided attention in such a long time, it was for the best. He didn't need any complications.

"Why don't we change the subject?" Jessica suggested. "Let's discuss next week's Melbourne PR trip in more detail." She leaned back against the seat and folded her arms. "Zoe and Brooke have booked all the accommodation and flights and I'll have the week's schedule of TV, print and radio interviews ready on Friday afternoon."

As he listened to her from across the table he only had one subject on his mind, and it had nothing to do with work. He wanted to crawl over the tabletop and have his way with her, feel her underneath him again. What had she done to him?

But no. He'd respect her wishes. Somehow he'd get himself under control so they could continue to work together.

"Please be assured that I'm happy to work in with whatever you've organized on such short notice," said Nate. "So, now let's put our little encounter behind us and look forward to the next few months. Can I buy you a drink as a means to a new start?"

"Alcohol and us is a bad combination. So unless there's anything else you need to discuss, I think we're done." Jessica wiped the corners of her mouth on her napkin and grabbed her handbag. "I have a huge hotel launch and promotions campaign to work on before my client kicks my ass."

* * *

Jessica was beyond frazzled when she returned to her office. She pulled at the collar on her knit top; it felt uncomfortably tight and hot. Nate's admission that the sex they'd had was phenomenal had set her pulse racing at lightning speed. In fact, his whole presence excited her. His velvet voice. His charisma.

His kiss had sparked a long-dormant flame back to life.

Nate, however, was only in the country for a few months and then he'd be gone. She couldn't risk her work or her heart for him. Her mind wandered back to last Thursday evening. Their crazy, hot sex had been so damn good. Her body temperature started to rise just thinking about it. She closed her eyes and furrowed her eyebrows as she tried to clear her thoughts. She controlled everything in her life—surely she could control herself around Nate Somers.

Goddamn it! Jessica grabbed her handbag and jacket and swept by Zoe's desk on her way out. "Something urgent has come up. I'll be back in time for my four o'clock meeting." Without breaking her stride, she walked out of the office. With Nate on her mind she was not thinking straight.

Jessica clenched her hands tightly around the steering wheel as she pulled into the visitors' car park at Somers Residential Towers. After a quick check of her lipstick and hair in the rearview mirror, she dashed from the car and into the foyer.

"Nate Somers, please," Jessica asked Amy, the receptionist at the counter.

"Yes, Ms Mason. He just went up to his apartment. I'll ring through for him."

Before Jessica had time to gather her senses, Amy gave her the all clear to head on up.

"Thanks." She walked over to the elevator and stepped inside. She leaned her head back against the wall as it ascended, closing her eyes in an effort to find some clarity. But there was none. She was out of her mind. What on earth was she doing?

When the elevator doors opened on Nate's floor, her feet somehow carried her up the hall to his apartment. She hesitated before knocking. The few seconds it took for him to reach the door seemed to drag on endlessly. But then it opened, and his eyes locked on to hers.

He cocked one eyebrow at the sight of her. "It's been so long, Ms Mason. Forty-five minutes to be exact. I didn't know we had a meeting planned for this afternoon?" A smile touched the corner of his lips.

"Are you alone?"

"Yes."

Before Nate could utter another word, Jessica placed both her hands on his chest and pushed him hard, back into his apartment, swinging the door shut behind her. He backed into the wall behind him as her lips found his without a moment to waste.

Her bag fell to the floor with a soft thud. Heat surged up between their bodies like lava up the chute of a volcano. Their mouths were desperate to taste each other as his hands knotted into her hair, drawing her closer to his chest.

Without breaking their kiss, they stumbled their way into the dining area. Jessica felt the table press up behind her. Nate shoved a pile of papers out of the way and grabbed her hips, picked her up and slid her onto the surface of the table. Jessica arched into his touch and her heartbeat escalated even further as his fingers ran over her breast. She felt her hardening nipples strain against the fabric of her bra. He grabbed the lapels of her jacket, slipped it off her shoulders and flung it onto the floor in a heap.

How could years of professional conduct be vaporized in the presence of this man? She had used up all her willpower trying to cover up her burning desire for him. All through lunch she'd sat listening to him, wanting to throw herself over the table and do him right then and there. Now he had her on his table doing her just as she had fantasized.

"God. Do you know how much I want you?" he whispered as he nuzzled into the base of her neck. The spicy scent of his cologne filled her senses as he kissed his way frantically back to her mouth.

Jessica yanked off his tie and hastily unbuttoned his shirt so she could run her nails across his bare skin, feel his muscles tense beneath her fingertips.

Sliding his hands up her slender thighs, Nate drew her skirt up to her hips, squeezing her buttocks when he reached the top. She needed no encouragement to part her legs even further as Nate pushed his hips into hers. His erection was hard and bulged within his trousers. At the feel of his body against hers, Jessica's muscles tightened, begging for more of his touch. Her hands found his belt and opened his pants, ripped down his trunks and rubbed her hand along his firmness. Nate groaned deeply as he grabbed the edge of her panties and slid them from her legs.

The black glass of the table felt cool against her bare skin as Nate's fingers trailed back up along her thighs and settled between her legs. Her skin blazed with fire under his touch. She was already aroused. Wet and ready for him. At the murmur rolling deep in his throat, she knew he liked what he felt as he fingered her deep inside. One finger. Two fingers. *Oh God, yes.*

Her hips started to rock in time with his motions. Her breaths came shorter and faster. Just as she was on the edge of exploding, Nate reached for his wallet on the table behind her, ripped out a condom, tore the packet open and rolled it on his stiff erection. His lips locked with hers again as he pulled her hips forward on the table.

Then he plunged inside sending a shockwave of tingles up her spine.

Again, Nate thrust into her, his buttocks flexing hard underneath her hands as he buried himself deeper inside. Jessica gasped breathlessly and wrapped her legs tightly around his waist as he hammered into her, sending pure ecstasy curling through her entire body.

He slid one hand down between them and rubbed against her clitoris. His firm fingertips worked their wonder on her arousal, leaving her at the mercy of his touch. His relentless thrusts sending her to the point of no return.

"Ah!" Jessica cried out as her orgasm ripped through her body. Her heartbeat hammered in her chest as the want for him had finally been met. Every inch of him fit into her effortlessly, filling her up. This was insane. Hot. Oh ... and just what she needed.

"Oh, Jess," Nate groaned as he came. Jessica clenched her thighs around him tightly, savoring the feel of him inside her.

It took a moment for her to catch her breath. Nate held her against his chest and she could feel his heart racing. He chuckled as he looked down at her. "I thought you were adamant about keeping our relationship strictly professional."

"I might have to change professions," Jessica said matter-of-factly.

Nate smiled as he released her from his arms. "I'm glad you changed your mind about the sex thing. I hate to admit it but I was suffering under duress."

Jessica shuffled off the table onto wobbly legs. Yes—she certainly felt like she'd been fucked.

"Do you have to go back to the office?" he said as he pulled his pants up and buckled his belt.

"Yes, I have a four o'clock." She realigned her skirt and looked around for her panties.

"Cancel it."

"No, I have to get back."

"How about a cup of tea before you leave?" he asked as he slipped on his shirt.

"Look, I think I should go. Let's not make this complicated, okay? It'll make it easier on both of us."

"So was this just '*once more*' or is this going to be a regular occurrence, Ms Mason?" He smiled at her, making her legs feel unsteady at the seductive sight of him. How could she have sex with a man and not get involved? Could she do it? Max assured her it was possible.

"Nate, I'm not sure what to make of it. Maybe I should get Alex to look after your launch."

"I don't want to work with Alex. I want to work with you."

"But we can't go on like this. You're my client. I can't be involved with you; it'll make working together uncomfortable ... well more than it already is. I don't need my staff getting suspicious, and I don't want emotions to get in the way of decisions that need to be made."

"Me either. But, I find it very difficult to keep my hands off of you."

She sighed because she had to agree. Something inexplicable attracted her to him.

"So what do you propose we do?" she asked as she slipped on her stiletto pumps.

He stood in front of her, his eyes zeroing in on to hers as he tucked her hair behind her ears.

"We either have to stop this, or ... I'm only here for a few months." His words full of suggestive connotations.

She gasped. Was she drawing to the correct conclusion?

"You really want to have an affair? With me? She blushed at the notion.

Nate's subtle nod and sparkle in his eye sent her head into a spin.

"Nate, I've never done the casual thing. You're only here for a while and neither one of us wants to risk getting hurt. I'm sure you agree."

"Wholeheartedly." He hesitated as if deliberating on many ideas before his expression turned serious. "Let's consider this like any other business proposition ... a negotiation if you will. If we agree, great. If not, we'll have to find some way that we can work together. Okay?"

Jessica couldn't believe her ears. But more shocking, was that she was contemplating the whole idea. "Okay."

"If we continue to see each other, my number one priority would be discretion." Nate said as he put on his jacket. "I'm sure you can appreciate where I'm coming from considering recent events surrounding my father. Unfortunately there are people out there, like those at the gossip magazines, who think my life is interesting, so the paparazzi often hang around when I attend functions."

She nodded in agreement because she didn't want to be front page news for the wrong reasons. "Discretion is a must." She paused, wondered what on earth she was doing discussing terms of having an affair with this man. It was such a crazy concept. "And I don't need any gray areas, so let's keep the intimacy out of it—no staying the night, romantic dates or weekends together." Jessica looked at him anxiously. She didn't really know what she was saying, but anything to protect her heart from being hurt when he left.

"I'm not opposed to that idea." His fingers fumbled nervously with her collar. "So where? ... How often, do you think?"

She tried not to laugh as Nate's stumbled over his questions as she straightened and tucked her shirt into her skirt.

"Um, I'm not sure." She grinned softly at him. "I'll have to check my calendar and see when I can schedule you in. I work most weekends, late nights, and I start early."

"Me too." A cheeky grin touched the corner of his mouth. "But I'm sure we'll be able to find some time here and there."

His eyes blazed with heat as he looked over her body. He swept in close, wrapping his arms around her waist as he pressed himself firmly up against her. And then he kissed her.

His mouth molded to hers perfectly; the taste of his tongue was delicious and made her head spin. She could easily opt for another round ... but no, she had a meeting to get attend.

"So is this what I think it is?" She rested her hands upon his chest. "Sex, with no strings attached?" Jessica could barely believe the words as they left her mouth.

"I do like the sound of your proposition, Ms Mason. And believe me, I will be looking forward to our next encounter." His eyes shone with mischief as his gaze dropped to her cleavage.

"I have to go or I'll be late for my meeting."

"Okay, I won't keep you any longer," Nate relented. "Why don't you come with me to Melbourne next week?"

"I can't." She managed to wriggle free of his hold. "I have some other business to attend to."

"Other business? I thought I was your first priority at the moment." He smirked as he straightened his tie.

"Your hotel launch is. This other business is personal, so please don't ask."

"Oh. Sounds serious."

"Baggage. That's all."

"Are we talking walk-on or trunk cases?"

"Trunk cases."

"And that's what's dragging you away from my business?"

"You don't let up, do you?" Jessica was hesitant about revealing too much personal information. Would it matter if he knew about her past? She had felt so much better after telling Max and being freed from the burden she'd carried for so long.

Nate stood there waiting for her to speak.

She exhaled. "I have a meeting with the father of my son." Jessica tried to sound nonchalant about the whole situation and act like it wasn't bothering her, but on the inside she was a quaking mess.

"You're meeting with your ex-husband? Why is that so

important?" Nate creased his forehead.

"What? No. Not Graeme. Conner's biological father's name is Troy. We were never married. I haven't seen this guy for twenty years. I'm not particularly looking forward to it either. But please be assured, my personal life never affects my work. The two are entirely separate—no fuzzy gray areas."

"Fair enough."

She smiled gratefully as Nate walked her to the door.

He opened it and leaned against the doorjamb. "So I guess I'll see you after Melbourne."

"Until we meet again." Jessica nudged past him and made her way to the elevator. She glanced back over her shoulder. Nate's eyes still blazed with desire as he watched her. It made it hard to resist the temptation to return to his arms.

The elevator arrived; she stepped in and the doors closed behind her.

She stared at nothing as their proposition replayed through her mind.

Oh God! What had she got herself into?

Chapter 7

Bitter winter blanketed everything with frost. Thick fog hung low and snaked along the rolling valleys. It was midmorning when Jessica pulled up her black Audi outside the homestead at Gumtrees Winery. Wrapping her woolen coat and scarf tightly around her neck and shoulders, she stepped out into the crisp mountain air. The smell of burning timber and the sight of smoke curling out of the cabin chimneys were easy reminders of why she loved coming here—to relax and unwind. However, this time was different. She took a deep breath and prayed that once she lit the fire inside the cabin, the twisting knots of nausea inside her stomach would disappear.

"Hey!" Nick came out of the office to greet her, key in hand. "Good to see you again."

"How's things?" Jessica hid her feelings behind a warm smile.

"Good. Busy," Nick said as he gave her the key, then rubbed his hands together to ward off the cold. "Both the guestrooms and the cabins are filled with couples wanting dirty weekends away. It's great—they all buy food and lots of booze from the restaurant and cellar door, and I hardly see them at all. It makes my life easy." Nick's breath misted in the cold air as he spoke. "You're lucky we had a cancellation to fit you in. So what brings you back to this neck of the woods so quickly?"

Jessica looked around nervously and scuffed her Ugg boot against the gravel on the ground. "I'm here to see Troy. Marie said he'd be here."

"He had to go over to the Finlay's farm to help fix a tractor. I don't know when he'll be back."

"Oh. Okay."

Jessica glared at Nick. She could see his eyes were full of suspicion and curiosity. "Don't look at me like that, Nick. Troy and I go a long way back. We went to high school together and I just want to catch up."

"I know. He told me. I'm only looking out for you." Nick smiled innocently as he picked up Jessica's bag and walked with her to the cabin. "Well, I'll leave you to it. I have to go and bring up some more firewood for the cabins. Catch you later." Nick strode off toward the sheds, whistling as he went.

* * *

In the evening, Jessica couldn't wait for Troy to return any longer. Her belly was grumbling with hunger and she didn't want to stay in her cabin and think about all the other loved up neighboring couples. So she headed off to have dinner at Harrigan's, the only pub in the district. She bound up the steps and into the restaurant shortly after eight o'clock. The log fire in its hearth burned brightly, sending warmth across the room and making the stone-walled venue feel cozy and inviting. Music from the band drowned out the sound of the football screening on several televisions mounted from the ceiling. The smell of beer intermingled with the aroma of roasting dinners wafting from the kitchen made Jessica's mouth water. She found a spare table, then ordered a steak and a nice glass of local red wine.

The meal was filling, and she was about to swig down the last mouthful of her wine when she saw Troy walk through the door. Her grip tightened around the thin stem of her glass. *Goddamnit!* She didn't want to meet him here. She wasn't sure if she could keep her mammoth load of emotions under control in public.

But then again, maybe a chat over a drink would help keep her calm, and be a good way to confront him once and for all.

Troy lumbered over to the bar and leaned on it, resting one boot on the foot rail. He was wrapped up in his moleskin coat, faded blue jeans snugged firmly around his sturdy legs. He ordered a drink and took a few sips of his beer as he talked to the barman. Jessica watched him as he slowly turned around and surveyed the pub. Then his eyes found her.

His face lit up at the sight of her and he made his way over to her table. "Hi. I'm surprised to see you here. May I join you for a drink, or are you going to run away on me again?"

Jessica sneered at him. *Remember—I'm here to talk to him.* "No. I'm not going to run away." Another drink might take the edge off everything that was bottled up inside.

"What can I get you?"

"Shiraz, please."

Her eyes followed him as he went to the bar and bought her a glass of wine, and then returned to the table. His appearance hadn't changed much in twenty years, was just a little more weathered, with creases touching the corners of his eyes. But Jessica couldn't stop herself from scrutinizing his every move. Would he show any remorse for what he'd done to her?

"Jess, you look amazing," said Troy, after he'd sat down. "Still beautiful, even though twenty years has passed under our belts. Even if the ol' belt is a few notches wider—on mine anyway." He chuckled as he pulled his chair in closer to the table. "So, give me the speed dating version, what's been happening for the past twenty years?"

Jessica was startled by his approach. But that was the Troy she remembered. *Just give me the facts, not the bullshit.* Okay, if that was how he wanted to play, she'd go along with it for now.

"I run a marketing and events management company in Sydney," she began. "I was married, but that ended about two years ago. And of course, I have one child ..." She paused, waiting to gauge Troy's reaction.

Nothing.

Troy seemed undeterred. "Wow. Me—I've been in the States until about six months ago. I was married and lived in Texas for ten years. My last stint was in the Napa Valley before finally deciding to come back home."

Jessica took in what he was saying. But with every word, she felt her eyes narrow into tiny slits. She wished they were daggers. Her throat started to burn as she withheld a scream. How could he be so heartless and not ask about his son? Had he forgotten? How could he be such an asshole?

The music changed to an old time classic, 'Love Is All Around Us' by Wet Wet Wet. A couple of locals swayed in time on the small dance floor.

Troy smiled. "Do you remember this song from high school? It was such a hit. Come and have a dance for old times' sake." He held out his hand.

Jessica stared at him in disbelief. Was he for real? Troy ignored her shock. He hooked his palm underneath her arm and dragged her to the floor. He swung her around effortlessly and then held her gently in his strong arms. She couldn't believe she allowed him to do this without causing a scene. But then he looked into her eyes. The pain that swelled in her chest was almost too hard to bear.

"Jess, it's been so long. Of all the places on the planet, I run into you at Gumtrees."

"Of all places." She barely managed a whisper. The bewilderment she felt with Troy standing here before her started to crack through her tough exterior. She felt a tear fall from the corner of her eye.

"Jess, what's wrong?"

"I ... I can't do this." She was at breaking point. "I can't be all nice and pretend as if nothing happened. I gotta get out of here." She turned on her heels, grabbed her bag from the chair and ran as fast as her legs could carry her out through the door.

She sprinted across the bitumen parking lot. Her hands trembled uncontrollably—in fact her whole body did as she tried to find the car keys deep in her jacket pocket. The cold night air stung against her face and her fingers would not cooperate. Tears rolled down her face and her breath misted in the air. She wanted to get away from here as soon as possible. *Come on, Goddamn it!* She cursed as the keys caught on threads.

Troy raced out the pub door a few seconds behind her. "Jess? Did I do something wrong? What's going on?"

"Everything's wrong. You're wrong, you heartless son of a bitch. Even after all this time you don't care," she cried.

"About what?" He raked his hands through his sandy blond hair. "Is this about us twenty years ago? I didn't know you felt so strongly about me back then. You were only sixteen. Things changed so much when I went overseas."

"This isn't about me, you fool," Jessica blurted. "I can't believe you don't even have the common courtesy to ask how he is or how he's doing. What is with you? Do you have no soul?" Her blood boiled in her veins as she tried to control her anger.

"Jess, you're sounding like a crazy person. What are you talking about?" He held his palms out as if in surrender.

"Conner."

"Who's Conner?" Troy asked, exasperated.

Jessica gasped in disbelief. Pain stabbed her chest like he was ripping her heart out with his bare hands. "Conner. My son ... Your son ... Our son."

Troy stopped in his tracks as if struck by a taser. He stumbled and took a step back, leaning on the car next to him to steady himself. The color appeared to drain away from his face. "What are you talking about?"

"Conner," Jessica said plainly. "I just want to know why you never came back? Why you never had the decency to even call me?"

"Jess, this doesn't make sense. Is this some kind of sick joke?"

"How could I joke about something like this? Conner was born nine months after you left."

Troy ran his hands across his face. "I didn't know."

"But ... I sent letters. So many letters. What happened to them?" She could see the anguish in his eyes as his shoulders slouched.

"Nicola. I can only assume my wife back then, hid, or more likely destroyed them. I never found anything like that in her belongings. Jess, she wasn't well. It took a long time for her family and I to realize she suffered from mental illness."

Jessica had not expected this at all. She was finding it hard to fathom. She'd thought he was a cold-hearted prick for so long. Now, to be standing in front of him as he heard the news for the first time had her mind wheeling out of control. It was gut-wrenching to see Troy crumbling to pieces before her.

Troy had tears in his eyes as he stepped closer and hugged her tightly. Jessica was dumbfounded and stood there frozen, unable to hug him in return. This was not how she had envisioned this reunion.

He took a step back and wiped his eyes on the sleeve of his coat. "Jess ... all this time. I ... I have a son ...? With you?"

She clenched her arms around herself and looked away from him to avoid his eyes. Those eyes.

"Yes you do. I know there are so many questions and things to discuss, but I'm exhausted. It's late and I'm freezing cold. Can we please call it a night and talk in the morning over breakfast?" She needed a breather. A timeout to process everything.

"But I need to know everything."

The desperation in his tone was tearing at her heart.

"And you will. But please, let's talk tomorrow."

Troy didn't look too happy with the idea but nodded in agreement. "Okay. Will you come to the restaurant 'round seven o'clock?"

"Sure. See you then." She turned and hopped into her car. She forced a smile at him and drove off, leaving Troy standing shell-shocked in the center of the parking lot.

She'd dropped a bomb of information on him, now she had to prepare for the aftermath.

* * *

Jessica woke after another restless night's sleep. The look on Troy's face when she'd told him haunted her all night. *He didn't know about Conner? Even after all her efforts?* She dressed and headed across the driveway toward the restaurant. She looked out over the valley where the fog hung low. The sky was the color of lead and the blackened vine tendrils spread out across the hills, giving a sad, gloomy feel to the morning. It matched Jessica's mood perfectly.

Quickening her pace to get out of the cold, she walked up the steps into the dining area. The place was vacant except for Troy sitting at a table by the window with tea in hand, staring out across the paddocks.

"Morning," Jessica said quietly so as not to startle him.

"Hey." He stood and pulled out a chair for her. "What can I

get you? Coffee, tea, food?"

"Tea to start with. White please. And what's Marie cooking this morning? Bacon and eggs would be good."

Troy walked out to the kitchen to confer with Marie. He returned with an oversized red mug. Steam rose from it and the aroma of tea filled the air. As he sat, Jessica noticed his eyes were red. It looked like he hadn't slept at all last night.

"So, how're you doing?" Jessica asked as she slowly stirred her tea.

"I don't know where to begin." Troy's shoulders hung low as he slouched over his own mug. "It's like I'm in some sort of surreal dream. Here I was expecting to have a catch up over a drink and reminisce about the good old days of high school, not find out I had a son."

"I still can't comprehend that you didn't know about Conner."

Troy winced. "The letters you say you sent, I'm convinced Nicola would have done everything possible to get rid of them. Maybe she read them and knew about Conner. She always threatened to hurt herself if I left. At first, when I met her, I thought it was a joke—part of her quirky humor, but then it got serious when she started self-harming. I can only imagine how intimidated she was by my ex-girlfriend back home."

Well, I wasn't your ex when you left, Jessica thought. But she could see the pain in Troy's eyes as he talked about his wife. "I'm sorry to hear she wasn't well."

"I remember when I left I got so wrapped up in the excitement of traveling. I met Nicola on New Year's and everything changed. I fell for her straight away. I wound up at her parents' cattle ranch and picked up work. I married her when I was twenty-one and we had a few good years before she grew more unstable." He paused and looked away like he was struggling with his memories. "She died in a car crash one day on her way into town. I'm still not convinced it was an accident."

Whoa! Jessica stopped with her tea halfway to her lips. She wasn't expecting Nicola to be dead. Locked away in a mental institution maybe, but not dead.

"When was the accident?"

"Just over six years ago."

"Do you have any children?"

Troy shook his head. "No. She never wanted kids." Jessica watched him closely as he sipped his drink. "After she died, I wanted to come home. It just took a lot longer than I thought. Mom had moved to Newcastle shortly after I left, but she died from ovarian cancer when I was twenty-six."

Jessica felt her heart lurch painfully within her chest. She'd really liked his mom. She was a dedicated nurse, she did yoga before yoga was cool and she never seemed worried about not having a man in her life.

Troy moved around, looking uncomfortable in his chair. "Did ... did she know? About Conner?"

Jessica shook her head and explained the whole fiasco of her parents moving her to Melbourne and how hard it had been trying to track him down.

Marie interrupted their conversation when she brought out plates of steaming hot food. She gave them both warm smiles and left quickly back for the kitchen.

"Conner. Please tell me about him?" Troy pleaded.

Jessica took a mouthful of scrambled eggs, not really knowing where to begin. "He was born on July twenty-fifth and turns twenty next month. He likes his sport. He was good at school and loves the outdoors." It dawned on Jessica just how similar Conner was to Troy in his younger days. "He's now studying architecture at university and lives with a friend near campus."

Jessica took a moment to butter her toast. What else should

she tell Troy? Should she talk about the good times—Conner's first steps, school days, holidays or birthdays? What about the bad times—not knowing where Troy was, the tantrums Conner could throw when he was young, or how he hated to eat pumpkin? She took a bite of her toast as she sifted through the thousands of stories rattling around inside her head.

"Conner was a good kid," she said when she'd finished her mouthful. "And I think he's grown up to be a decent young man. Graeme, my ex, was a great father and still is. Troy, you have to understand, I thought you left me and wanted nothing to do with Conner. He's never wanted to know you, or find you, for that matter."

"I realize I can't turn back the clock, but I never would have left you and our son if I'd known. Things would've been so different."

"Yeah, well they aren't." The memory of the two of them doing it in the park the night before he left flashed through Jessica's mind. All so long ago. "You broke my heart. I never thought it would heal. But it did with time."

"I'm sorry. Believe me. I'll never be able to forgive myself for not contacting you. I feel worse than shit, Jess."

"You look it, too."

"Thanks for that." He smirked. "Do you have a photo of him? Of Conner?"

Jessica pulled out her phone from her jacket pocket and scrolled through her photos. "Here. This is Conner at Easter time with his girlfriend, Becky."

Troy held the phone in his hands and a tear escaped from his eye. He quickly wiped it away.

"He has your eyes, Troy," she said. "Every day of my life I thought of you and couldn't understand how you could not want to be part of his life. He's such a wonderful kid."

Troy straightened his shoulders and looked directly into

her eyes. "When can I meet him?"

"I don't know. I'll have to talk to him—"

"I'd appreciate that. God, Jess! I want to meet my son."

Chapter 8

On the long drive back to the city, Jessica's fingers tapped nervously on the steering wheel while she processed her thoughts. How the hell was she supposed to tell Conner? How did one approach such a conversation?

Hey Conner, your dad's turned up out of the blue.

Conner, your biological father wants to meet you.

Hey—you wouldn't believe it, but guess who I ran into today?

All of them sounded crazy. The very essence of it all still shocked her to the bone.

Jessica couldn't delay the inevitable any longer. Her fingers shook as she found Conner's number on her phone and hit dial on the Bluetooth connection.

"S'up," Conner said as he answered the phone.

"Hey." Jessica felt a cold sweat break out on her brow. "How's my boy doing?"

"Studying hard. Two more exams to go until the midyear break," Conner mumbled.

Jessica could hear a crunching noise through the line,

like he was munching on potato chips. Music was playing in the background and several loud voices were shrieking with excitement. It didn't sound like much studying was getting done. She smiled to herself, secretly glad her son was having fun with friends. She had missed out on all the young adult years of going out, drinking and attending football games. Rather than going to friends' parties, she'd fed her baby his bottles and changed his diapers.

"I need to talk to you about something important that's come up," she said. "It's urgent. Can I swing on by your apartment?" She struggled to keep her voice steady.

"Um, now?" Conner hesitated. "Can I meet you somewhere instead? How about at Pepe's Pizza on the corner for dinner? It's just that ... the apartment's a mess."

"Studying, right?" Jessica knew perfectly well that his mates were over drinking and watching football. "No worries, I'll meet you there in an hour."

* * *

Pepe's Pizza was warm and inviting on a cold Sunday evening. Half of the restaurant was full of families having early dinners with their young children. Italian opera music hummed from the sound system a little too loudly for Jessica's liking. She realized she was famished as the aromas of garlic, parmesan and pepperoni wafted from the wood-fire ovens. She took a seat near the window at a table covered in a red-and-white checked tablecloth. She'd started to check her emails and messages on her phone when she looked up and saw Conner bounding through the door.

Jessica couldn't help but admire how handsome her son was. She even noticed a group of teenage girls at a table gawk and giggle at seeing him. His bronzed skin set off his amazing blue eyes—just like his father's. He dressed well, compared with many of his friends, looking quite the catch in designer jeans and woolen sweater. After spending time with Troy this weekend, she was astounded by how much Conner resembled his father.

"Hey, Mom." He leaned down and kissed her on the cheek before flopping into the chair across from her. "S'up?"

Jessica swallowed hard. Her mouth felt dry. "Let's order first, hey?"

They ordered pizza and a couple of beers. Conner rambled on with news about university, sport and outings with Becky and his friends. Jessica listened as best as she could but her mind was on other matters.

"So, what's so urgent that you had to see me?" he asked.

She flipped her phone round and round in her hand as she pondered how best to approach the daunting subject. But there was no point in dancing around it any more. "I have some news about your father."

"Why? What's happened? Is everything all right?" Conner looked at her with concern.

"Not Graeme. Your biological father, Troy. I know where he is." She held her breath.

Silence dropped like a weighted lead balloon between them. For ages he sat there staring vacantly at a spot on the table, his only movement was the furrowing of his eyebrows and the odd twitch of a muscle in his jaw. Jessica's heart thundered in her chest as she let him absorb her words. All she wanted to do was reach out and hold him and tell him that everything was going to be okay.

Conner grabbed a table napkin and twisted it into tight knots. "I don't want to know anything about him. He left."

"Conner, please?"

He slumped back on his chair and blew a puff of air at the blond hair that had fallen across his eyes. She could see so many emotions playing across his face. Rage, anger, hurt, shock—all of the same things she had experienced.

"You're not going to believe this, but he's only recently got back from America and started working at Gumtrees. I've just come from there after we talked." She braced herself for the next reveal. "Conner, he didn't know about you. He never knew you existed—even after all the efforts I made."

Shock flashed across his eyes, filling her heart with sorrow.

"I don't care. I already have a father," Conner snapped, and his eyebrows furrowed more deeply. She could see the pain in her son's eyes.

"I know it's a lot to take on board. I'm still trying to comprehend it as well."

He shrugged. "I don't care where he's been or what he's been doing. It doesn't change anything. I don't need him. Graeme's my dad. I don't want to have anything to do with Troy."

Deep down Jessica knew curiosity about his biological father would get to him eventually. He just needed time to absorb it all. "I know. Please take some time to think about it because Troy really wants to meet you."

Conner's back straightened as he sucked in a sharp breath. "What? I don't want to meet him."

"Please. Just have one meeting with him. Then you can decide whether or not you want to continue to get to know him," she went on. "He doesn't have any other kids, and I don't think I'll be able to keep him away from you for very long now that he knows."

Jessica heard Conner mumble some profanities as she took a sip of her beer.

"I'm not making any promises." He crossed his arms in front of his chest.

The waiter appeared with their meal and placed the pizza and garlic bread on the table. Jessica sighed, but was thankful for the interruption. Conner grabbed a huge slice of scalding hot pizza, stringing melted mozzarella cheese across the table as he dropped it on his plate. "Enough about Daddy dearest. What's been happening at work? How's the hotel stuff going?"

Jessica relaxed a little, feeling the tension dissipate from her shoulders. "It's keeping me on my toes."

Conner licked his fingers and took a swig of his beer. "What's Nate Somers like? Like … I mean … he's mega rich?"

Jessica gulped. "I suppose he is. To me, he's just another client and business as usual. I mean he's nice enough." She felt color rise in her cheeks as images of his nice, firm, naked body flashed through her mind. "He's got a lovely accent, he's tall, handsome—"

Conner coughed. "Alright. I've heard enough. Sorry I asked." Then he shoved another slice of pizza in his mouth. "You're all red, Mom. Do you have a thing for Nate Somers?"

Jessica moved uncomfortably on her chair, caught off guard by her son's observations. "No. Not at all, why?"

"I don't care." He shrugged again. "It's just that I know you haven't been with anyone really since Dad, er, Graeme. Maybe you should start dating?"

Her heart melted. He was such a sweet young man to care or even notice. Oh! But there was definitely no need for him to know what was really going on with her and Nate. *At all!* Conner was entering dangerous territory and she'd had enough of emotionally charged conversations for one day.

"One day maybe, when I have time. You know me—it's all business, no pleasure."

"Yeah, right, Mom. Whatever."

* * *

Sunday evening in Melbourne was cold and drizzling with rain when Nate and Brooke arrived late after their delayed flight.

They checked in at the Crown Hotel, and Nate immediately retired to his room. He had worked sixteen-hour days for the past week. Nothing unusual. He couldn't wait to have a hot shower to soothe his tired muscles and he looked forward to his first early night's sleep in ages.

After soaking under the steaming showerhead, he hopped out and toweled himself dry. As he walked out of the bathroom, the king-sized bed loomed in front of him, and thoughts of Jessica filled his mind. He was disappointed that he'd been unable to catch up with her before he had to fly to Melbourne. Work got in the way as always, as he had to oversee the installation of the communications system and staff training exercises. As he ran his fingers through his wet hair, he glanced at the bedside digital clock. 10:10. It wasn't too late to call her now.

He reached for his cell phone off the nightstand, hit her number and paced the floor while he waited for her to answer.

"Hello." The sound of her soft voice made his groin twitch against the fluffy white towel.

"It's Nate."

"Yes, I have Caller ID. Are you in Melbourne? Is everything okay?"

"Yes, everything's fine. Brooke keeps me in line."

"You and Brooke, hey?" she asked. He detected a serious note to her question.

"Oh, don't even go there. Definitely not." Brooke was certainly not his type. "How was your weekend? Did you have your meeting?"

He heard Jessica sigh heavily. The sound of her breath sent shivers down the side of his neck.

"Draining, to say the least. It was a very different outcome than what I expected. But everything will be fine."

"Good to hear." He paused. She sounded tired and suddenly he felt bad for calling so late. "I'm sorry we didn't get to catch up before I left."

"No harm done."

"Well, I aim to make it up to you." He was suddenly feeling bold and playful. "Are you in bed?"

"Yes. I try to get to bed before midnight at least once a week."

"What are you wearing?"

"What?" She gasped. "Is that the tackiest line ever in an attempt to seduce me over the phone?"

Nate smiled. That was exactly what he had in mind.

"I've just had a shower. I'm still wet. I'm wearing nothing but a towel. Just hearing your voice and picturing you naked has given me a hard-on. You have my undivided attention. So let's have a little bit of fun. So, once again what are you wearing?" Nate had never done anything like this before ... over the phone. But with Jessica, he was in unchartered territory anyway.

"Pale blue flannelette PJs," she replied.

Nate closed his eyes. Jessica could be wearing a hessian sack and she'd still look amazing. The thought of unbuttoning her top made his dick grow even harder.

"Unbutton your shirt." He lowered his voice in an attempt to be flirtatious. "I want you to imagine I'm undoing one button at a time ..."

"Nate? What are you doing?" Jessica giggled.

"Shh. I want you. Now."

"But we're five hundred miles apart!"

"Close your eyes. Visualize." Nate walked over and knelt on his bed and let the towel fall away. "I'm kneeling on my bed. My cock is in my hand and I'm rubbing it up and down."

Nate heard Jessica's heavy breath come down the line. It sent tingles all over his body. The vision he had of her touching herself was so hot. Her full breasts arching toward him, her smooth stomach, her legs spread wide open for him. *Holy crap!* He was turned on. The phone sex was definitely working for him. "Jess, you're driving me crazy. I want to bury myself inside you again. I want to fuck you till we both can't walk."

"Nate? Seriously stop." Jessica laughed loudly. "You're crazy. I'm not having phone sex with you."

"Come on, baby." His breath was heavy. "Tell me ... where do you want me to kiss you? Where can I touch you? What does it feel like?"

"Nate. Enough."

All he could hear was her laughter while he knelt there alone with his dick in his hand. It took a moment for him to regain his composure. He was really starting to get into it.

"Spoilsport," he grumbled. Okay, phone sex might not be her thing. It had been worth a shot.

"Nate, it's late," said Jessica. "I'm tired. And you have an early start in the morning."

"Yeah, I know. You've certainly set up a full week for me. I'm back late on Friday night, but no doubt I'll talk to you before then."

"I look forward to it. Goodnight, Nate."

"Night, Jess." He clicked off the phone and threw it down on the bed. He looked down at his hard cock and sighed as images of Jessica still swarmed in his mind. Phone sex might not have worked on Jessica, but it did on him. *I need another shower. A cold one this time.* Nate stood up off the bed and headed to the bathroom once more.

Chapter 9

Another Friday night. Another function to attend. At least this time Jessica was grateful to be a guest and not the host. She was standing at a bar table in the foyer of the ballroom waiting for the Sydney Harbour Foreshore Authority event to commence and for Max to join her. It was early, so Jessica took a sip of her wine and savored the quiet moment before too many other people arrived.

She still couldn't believe how crazy life had turned in the past few weeks — first, meeting Nate and second, reuniting with Troy. A mischievous smile tugged at the corner of her mouth as she thought of Nate and how he made her feel. He lit her fire in a way she never thought was possible. So much more than she'd ever experienced with Troy—from what she could recall. And miles ahead of Graeme—well that was a no-brainer.

In her head, she was still trying to work out the logistics of how her arrangement with Nate would work. Secrecy and lies had caused her so much angst in the past; more could only lead to no good. Maybe she should end this affair with Nate before it even started.

Would she regret not relishing in more of his kisses, his voice seducing her and his lovemaking blowing her mind? She shook her head feeling so confused and conflicted. Because if word got out that they were together, the consequences could be ugly. Her business and respectability were at stake. Too much was at risk. She couldn't ruin her reputation, jeopardize the success of the launch or cause grief to Nate.

Jessica was startled when someone slid an arm around her shoulders. But the touch made her smile. She looked up and saw Max, looking tired at the end of a busy day.

"Sorry I'm late. Court went overtime. And then walking five blocks in new shoes wasn't smart. My feet are fucking killing me."

"Here," Jessica grabbed a glass of red wine off a waiter's tray and plonked it down on the table in front of her. "Get this into you."

"Look, the doors have just opened. Can we go inside and sit down at the table? I really need to get off my feet."

With glass in hand, Jessica led Max through the array of tables in the function room and found their seats.

"Oh that's better." Max looked relieved as she sat down. "Shouldn't you be schmoozing all these potential clients?"

Yes she should be, but she just wasn't in the mood. All she wanted to do was sit back and enjoy hearing about Max's hectic week and have a drink or two to get her mind off work … and other things. "Later."

"Good. So before this presentation gets underway and we are all bored listening to the Harbour's development plans, tell me, what's going on with your love life?"

Jessica rolled her eyes. That was just the topic she had wanted to avoid. But Max wouldn't let up until she spilled the beans. Damn lawyers—they were too good at interrogations!

"How's the whole Troy debacle going?" Max asked as a waiter refreshed their glasses.

Jessica placed her napkin across her lap. Every time she thought of Troy, she could see his piercing blue eyes in her mind. But then telling Conner and seeing the painful reaction spread across his face made her heart ache. Where to from here? She had no idea. "One day at a time is all I can say. Time will tell."

"So ... What about Nate?"

"Shh. There are way too many people in this room who know him." Jessica's eyes darted nervously around the room as it filled with guests taking their seats.

"Okay. Let's call him Mr ComeFuckMe then."

Jessica laughed. Talking about Nate sent a sizzling reaction through her body.

"No more encounters?"

"No. None. And before you ask, there are none planned either. He's been away all week. The more I think about it, the more I shouldn't do what you suggested. Before it even starts ... or should I say progresses further ... it has to stop."

Max shook her head. "Are you crazy? Casual sex with someone that hot, no strings attached and then he's gone."

Maybe she should? It would be nice. The sex was fantastic. He's hot. She sighed. Yet again she was toing and froing with the idea. Why could she not make a clear decision, stick to it and move on? This was driving her insane. Jessica shook her head because she just shouldn't do it. He was her client. "Believe me, Max, his proposition is very enticing but there's just too much risk and too many complications."

As her eyes surveyed the room, she nearly got whiplash when she felt a pull, a disturbance in the air that grabbed her attention. She turned toward the entrance. Her breath caught in her lungs.

There he was.

Nate.

He was talking to people around him and as they cleared from his path, Jessica swore under her breath. Meredith Bowen from EyeOn was by his side.

She nudged Max. "Speak of the devil." She nodded toward the door. "There's Nate."

"Where? I so want to meet him."

Jessica restrained Max from jumping out of the chair. "No. Look who he's with; it's Meredith."

"What the hell is she doing here?"

Jessica didn't want to jump to the wrong conclusions. Meredith's company did a lot of work for the Harbour Authority. Some of her clients were here, as were Jessica's.

"Oh my God! Is she his date?" Max gasped "Do you think Nate's screwing her too?"

The thought made Jessica's skin crawl and nausea loomed in her belly. "Thanks for that horrid vision." She shuddered. "Surely not." But doubt had been planted firmly in her mind. "I didn't even know Nate was coming. The invites for this function were out months ago, before we even won the Somers account."

Jessica couldn't take her eyes off Nate. He looked up. Straight at her. Then a smile crept across his face that made butterflies take flight in her stomach. The longing to be with him blazed to life, overpowering any form of reasoning. All her thoughts of calling off their affair dissipated into thin air. That smile of his should be made illegal.

Max was kicking her under the table. "Here he comes. You were right. He's so much better looking in person."

* * *

Jessica was here. Nate inhaled deeply, intoxicated by the very sight of her from across the room. He ignored the people he was with and made a beeline for her table.

He couldn't help himself. His body was drawn to hers in some mysterious manner. As he approached her table, Jessica rose from her seat, moved behind her chair and met him face to face. Her hand slipped into his. Her skin was so soft it made the rest of him ache, because now he wanted to touch her all over.

"Hi," she said, a girlish smile inched across her lips.

He took a moment to absorb her attractive features. Her mouth looked irresistible and he longed to taste her lips against his. And as he stared into her eyes, there was no doubt in his mind that they reflected his own burning desire.

"Ah-hum." A woman cleared her throat loudly as she joined Jessica at her side.

"Um. Yes. Max, I'd like you to meet Nate Somers." Jessica introduced her friend without breaking eye contact. "Nate, Maxine Gordon."

He reluctantly drew his attention away and shook her hand. "Nice to meet you."

"And you. But please call me Max. FYI, I'm the friend who knows *everything*."

Nate raised his eyebrows in surprise. Jessica winced and nodded. "She's right. She's my best friend."

What happened to discretion? Should he worry about Maxine?

"You two are like bunnies on heat, aren't you?" said Max.

Nate couldn't believe his ears at the bluntness of this woman. He took a step back from Jessica, fighting against the desire to keep contact with her skin.

A group of people gathered around them in the clearing between the tables. A woman's nasal voice drew his focus momentarily away from Jessica.

"Ah! There you are, Nathan."

Meredith!

"Well hello, Jessica. Maxine."

It was as plain as day, Jessica stiffened. Every muscle on her face tensed and her eyes narrowed. There was no handshake, no friendliness in their manner. The warmth in the air seemed to drain away.

Jessica looked suspiciously at him. "So, how do you know Meredith?" There was a definite sting in her voice. "Did you two come together?"

"No. We just bumped into each other outside in the foyer and we seem to be at the same table with the Harbour Authority representatives. I met Meredith when EyeOn did their presentation during the tender process for the launch."

"Fancy seeing you here, Jessica," Meredith said. "I wondered if you'd make an appearance, especially after this afternoon's announcement."

"What announcement?" Jessica asked dubiously.

"EyeOn are taking over another one of your accounts. The national food chain giant, *Garcon's.*"

"No. I hadn't heard. I was out all afternoon at meetings." Jessica flinched, as if she'd had a quick blow to the stomach.

That was cruel of Meredith. He could see the hurt in Jessica's expression, even though she still held herself with an air of grace. He knew the feeling of losing business all too well. All he wanted to do was reach out and put his arms around her and tell her it would be okay.

He noticed a triumphant smile extend across Meredith's face. She seemed to puff out like a peacock on display. The nerve of this woman to gloat about winning an account in front of others, at the expense of someone right there, was downright rude and unprofessional in his opinion.

"See, Mr Somers." Meredith turned to him. "We're an international company, expanding and growing. Excelling in everything we do. We would've put on one outstanding show for you if you'd chosen us to help you open your hotel."

Did she just flutter her eyelids at me? Oh, that's so wrong!

"Jessica's organization is doing an outstanding job for us. Their professionalism and creativity has been beyond our expectations. It was their proposal that outdid all other bids by far. It was not about their company's size or growing client list."

That shut Meredith up.

He didn't want to be in the middle of an escalating territorial war between these two businesswomen.

The screech from the microphone saved him, diverting everyone's attention as the MC announced that the evening's function was about to begin, and requesting the guests to please take their seats.

"I'll see you after dinner." Nate placed his arm on Jessica's to offer a friendly show of support.

"Maybe." Jessica turned away from him without so much as another glance and returned to her chair. Meredith, still looking like she'd won a prize, bustled him off through the crowd to find their table.

* * *

"Well that was boring as all fuck." Max said as they had a drink at the bar after the function. "You really need to talk to these guys about doing a much better event for them. Seriously, I was digging my fingernails into my thigh just to try and stay awake."

Jessica giggled. "You crack me up." But she'd hardly focused on the speeches; her attention certainly lay elsewhere in the room.

"No, wait. The ice-cold glares you kept giving Meredith and Nate were entertaining. I think you scared half the people at our table. "

"I'm sorry. But Meredith rubs me the wrong way."

Seeing Meredith—her arch-enemy—next to Nate made

Jessica want to draw her talons and scream *"Back off bitch, he's mine"*. In more ways than one! She didn't like Meredith's approach to business and gossipy tactics. She didn't like their campaigns and didn't want Meredith's hands on any more of her clients.

"Thanks for the evening out, but next time I think locking myself in a room full of geriatric lawyers would be loads more fun." Max finished off her drink.

"Sorry, I didn't think it was going to be this bad," said Jessica. "The food was nice though!"

"True. I'm going to head off and catch a cab home. You stay here and have some fun. Find that Mr Somers, and stay out of Meredith's firing line." Max said as she hugged her goodbye.

Jessica finished her drink and placed her glass on the counter. She was in no mood to network with the mob of suits that lingered around after the event. She gathered up her coat and scarf, hitched her bag on her shoulder and made her way out of the bar to the bathroom for a quick visit before heading home.

She toweled off her hands and opened the door back out into the hallway only to run into a wall. A wall made of man. She knew that scent. She knew the shape of that chest. She looked up, straight into Nate's eyes.

"Why didn't you tell me about Meredith?" he asked.

Jessica gasped. "Tell you what?" Oh crap. Did blabbermouth Meredith tell him all about their history. Even when she tried to take them over? It seemed so. "Excuse me." She tried to side step around him but he blocked her path.

"She wanted to buy you out to avoid being your competition. That's a smart business tactic, but I for one am glad that didn't happen. We may have never met otherwise," he said. "But I think she'd still want to take Kick if you gave her the thumbs up."

She couldn't hide how crushed she felt inside at the thought of selling, "I know she would, but my company is not for sale." Would Nate think that Kick was unstable and unable to carry off the launch?

"So why the tension between you two?"

This was not the conversation they should be having in the bathroom hallway, but Jessica couldn't help herself from babbling.

"It's so much more than that." She lowered her chin and looked away. "She's like an annoying woodpecker pecking continuously. Or a vulture trying to eat you. She has her eyes set on us and is willing to do anything to steal, win or chisel our clients away. I just don't like the way she conducts business and she won't accept no for an answer."

"If it's any consolation, I know where you're coming from," Nate lifted her chin with the tip of his finger. "We've been the target of several ruthless takeover attempts in our time. Look, we wouldn't have selected your agency for our launch if we didn't believe that you had the financial capability, the unique creativity, and that you operated in a manner that suited our style. We did our research. Besides, I personally prefer to deal with smaller organizations like yourselves rather than massive multinationals like EyeOn."

Nate put his hand on her arm and rubbed it to comfort her. Heat started to flare inside her from his touch. She heard his breath shorten. His close proximity to her was altering her train of thought.

"Want to get out of here?" Nate asked as he looked at her with pleading eyes.

"I can't be seen leaving with you from here. Meredith? Cameras? Gossip?"

He stepped closer. "You make me want to throw discretion out the door."

Jessica closed her eyes as his breath feathered in her ear. Warmth spread down the right side of her body and her knees went weak.

But no ... not in front of everyone. She still had her dignity. Her eyes shot open and she looked around nervously. She stepped back against the wall, away from Nate.

She blushed at his suggestion. His cheeky smile and the hunger in his eyes made her falter. Her earlier battle with her confused feelings had been worse than relying on the outcome from a coin toss. It had been *heads*—stay away, *tails*—stay with. Every time she thought she'd decided not to be with him, something came up and it flipped back the other way. What was with that? But now, seeing him before her, the coin had definitely landed on tails. She inhaled deeply as the scent of him filled her senses. The idea of being whisked away sounded kind of fun.

She met his waiting gaze. "Let's get out of here."

He placed his warm hand on her cheek and was about to step in to kiss her, when she froze at the sound of footsteps coming from the corridor. Nate quickly stepped back and shoved his hands in his pockets. Jessica struggled to breathe as she saw Meredith walking toward them.

* * *

"There you are, Nathan." Her eyes rudely shot daggers at Jessica. "Discussing business, are we?" She raised a penciled-on eyebrow at him.

Guilt washed over Nate. What was he doing trying to seduce Jessica in the hallway? He had to be careful with the likes of Meredith Bowen about. "Just ran into each other in the hallway. That's all."

"I'm heading off to catch a cab. Night, all." Jessica turned and headed out to the foyer.

"I'm heading off as well. Good evening, Meredith." He went to walk around her but she stepped in front of him.

"Would you like my limo driver to give you a lift? You're staying in the Tower, aren't you?" Meredith said with a twinkle in her eye. "I'm heading past there and could drop you off."

He shuddered at the evocative tone in her voice. "No, thank you. My driver is waiting for me. Goodnight."

Before she could utter another word, he rushed out into the foyer, through the revolving door, and glanced frantically up and down the street looking for Jessica. Where had she gone? Had she really left for the night? He started down the street for the taxi rank, and relief washed over him when found her toward the end of the line. She looked cold and out of sorts.

"Jessica, would you like a lift?"

"No, thank you. I'm fine. I'll just get a taxi."

Meredith had obviously unnerved her. Oh, he wanted to throttle that woman. Jessica's notion of calling her a woodpecker certainly rang true.

"You look cold," Nate persisted. "My car's waiting just up the street there." He thumbed in the direction of his limousine.

He saw her shoulders relax as she smiled at him and nodded. "Okay. That would be nice. This line looks like it's going to take ages."

Jessica walked next to him as they made their way down the street. As they were about to pass the entrance, Meredith barreled out in front of them. Her eyes snapped from him to Jessica. "Where are you two off to now?"

"Just giving Jessica a lift, because she looks freezing."

"How gentlemanly of you." The suspicion on Meredith's face stretched Nate's tolerance to the limits. He could see the headlines in tomorrow's news: *Nate follows in his father's footsteps—sleeping with women around the world.*

God, the thought made him shudder. He hadn't slept with a

string of women; he couldn't be more different from his father. But the tabloids wouldn't care about the truth. Yes, this was a short-term fling, but no one was going to get hurt as a result of it. There was something different about Jessica; he just couldn't put his finger on it yet. But damn it if someone like Meredith was going to be the one to put him in the headlines.

Nate ushered Jessica away to the string of limousines and drivers waiting in the cold night air for their clients. His driver opened the door on his approach. As Nate placed his hand on the small of Jessica's back to aid her into the car, a shiver ran down his spine. It felt good to finally touch her. He'd being struggling to resist the temptation all night.

Without thinking, he glanced back toward the doorway. There was Meredith. Watching his every move. *Shit!* He turned away and slipped into the back seat after Jessica.

It was welcoming and warm inside the car after standing out in the brisk air. The driver took off down the street. Nate leaned against the back corner of the car seat. Everything was going to be fine. Nothing he could do about it now.

The feel of Jessica next to him drew his attention.

"I know it's been a rough night. Do you want me to take you home or ... do you want to come back to the hotel?"

Her eyes glowed warmly and a smile curled on her lips. "Hotel," she whispered.

It took all his willpower not to take her then and there in the car. He couldn't wait to run his hands up and down along the smooth skin of her thighs. Kiss her red lips. Taste her skin. And embed himself inside her. He swallowed hard trying to get his thoughts under control and loosened his neck tie in an attempt to lower his body temperature.

"How was Melbourne?" Jessica asked him suddenly, in a businesslike tone.

Yes! Distraction conversation for a moment would be

good. "We should get the video edits back in the next few weeks. We have two weeks to make any changes before the programs start running on various channels in Australia and Asia, and at our next meeting, we need to discuss ..."

Nate couldn't help but grin as she rattled on. He'd noticed she did that when she was nervous. "I'm amazed you pulled all those meetings together for me at short notice," he said, when she took a breath. "You're doing a fantastic job."

"And don't you forget it."

Her passion for her job and her company excited and rejuvenated him. It made him realize that he loved what he did too. He'd been running flat for months. Just working day to day. But Jessica's enthusiasm was contagious and had reignited his drive to oversee the growth of the Somers organization.

"I've worked with heaps of agencies around the world and your flair is a rarity," Nate said. "You'd do well in Europe."

"Europe? I'd have an uphill battle convincing Alex on that one." She smiled, but he could see sadness in her eyes. "Alex is driven by money, making it, not spending it."

Nate remembered the many times he'd been excited about ideas for growing their business and had continually been blocked by his narrow-minded father. Yet again, he noted that he had more in common with Jessica than he could have ever imagined.

He couldn't take his eyes off her as she turned her head to see the city pass by outside her window. Silence hung in the air as he watched the night lights dance across her skin. She was simply beautiful.

As the car got nearer to the hotel, Nate looked down at Jessica's hand resting on her lap. Within the short drive, their bodies had slowly edged closer together. Their legs were now barely an inch from touching. They were drawn toward each other like magnets. He'd never found anyone who seemed to be the whole package—elegant, sexy, intelligent. Snapshots flashed through his mind of all the crazy places in the world he would like to make love to her. Places where she could wrap those long legs around him. Places where he could look at her and drown in her gorgeous brown eyes forever.

Don't be stupid! That's not going to happen.

Nate pulled himself up short, clenching his jaw. He closed his eyes to refocus on what was truly happening here. *Just sex. This little get-together is just for sex!* Nothing more. Nothing less.

* * *

Nate called out to the driver. "Can you go down through the carpark to the elevators, please?" He turned back to Jessica. "Away from too many prying eyes."

Jessica managed a few calming breaths. "Thank you." Yes, keeping their encounters private was necessary. She didn't want to be a headline scandal.

The chauffeur pulled up by the elevator bay, hopped out and opened the door for them. Nate collected his luggage from the trunk of the car and bid the driver goodnight. As they entered the elevator, Nate pointed out the security camera as the doors closed behind them. Did he seriously think she was going to jump him in the elevator?

Jessica sighed. *Probably would have if he didn't point them out.*

As they stood like statues facing the doors, Jessica could hear Nate's heavy breathing. In. Out. In. Out. The thought of that warmth rushing all over her body made it a struggle to remain standing still as the elevator sped toward the thirty-second floor.

She followed Nate down the short hall to his apartment. He swiped his door key in the card reader and stood aside for her to enter. The door closed behind them with a click. With a flick of a few switches, Nate turned on the downlights before he abandoned his suitcase and flung his arms around her. His lips took instant possession of hers. His body finally pressed against hers, making her skin tingle from her head down to her toes. All her senses were finally aligned and focused on him.

Skin. She wanted Nate in the flesh. Too much fabric hindered her way. With hasty fingers she unraveled his tie and made quick work of unbuttoning his shirt. As she glided her hands back up over his chest and down the lengths of his arms, she pulled his shirt and coat along in their wake. For someone out of practice, she was certainly good at getting his gear off. A skill she was very grateful for.

"Jess, what have you done to me?" he whispered as he nuzzled her neck.

"Nothing just yet. Give me a sec." She struggled to unfasten his belt, before it released and she slipped it free from his trousers. She held it up beside her and dangled it playfully before she dropped it to the ground. "Well, I've already had dinner and a few drinks. So there's no need for you to wine and dine me. Let's just get to the sex. I want you inside of me now."

She wanted to forget this evening—the boring dinner, Meredith and her troubles. Hot sex was just what she needed.

Nate's eyes blazed. "I'm only too happy to oblige. Besides, I'm not sure if I'd make it through a whole date with you." He pulled her back into his arms. His hands ran down over the curves of her back, found the bottom edge of her top and peeled it up over her head. She arched her chest toward him as his thumb circled over the front of her silky bra. Her nipples peaked beneath the fabric as he cupped her breast.

She knotted her fingers up through his hair and pulled his lips back to hers. She savored the taste and the dance of their tongues. He reached up to take her hand and drew back from her kiss. His eyes burned into her with a fiery desire that made Jessica catch her breath.

"Come on," he whispered.

Kicking off her shoes, she let him lead her to the bedroom. Standing before him at the edge of the bed, Jessica ran her palms over the hard plain of his chest. Following his light dusting of hair, her fingernails trailed to the top of his trousers. Slowly, she unzipped them. That was Nate's undoing. He kicked off his shoes, rid himself of his clothes and pushed her down onto the bed.

In his naked glory, Nate arched over her as she lay beneath him. As she rubbed her hand up and down along his shaft, a deep groan of pleasure rumbled in his throat. He kissed her. The touch of his lips against hers sent ripples of heat all through her body. She grasped onto his hips and drew him in closer to her. She felt like she would explode if he didn't enter her soon.

She groaned when he pulled away. It was just starting to get really good!

"Wait, I've got to get to my drawer," he said.

Jessica giggled while admiring the view as he leaned over her and opened up the drawer of the bedside table.

"It better not be handcuffs."

Nate chuckled and flashed her a gold-foiled condom packet in front of her. "So what ... no toys, whips or leather straps?"

"Not my thing." She wrinkled her nose at him. "I just like your dick."

The fire that burned in Nate's eyes made Jessica's heartbeat soar.

"I'm very glad to hear that," he said. She felt like she was melting into the bed as Nate returned to kissing her. "Besides, I think we'd break too many things the way we're going."

Jessica had to agree.

Nate sat across her hips. His cock standing up like a flagpole made her want him to hurry up. He grunted with frustration as he struggled to open the packet. She placed her hand over his to stop. "I'm on contraceptive injections." Yes, they should've had this discussion before they were both in such a compromising position. "For controlling my cycle, not a rampant sex life. So, if you're not riddled with STDs, how do you feel about no condoms?" She'd rather do away with them if they were going to do this on a regular basis.

"You don't have to ask me twice." He threw the packet onto the bedside table. "And for the record, no, I don't have any diseases." He took her hand in his and pressed his lips against her palm. His eyes, full of what looked to be adoration, captured hers. Or it could have been downright lust. Jessica's pulse picked up to its former pace. Nate leaned forward over her and lowered his body down against hers. He connected with her once again. Every cell of her body hummed and felt alive as she wrapped her legs around his waist.

Nate smiled as he pressed his hips firmly into hers. His penis bulged hard against her opening, teasing her arousal into overdrive. "You feel so good. I want to savor you for just a moment longer."

Jessica rubbed her hands over his firm buttocks. She pulled them to her as she wiggled her hips beneath him. "Is that long enough?" she asked as she kissed across his shoulder and collarbone.

"Mm. I think so."

Slowly he slid into her, filling her with every inch of his sturdy length. Tantalizing shivers shot to every one of her nerve endings. Jessica felt Nate quiver as he buried himself deep inside her. Her core clenched tightly around him. It would be so nice to make love to him all night and wake up next to him in the morning. She could imagine the tenderness on his face as the sun peeked through the curtains.

No! This was not about tender lovemaking, this was about sex. Damn good, hot sex.

Nate's quick, erratic hip movements brought her back to the moment. His body pulled back and he plunged into her hard. Faster. Deeper.

"It's been way too long, Ms Mason," Nate's heated breath brushed across her face. "I highly recommend we do this more often."

* * *

After round two in the shower, Nate's legs could barely hold up his weight. What was it about sex with Jessica that made his whole body feel like rubber afterwards? The stress in his mind and body had all but gone. He slipped on his robe and walked out of the bathroom, only to find her sitting on the side of the bed getting dressed. He glanced at the clock on his bedside table and saw it was nearly one o'clock in the morning.

He ran his hand through this wet hair. "What are you doing?"

"I'm going home."

His gut clenched as if he'd been punched. He froze and tried to think of something to get her to stay. He wanted her to spend the night, have a lazy breakfast in the morning with her and make love to her again. He sat down beside her as she did up her boots. "You don't have to."

"I can't stay. That complicates things, Nate, you know it does. We've discussed this … situation. Besides, I have Conner's football game at ten o'clock." Jessica stood up and straightened her clothes. "So … I'll see you on Tuesday at our next meeting."

Nate had never felt so helpless as he followed her out to the door. "Wait."

Jessica stood with her back to him for a moment before she turned around. The look on her face caught him off guard. She was all composed and difficult to read. He wanted to say something to get her to stay, but words escaped him.

But then it dawned on him. This is what she wanted. This is what he said he wanted. *Wasn't it?* No strings attached. All he could offer was a warm smile as he reluctantly opened the door. "I'll see you Tuesday and look forward to our next ... rendezvous."

Chapter 10

Jessica closed her eyes and rubbed her fingertips over her temples. The month of July so far had been a whirlwind for her. Over the past few weeks she'd managed to see several campaigns and events roll out the door, even while the majority of her time had been spent working on the opening of Somers Hotel.

She'd hoped after a few weeks the fire between Nate and herself would have extinguished, but that had not been the case. A smile crept across her face as she thought about the times they'd successfully hooked up after meetings, dinners and lunch dates. His office. Her office. His apartment. The quickies. The head-jobs she'd given him at his desk. The things he did to her on the couch in her office. The sex was incredible. But this game they were playing had her continually on edge—trying not to get caught, trying not to act suspicious in front of staff and trying to keep her heart protected.

Every day she tried to convince herself to end the affair, but she kept going back for more. He was like an addictive drug—she couldn't wait for the next hit. She glanced at her watch. Could she sneak a quick visit to see Nate now? No. Not today. There was simply too much work on her plate. She had this weekend off, catching up with him would have to wait until then. A weekend at Gumtrees would be ideal.

The idea of spending a weekend between the sheets with Nate, locked away in a cabin, played out in her mind. The log fire would be blazing. They'd be naked, wrapped up together in a warm blanket, watching the flames dance in the hearth. They'd drink wine, eat some divine food ... *But no.* What was she doing fantasizing about romantic getaways that could never happen? That was not on her dance card. Yet again she had to pull herself into line. Nate was short-term. Temporary. She wasn't going to open her heart and risk being hurt.

And there was Troy. The thought of him brought her back to harsh reality. At least her mind no longer spiraled out of control when she heard his voice on the phone, as he called now on a regular basis. Slowly it had sunk in, that yes, he was well and truly back, and she was not having a repetitive nightmare. Conner remained adamant about not wanting to meet his father every time she brought up the subject. Excuses of exams, sports and his part-time job taking up all of his time. Troy had been incredibly patient, but Jessica knew he was desperate to meet his son. She decided to try Conner again. She reached for the phone and dialed his number.

"Conner, it's Mom."

"S'up?" He sounded sleepy. Had she woken him up at three in the afternoon?

"I was wondering if I could take you out for dinner on Wednesday for your birthday? Your choice of restaurant."

"Thanks, but I already made plans to see a band play at the uni. Sorry."

"Oh. Okay. Well ... Um, I'm thinking of going out to Gumtrees this weekend and I was wondering if you wanted to come with me. It'd give you a chance to meet Troy."

'*Mom!*'

"Conner, I just have the feeling he's going to wind up on your doorstep unannounced if you don't agree to see him soon."

"Mom, we've discussed this."

"I know. And I understand how you feel, I really do," said Jessica. "But you won't be able to go on ignoring him forever. He calls me every week to ask about you."

Silence stewed between them as she heard Conner punch something like a wall.

"Fine. One meeting."

"Thank you," said Jessica. "Would you like to bring Becky along? I'll book you a separate cabin if you'd like."

She heard him sigh down the phone. "Yeah. We'll drive up by ourselves on Saturday after lunch."

"If it's any consolation, I'm just as nervous about this as you are." Not only for Conner, but a strange coil of mixed emotions swirled inside her stomach knowing she too was going to see Troy again.

"Not helping, Mom."

"Probably not, just want you to know I'll be there for you. No matter what. Ok? I'll go ahead and book the cabins."

* * *

Jessica parked outside her usual cabin at Gumtrees and climbed out of the car. She stood and stretched every inch of her body—from the soles of her feet through to the tips of her fingers.

She turned around to see Troy walk out of the cellar shop. His bow-legged walk showed he spent way too much time horse riding. His dark brown moleskin jacket made him look like a big, warm teddy bear. His eyes reflected her anxiety.

"Jess." He touched the edge of his Akubra hat, and then, as if on second thoughts, he gave her a hug.

She smiled at his awkward embrace. "Troy, nice to see you again." Disbelief still rippled through her veins at the sight of him. Her heart didn't know if it wanted to burst with joy or bleat in pain as his vivid blue eyes looked into hers.

"Do you want me to go get the key for you?"

"No, I'll get it. I want to say hi to Marie and Nick. Conner won't be here until after lunch. I'm going to go settle in and maybe go for a quick ride on Stirling, if that's okay?"

"Sure is. Let's go. I'm was just heading up to the office as I've got some paperwork to do this morning. I'll catch up with you at lunch."

* * *

After changing into her riding gear Jessica sat on the side of the bed holding a folder on her lap and running her hands over the smooth plastic cover. The silence of the cabin was welcoming and gave her a moment to collect her thoughts. Conner was finally going to meet his father. After so many years. She had wanted this for so long and now the moment was nearly upon her, all she could do was feel petrified. How was Conner going to react? She sighed, knowing it wouldn't be long until she found out.

But first things first. She stood up and headed out the door for the homestead. She climbed the few sandstone steps into the office and went inside. Troy sat behind the desk typing with one finger on the computer. Jessica smiled at him, amused. Yes, there were some things about Troy that had definitely not changed in twenty years.

"Hey, what's up?" he asked.

"Here." She handed him the folder.

"What's this?"

"It's an album I made of photos of Conner growing up. Baby photos, school, holidays, etcetera. I had Zoe, my assistant, scan and copy a heap of things I thought you might want to see."

Troy hesitated, then took it from her. "Wow, I don't know what to say."

Jessica glanced away to avoid looking at his eyes. "I've written some quick notes—the year and stuff—on each page for you, too. It's no scrapbooking masterpiece, but I think it covers everything."

Troy, seemingly lost for words, ran his free hand through his thick hair. "Geez ... Thanks."

They stood in silence as Troy opened up to the first page. Jessica knew it was a picture of Conner at birth. She saw his eyes fill with tears and felt her own eyes start to sting. She had to get out of here before she was too overcome.

"I'll leave you to it. I'm going to go for a quick ride." She turned and headed briskly back out the door.

* * *

After putting Stirling and all her gear away, Jessica walked out of the stables. She was meandering back to her cabin, absently kicking the odd large stone with the tip of her riding boot, when she looked up and saw Troy sitting on the steps to her cabin. As she drew closer, she could see his eyes were red, as if he'd been crying.

"Hey." She spoke softly. "You all right?"

"Thank you for the folder. It's amazing. It looks like you've been a wonderful mother. You look so happy in all the photos."

She smiled. "I'm very proud of him. Believe me, it hasn't all been smooth sailing, but I think he's turned out all right."

"I can't fathom what you went through thinking that I didn't want to be a part of his life. But God, Jess. I would've if I'd known. I was so stupid not to call you and tell you about Nicola.

I was too ashamed and gutless to face you."

She resisted the urge to roll her eyes. "You can beat yourself up for all your wrongdoings when I'm not around. I don't want to hear you're sorry anymore. I don't want to hear you wish things were different. What's done is done. It's all in the past."

Together, they had to get beyond the hurt, heal old wounds that had reopened and move forward somehow. As friends, as past lovers, as parents of a grown child.

After a moment, Jessica sat down next to him. She was still trying to piece everything about him together. "So, you've never told me, how on earth did you end up working for Nick?"

Troy straightened his legs and crossed his ankles. "After Nicola died, I ended up in the Napa Valley. I think after growing up in the Hunter Valley, the wine industry has somehow always been in my blood. I studied viticulture, learned the ropes of winemaking, and made a few contacts back here to touch base with. One day, I was having lunch and talking to Grace, the manager at Harrigan's, and I ran into Nick. The rest is history. It all came down to good timing."

"So what exactly are you responsible for around here?"

"Since this is only a small vineyard, I do a bit of everything. I manage the vines ensuring they'll fruit well ready for harvest early in the new year. And I will oversee production of all the winemaking. Nick's trying to focus on expanding the accommodation and functions side of the business with Marie. I help out in the cellar shop and do the odd tour group if they need me, but I'm mainly out in the field."

"So what's your plan? For the future I mean?"

"Plan? What plan? This is it." Troy shrugged a little. "Working for Nick is great. He's a good boss. I love what I'm doing. Would you believe, I have more money than I'll ever know what to do with, thanks to Nicola, but just haven't found anywhere to settle down yet? For now, I'm really happy here. I get accommodation in the old cottage and meals in the restaurant. What more do I need?"

Jessica eyebrows furrowed. "Do you want your own vineyard one day?"

"If one came up for sale, maybe I'd consider it, but otherwise I have no such grand plans. I'm a man of simple means."

What? Troy was content with his life? How could that be possible? It was just something that Jessica couldn't comprehend. He seemed to have no goals, no plans, no ambitious dreams. Hers were never-ending. Adding Somers Hotels to her business portfolio was starting to attract new attention and was keeping Alex happy. With renewed fervor, she wanted to expand her business with new office locations, add more clients to her list and, for a treat, go on a shopping holiday with Max in Hong Kong. And that was just what she'd thought of in that split second in time.

Jessica turned to look as she caught sight of a car pulling off the main road and heading up the driveway toward them. The silver Audi crept along, its engine purring like a sleeping lion.

Time seemed to stop.

"That's Conner," Jessica managed to say as her stomach twisted into knots.

"Conner drives an Audi?" Troy said.

"Yes. I bought it for him for his eighteenth birthday. Why?"

"Do you remember the piece of scrap metal I used to drive in high school when I was seventeen?"

"Yes, I do. How could I ever forget?" She closed her eyes recalling all the sex they'd had in that car. "Audi is one of my clients. I can get a good deal on one if you're interested."

Troy shook his head. "I'll keep that in mind, but they don't make work trucks, now, do they?"

"No. Definitely not." Jessica drew her attention back to the driveway to where Conner was parking. She stood up and stuffed her hands in the back pockets of her jeans. Her heart rate escalated and she felt sick to her stomach. "Well, here goes nothing."

As she looked back at Troy, his face was ashen. "I'm panicking. What if he doesn't like me?"

She laughed. "He's one up on you there. He hasn't liked you for twenty years. Come on, come and meet our son."

"Will do. Just give me a sec." Troy remained seated. Jessica could see him wringing his hands together and that his legs were shaking.

She took a gut-filling breath, turned and slowly made her way over to the car, the gravel crunching beneath her boots.

As Conner stepped from the vehicle, his blond hair danced in the breeze. While he had Jessica's olive skin and her mouth, everything else about Conner was clearly from Troy's gene pool.

"Hey, Mom." Conner kissed her cheek as always, and Becky came around and hugged her too.

As she turned her attention back to Conner she could see his striking eyes were full of anxiety. "You okay?"

He nodded, but she knew better. This was really hard for him.

"You ready?"

Jessica glanced back towards the cabin and saw Troy finally approaching.

This was one of the most surreal moments of her life. Her stomach felt like it had tied itself into one massive ball of knots. Her heartbeat pulsed in her ears and she felt like her knees might give way at any moment.

Conner flicked his head back, brushing away the hair from is eyes and took a sharp breath, trying to keep his cool as Troy came to stand in front of them.

"Conner, Becky," Jessica said. "This is Troy."

She could tell Troy was trying to be strong, fighting to contain tears that were evident in his eyes. He held out his hand to shake Conner's, but swept him into a full embrace instead. He lost the battle with his emotions as he held his son in his arms for the first time.

Watching them together was overwhelming and Jessica found herself having to swipe away a few tears of her own with trembling hands. Maybe not knowing or having his biological father affected Conner more than he ever let on.

Conner tried to step back, but Troy placed his hand behind his neck and drew their foreheads together. "I am so sorry. I never knew."

Conner sniffled as he pulled away and brushed away his own tears. "S'okay."

Jessica heart was thumping in her chest. It was both beautiful and agonizing to witness. She hated seeing Conner in pain and fighting to be strong. Seeing Troy so overcome was bewildering; his very presence still blew her mind.

Both men stood looking at each other in disbelief, she knew that this was their moment and that she needed to give them some time alone.

"Becky, let's take a walk and I'll show you around," Jessica suggested. "Let's let the boys catch up."

She touched Conner and Troy on their forearms for some subtle reassurance before walking off with Becky toward the winery sheds.

* * *

After an hour wandering around the vineyard, Jessica made her way back to the cabins with Becky in tow. Troy and Conner were sitting in the alfresco dining area of the restaurant, talking over a couple of beers. Men always managed to bond over beer. Jessica was relieved to see that they were chatting.

The girls left them be. Becky turned in to her cabin to rest, as did Jessica. She was sitting enjoying a nice glass of Shiraz when a knock came at her door. She opened it to find Troy leaning against the railing on the porch.

Even in the dim afternoon light, underneath the rim of his Akubra hat, his eyes made her breath catch sharply in her chest. "Hey, how did it go?" she asked.

Troy smiled sheepishly. "I think well. We've agreed to take it slowly and try to get to know each other. Step by step. It's so much more than I could have expected. You're right. He's a great kid. Well ... man now, isn't he?" Troy rubbed his hand across his chin. "Thanks. Thanks for setting this up. It means the world to me and I am really looking forward to getting to know our son. Running into you after all these years has certainly been full of surprises."

Chapter 11

"Why does everything have to go haywire just a few days before a function?" Jessica groaned to herself. She slammed the phone down into its cradle and buried her face into her hands. More budget blowouts for the industry representative event, with the performers canceling due to illness. The night to entertain and impress all the travel agent and flight operator executives and other booking agents was causing her a huge amount of grief.

Now, where was she going to find new entertainment on such short notice?

She jumbled figures in her head, brought up the spreadsheet of expenses for Somers Hotels on her laptop, and cringed at the narrowing bottom line. But there was no time to worry about it now. First, she had to call Nate to tell him of the latest development, then get together with Lin and find someone to fill the vacant spot on their agenda as soon as possible.

* * *

Jessica said a silent prayer, thanking the gods above as clear skies prevailed on the late August evening. Dressed in a warm coat, black cocktail dress and towering stilettos, she scurried across the loading ramp, boarded the boat and entered into her realm of running events.

She loved this moment just before a function was about to start. The nerves. The jitters. The excitement. The calm before the storm. She stopped underneath a gas heater and turned to absorb the spectacular view. In front of the vessel, the Somers Hotel and Residential Tower loomed above. It was exciting to know that this amazing construction would open its doors to guests in just over a month. Lasers and floodlights danced around and glimmered off the glass windows of the two dominant structures. Exhilaration inside her started to build. A shiver coursed through her body as the adrenaline kicked in. Her moment of serenity was short-lived as she turned on her heels and entered the cabin.

Waiters dressed in their Somers Hotel uniforms were gathered in the center of the room getting a final pep talk from William, the food and beverage manager, and readying themselves to tend to the invitees. Jessica weaved through the back of the crowd and found Lin by the podium performing final sound checks.

The air shifted and Jessica smiled. She didn't even have to turn around to sense Nate's presence as he walked up beside her. She knew the scent of his aftershave and her body temperature seemed to rise a degree or two whenever he was near. Her heart did that crazy flutter thing as she greeted him. *Damn, he looks good in a suit.Even better naked!*

"You look nervous?" Jessica said, noting the creasing in his brow.

"I am. Let's hope my presentation impresses them."

"It will. You'll be great."

Clicking into host-mode, Jessica ran through the evening's agenda one last time with Nate and Lin as the night closed in on them. Guests started to fill the boat and drank sparkling champagne before the proceedings got underway. She barely batted an eyelash when the hired entertainers were half an hour late, and a microphone failed during a speech. It was nothing she hadn't dealt with before.

After the formalities, the guests mingled and continued to drink too much alcohol. As she handed out promotional gift bags she blushed knowing Nate's eyes were on her. Watching her from wherever he moved about the room. All the industry representatives wanted to occupy his time and attention, but at every opportunity she found him looking at her. She liked that—him watching her work. His gaze made her feel ... sexy. Flirtatious. Powerful.

But she had to keep reminding herself that this was business. It was ensuring her client's function was a success. It was not about how he felt for her personally. She prayed that his seductive smile and the smoky look in his eyes meant Nate was enjoying the evening and not just trying to undress her with that stare of his.

After yet another glance his way, she smiled and turned away. Then it hit her. Like a firework going off in her chest. The sensation that washed over her stopped her in her tracks. She *was* concerned about how Nate felt for her. That warm glow deep inside her was getting stronger every day. The bodice of her dress suddenly felt too tight and made it difficult to breathe. She placed her hand on the table to steady herself. Damn it! This wasn't supposed to happen. She wasn't supposed to fall in love with him. She had to protect her heart at all costs, because he'd be leaving in a few short months.

She tried to pin down the moment it happened as she had memorized every one of their little get-togethers. Meetings turned into lunches that lingered late into the afternoon. Dinners and functions lasted half the night. Stolen kisses and quickies in his apartment seemed like fun at the time.

She recalled rolling around on the couch in his apartment, laughing as they listened to music to select for their functions. Nate singing and swooning as the tunes played would be something she'd never forget. His British humor mirrored hers, and his crazy tea superstitions kept her intrigued. Just yesterday, he had told her when he found sugar undissolved in the bottom of his cup that it meant *'someone had a crush on him'*. She joked along and suggested several of his staff members—men and women—but deep down she knew it was her all along.

Nate had weaved his way into her heart. She should've seen this coming and been more cautious. Because falling in love only caused problems. Troy left her, so had Graeme; and Nate was destined to as well.

Should she walk away from the affair now or face the heartache when he left in a few months' time? With a shudder Jessica shook off her thoughts and went about attending to the guests. More gift bags, promotional giveaways, and light chitchat about business. Now was not the time to think about it. Everything could be dealt with later.

The clock struck one in the morning as security helped the last intoxicated guests to disembark from the boat and into waiting taxis. Jessica couldn't wait to finish packing up, get off her aching feet and get home to bed.

"That went exceptionally well." Nate joined Jessica on the deck outside and offered her a steaming cup of tea. "I thought you could do with this after the long night."

"Thanks." She smiled at him as she took the cup. Why did he have to be so good and thoughtful with even the little things? "I hope you enjoyed the night."

Nate leaned in and kissed her on the cheek, his lips lingering on her skin. "The scenery was spectacular."

Jessica glanced down, hiding her smile behind her cup of tea. "Well, the night's not over yet. I've still got a fair bit of packing up to do. I better go and find Lin."

Nate followed her back into the boat. "I'll stay and help. I want to make sure you ladies get home safely."

After nearly an hour the room was finally cleared and they managed to call it a night. "You right to get home, Lin?" Jessica asked.

"Yeah, I'll catch a taxi."

"Lin, don't be silly." Nate followed them off the boat and onto the boardwalk. "Come up to the Tower and one of the limos can take you wherever it is you need to go."

"Really?" Lin looked excited as they all walked through to Nate's office, boxes of leftover goodies carried in their arms.

In the hotel driveway, Jessica and Nate saw Lin off; they waved goodbye as the car drove off and disappeared from sight. Jessica finally slumped her shoulders and walked back inside the hotel. It was dimly lit, vacant and peaceful in the early hours of the morning. Another event done and dusted and her staff all off home safely.

Nate moved in a step closer toward her. "Jess, it's late. Please stay here with me tonight." His voice was barely above a whisper. "There're only a few hours left until daybreak, and for once I want to wake up next to you in my bed."

The urge to wrap herself up in his arms was unbearable. Every fiber in her body wanted to entwine itself around him. *But no. Not out here.* Jessica was so conscious of observing eyes—the staff, the security and any hidden paparazzi that might be loitering outside the hotel.

The way Nate looked at her, the allure in his eyes, and the thought of finally having him alone all to herself suddenly recharged her batteries. Staying with him and not having to use every ounce of her strength to drag herself away after sex sounded wonderful, but it just couldn't happen. "I won't stay. But you look a little disappointed at the moment and I don't like unhappy clients. So I had better do something about that. I want to make sure you are *totally* satisfied with all outcomes this evening." Jessica turned to walk down the corridor to the residential tower elevator, swaying her hips and looking back over her shoulder with an inviting glance.

Nate followed without hesitation.

* * *

Up in his apartment, Jessica absorbed the peacefulness. She stood in the darkness by the full-length window that looked out over the twinkling nightlights of Sydney. From this height, the harbor waters looked like liquid ink stretching off toward the horizon. She kicked off her shoes, curled her toes into the plush carpet and stretched her neck from side to side.

The reflection of his apartment in the windows made her notice things differently. The pictures of his daughter on the sideboard. A pile of clothing on the chair that looked like laundry. Dirty dishes left on the bench. It made him more real if that was possible. So much more to like about him.

She felt Nate walk up behind her. His body brushed against hers. Ice clinked against glass as he handed her a drink from behind. With his free hand, he moved her hair back from her ear, baring her neck. She gasped at the sensation of his ice-cold lips pressing onto her skin. A quivering jolt of fire blazed to life all over her body as his breath blew gently against her ear. His fingers snaked down over her back, found the top of her zipper, and ever so slowly slipped it down. The silky fabric slid from her shoulders and shimmied down her body onto the floor.

"You are so beautiful." Nate's lips pressed softly against the tip of her shoulder.

Jessica placed her glass on the table. She faced him and laid her hands on his chest. The slow, rhythmic rise and fall of his ribcage and the steady beat of his heart washed a strange calmness over her. Tonight there would be no craziness. No uncontrollable lust. No need to rush. Enraptured by his smoldering eyes, she leaned in and kissed him. The sweetness of his lips and tantalizing taste of his tongue playing with hers quickened her pulse. But tonight she sensed a difference in his kisses. Instead of hungry and wild, they were soft and tender as he touched her mouth or nuzzled and nipped at her neck. It seemed like forever since she had been so loving and sensual with anyone.

One button at a time, she undid his shirt and slipped it away from his chest. She ran her fingers over his stomach and down to the top of his pants, watching his sculpted torso flex as he registered her featherlight touch.

The silence that hung between them as their eyes met made Jessica's heart race. This was too much. Too close. Too good.

As if she were standing on the edge of the bridge about to bungee jump into the ravine below, Jessica hesitated. Her heart was begging to let love in, but her head was trying to find a way out. There was no time for further doubt as Nate's lips captured hers, and he swept her up in his arms and carried her to the bedroom.

Every one of her senses was in overdrive as Nate lay her down on the bed and stood before her. Her eyes feasted on his magnificent physique. Her mouth craved to taste his lips against hers again. She could hear his deep breaths. Her fingers ached in anticipation to touch him.

Hunger for him built as she watched every one of his taut muscles move as he shimmied out of the rest of his clothes and threw them on the floor. She could never get enough of his ripped abs and sculpted arms. His wandering hands felt warm as they slid over her body and removed her bra and panties. As he lay down beside her, she closed her eyes when he started to kiss his way up her arm, down across her chest and then enclose his mouth over her nipple. Cupping the other, he sensually massaged it and playfully tweaked her hardened peak.

"You were amazing tonight," he said as he licked, kissed and tasted each one again before returning to her lips.

She snaked her hand over the smooth skin of his arm, across the arch of his hip and down to his groin. Eyeing his impressive erection, she fondled his testicles before stroking up along his firm, thick shaft.

He pushed against her grip and murmured in her ear. "God, that feels so good."

"I'm glad you approve."

"I won't be able to last long if you keep doing that," he said as her drew her hand away from him before nudging her down onto her back.

His soft hand skimmed up over her thighs and nestled between her legs. He stroked up and down her slit, massaged her clit and fingered her inside. He smiled contently, no doubt at her arousal, before rolling on top of her and nestling between her legs.

She brushed her hand down over his cheek, drew his lips to hers and let their tongues taste each other. She groaned with delight as he pressed his erection against her opening and slowly entered her.

Why did it have to feel so right when they were connected together? Running her hands over his shoulders and down across his back, she couldn't resist the urge and gently dug her fingernails into his flesh. Nate flinched, closed his eyes and gently rocked his hips into hers, penetrating her deeper.

"Now that ... feels good." She whispered enjoying the full length of his penis.

Jessica could not peel her eyes away from watching him. Pleasure built within her core. Every nerve ending in her body felt alive with electricity. With him buried deep inside her, she surrendered to him—body and soul. Even the mattress was unable to stop her from falling. She was lost to him in every possible way. How was she going to get her head and heart back under control after this? Tomorrow was another day because for now—Nate was hers and she belonged to him. She knotted her hand into his hair and brought his mouth down upon hers. He pulled back and stared into her eyes. His movements remained gentle, so tender and divine. He was rock hard and she could see he was struggling to stay in control. Seeing him turned on like this made the want for him burn even more. His breath hitched as she tried to pick up the pace.

"Jess. Slow. We're in no rush. Tonight, you're mine."

Her blood heated and curled through her veins as he worked his magic. Her fingers clawed at his back, drawing him closer to her so she could press her breasts into his chest. The friction of skin on skin, the contact of her body to his, ignited the air all around them.

His lips were everywhere. On her mouth. On her face. On her neck. His warm breath, playful nips and licks danced across her skin as he continued to thrust inside her. Near panting for her breath, she drew her knees up beside her so he could penetrate her even deeper.

The sound of the guttural groan within his throat sent shivers through her from her head down to her toes. Her insides throbbed uncontrollably, begging for more as he pushed into her. Her heartbeat pounded. Her muscles ached. She grabbed on to his butt cheeks and let him ride her to the edge.

Her back arched and she cried out his name as she came, her body convulsing and flooding with rivers of intoxicating bliss. Muscles relaxed in satisfied contentment. She opened her eyes to focus and realized Nate was coming too. As his body shuddered, his eyes never left hers. His gaze remaining dark, smoldering and intense, making her heart beat erratically in her chest.

That had been one of the most sensual, tender orgasms she'd ever had in her life.

This type of ... lovemaking ... was entering the gray area she so desperately wanted to avoid.

He fell beside her, wrapped his arms around her and drew her into his chest. She felt amazing, scared out of her wits and utterly exhausted. She rubbed her hands over his chest, feeling his heart beat next to hers. She just needed a moment to catch her breath. Yes. She'd get up and leave in just one minute.

* * *

Jessica stirred. She was dreaming of making sensual love to Nate until the dawn broke in the eastern sky. His kisses ... His touch ... The warmth of his lips on her shoulder curled her lips into a smile. The movement of his body as he snuggled into her from behind. It made her feel safe and secure. It felt so real. She could even feel the hairs on his legs brushing against hers, and the smooth skin of his chest pressing against her back.

Jessica's eyes shot open. "Nate?"

"Morning," he said, as he continued with his trail of kisses.

"Sorry, I fell asleep." Panic crept across her. "I'll be out of here in a sec."

As Jessica tried to wriggle out of his grasp, Nate draped his heavy arm over her chest. "You're not going anywhere." He rolled on top of her to restrain her even further. He laced his fingers with hers and pinned them back against the pillow. She started to melt like a marshmallow in a fire as he nuzzled his way down her neck.

"I shouldn't have stayed. You know that." Her body seemed

to have a mind of its own as it responded to the touch of his lips.

"Why do you insist on leaving?" He edged his way down her body.

She bit her lip as he reached her breasts, taunting her nipples to erection with the tip of his tongue.

Oh God. That feels so good. No ... Focus.

"You know why. This is too much." Jessica squeezed her eyes shut and tried to slow her racing heart.

Nate stopped and gazed down at her. A slight furrow etched his brow. Just as he opened his mouth to say something the doorbell rang.

"Are you expecting someone else for the weekend?" Jessica cocked one eyebrow up at him.

"No, not at all. I'll see who it is."

Jessica grabbed a spectacular view of his naked bottom as he picked up a thick black robe from his chair. He headed out the bedroom door, leaving it slightly ajar.

Jessica heard voices and panicked. *Oh shit!* It was Brooke, his assistant. What the hell was she doing here? Jessica's clothes were on the floor in the living room, and her bag and coat were on the table. Brooke would surely notice Nate had someone here.

Their voices came through the door.

"I have all your flight schedule and itinerary for you," Brooke said. "Your plane leaves tomorrow night via Singapore at one o'clock in the morning."

Jessica shook her head with disbelief. He was leaving? Via Singapore. To where? Why hadn't he told her?

Jessica heard the sound of a newspaper being rustled. "Your little party last night made page three in the papers. Who's this you're kissing on the boat deck. It's such a blurry photo taken from miles away."

"What?" Nate sounded stressed.

"Oh shit!" Brooke hesitated. "I didn't know you *still* had company. So you did have a lucky night. About bloody time!" There was a cheekiness in her voice. "Oh ... Oh my ... Isn't ... isn't that the dress Jessica was wearing? Oh ... Oh my God, you didn't. Did you? With Jessica?"

Jessica cringed from her hiding place in the bedroom. She wished she could be engulfed by the mattress and disappear. *Busted!*

"Brooke, it's not what you think," Nate said.

"I think a lot of things, Nate. What am I supposed to *not* think? So, it's Jessica in the picture? I've suspected there was something going on, but I've kept my mouth shut. Was last night the first time?"

Jessica heard Brooke gasp as, no doubt, Nate shook his head.

"No. You're right. It's been going on for a while." Nate sounded distressed.

"While I'm glad you're finally getting some—"

Jessica was stunned that his assistant talked to him so bluntly.

"—it's a good thing you're leaving. Maybe this whole thing will blow over without too much notice."

"Let's hope so. Not a word of this to anyone. Okay?" Nate said. "Thanks for the itinerary. That's all for now. I'll talk to you later."

"Oh, I'm gone. You don't have to ask me twice. You are so right, though. You will be talking to me about ... this ... whatever this is."

A moment later, Jessica heard the front door close. She flopped back down on the bed and pulled the sheet up over her head. She heard Nate walk back in to the room.

"Jess? You okay? Um, I guess you heard Brooke."

"Yep." She lowered the sheet. "When were you going to tell

me you were leaving?"

Nate looked distraught. "Please get dressed and we'll talk. I'll go put the kettle on."

When she walked out into the dining area, Nate had made two cups of tea. Jessica slipped into the chair beside him at the table. She curled her fingers through the handle of the white china cup and savored the first sip.

"I had a call from London yesterday," Nate began. "The board meeting has been brought forward to next week. Originally I was just going to Singapore to spend the school holidays with Lucy, but now she's going to stay with me in London while Rachael goes to a conference in Edinburgh and the nanny takes a week off." He swiveled his cup around in his hands, a solemn look on his face.

"Oh." Jessica was startled by the sudden news. "So when will you be back?"

"Two weeks. Not long."

She couldn't hide the disappointment in her face as she stared at her tea. Two weeks without Nate sounded like a very long time to her. She missed him already.

He brushed her hair back behind her ear, his soft touch filling her with warm desire. "Will you spend the day with me?"

Jessica turned her face toward him. His blue-gray eyes looked like an ocean that she could swim in forever. Alarm bells were going off in her head—but she ignored every one of them. Something had changed between the two of them last night. Something that meant a bit of time apart would do her good. But he wasn't gone yet. "I'm going to watch Conner play rugby later on this morning. How about dinner tonight—before you go?"

"Dinner?" He raised his eyebrow. "Dinner sounds wonderful, but it feels like I've eaten at every restaurant within walking distance of here. Can you recommend somewhere else we could go?"

"How long has it been since you had a home-cooked meal?" Was she really digging herself into a deeper hole? Surely one dinner before he left would be fine.

"Let me see. I left home when I was seventeen, so ... fifteen years."

"Are you serious?"

"Not quite, but it has been a bloody long time."

"Would you object to me cooking you dinner ... at my place?" She'd made the offer so she couldn't really back out of it now.

"You can cook?"

"I'm no master chef, but I can whip up a mean chicken and pesto pasta."

"I'll bring the wine."

Chapter 12

In her house at Point Piper, a few miles from the heart of the CBD, Jessica stood at her kitchen bench and fussed over making fresh pesto while she awaited Nate's arrival.

After Conner's game, she'd spent the afternoon shopping for groceries; her fridge was usually bare because she often ate out or ordered takeaway. She cleared the unopened mail off her buffet and had taken several magazines out of their plastic packets and put them in her magazine rack. She ran through a final checklist in her head. Yes, the dining table was set with polished cutlery, wine and water glasses, and she'd bought fresh flowers and placed them in a vase in the center of the table. Yes, she'd cleaned the downstairs bathroom and put out fresh handtowels. Yes, she'd tidied and vacuumed the floor, in spite of the fact her cleaner had only come three days ago.

Why the hell did I invite him for dinner? At my house of all places. It's like a date when we shouldn't be dating!

Jessica knew she'd crossed the line by inviting him to her home. But so many lines had been crossed, it now all seemed to be scribble on a page. Apprehension had taken up residence all day in every one of her muscles. Bringing him to her house felt too personal. But after she'd stayed with him last night, their casual sex was no longer just casual. Her black and white relationship with Nate was suddenly a colossal mess of color. Butterflies fluttered within her belly as she watched the minutes tick by and muttered an obscene number of profanities.

She jumped when the doorbell rang just shy of seven. She checked over the food once more, making sure everything was in place before she headed across the room and opened the door. Dressed casually in jeans that hung low on his hips and a long-sleeved black jersey sweater that stretched firmly across his chest, Nate's blue-gray eyes lit with warmth as she greeted him.

* * *

"For you." Nate handed Jessica a bottle of red wine.

"Thank you. Come in." She stepped aside and let him enter.

He glanced around the house. It was nothing like he expected. He had envisaged strong lines and contemporary furnishings like her office. But no, this was all neutral and urban country. Big wooden dining table and chairs, leather couches and timber blinds.

Coats hung on a stand by the entrance, and a few pairs of exercise shoes were lined up neatly in a row underneath it. A rack by the couch was overflowing with *Times* and *BRW* magazines that didn't look read. Color-coordinated cushions lay scattered across the couches. Photos and artwork of countryside scenery lined the walls.

It made him miss his home. It had been three months since he was at his house in London and nearly a year since staying in his apartment in New York. It had never bothered him until recently, but seeing this before him struck a chord. Was it that he wanted more stability in his life? Maybe even to settle down? *Like that's ever going to happen!*

"You have a lovely home." Nate said as he walked across the timber floor toward the kitchen.

"You should take a look of the view I have down over the harbor." She swept her hands toward the bi-fold doors that led out onto the patio. He took a quick glance but he preferred the view of her bottom swaying in front of him as she walked. The delicious smells from the kitchen drew him back from his wandering mind.

"I hope you didn't go to too much trouble for dinner. It looks like you're making a feast?" Nate observed the mass of food sprawled across the benchtop as he opened and poured the wine.

"Pasta for dinner and apple crumble with hot custard for dessert. I did cheat and buy the custard." Jessica smiled.

"I'm impressed. It looks amazing."

"Wait until you taste it before you make such a bold statement." She laughed as she took a glass from him. "Cheers to home cooking."

"Cheers."

It felt like for the first time they were truly alone. No staff loitering around outside closed doors, no sneaking in and out of his apartment. It was nice, for just a while, to not have to be the boss, or worry about being caught in a compromising position with Jessica. For the first time in a long time Nate was able to relax. He felt like a man on a date. *A date?* That put a serious note on things. He liked Jessica a lot. But seeing his picture spread across several papers and in the headline news today was not what he needed. It had given him a firm reality check. Two weeks away would do him some good. Without Jessica around he might be able to think straight with the head on his shoulders and not the one between his legs. He needed to refocus. But as he drank from his glass, unable to take his eyes off Jessica, he knew that was going to be extremely difficult to do. But he still had a few hours up his sleeve.

"Hmm. I have another proposition for you."

Her eyes sparkled with curiosity.

"How does wine, sex, then dinner sound?" Nate said as he curled his arm around her waist and pressed his lips into neck, just below her ear. He lingered there enjoying the feel of her skin on his mouth and the smell of her sweet perfume.

"That sounds like a grand plan." She took his hand and led him upstairs to the bedroom.

* * *

Jessica couldn't hide the playful smile on her face as she ate dessert on the couch with Nate. He stood and cleared the plates away and was returning to the living room with the bottle of wine when he stopped in front of an old family portrait on the sideboard.

"The family?"

"Yeah. I really need to move that photo. I don't need a picture of my ex-husband lying around anymore. I just never seem to get around to doing odd jobs around the house." Jessica watched him closely as he looked at the photo.

"You were so young when you had Conner." Nate looked uneasy as he held the frame in his hand. "How's it been going with Troy?" There was a sudden edge in his voice. "No old feelings for him bubbling to the surface?"

"It's been a crazy couple of months, but no." As if she'd tell him that she had many sleepless nights pondering that very notion.

"You're sure?" Nate's intense glare made her feel uncomfortable. Did she detect a hint of jealousy in his tone?

"Yes." Troy had certainly stirred many dormant memories

but she wasn't about to let Nate in on that. She was still trying to place how she felt about him. But regardless, it was nothing compared to how she felt about Nate. No other man had ever made her feel this way. "I'm occupied elsewhere at present." She bit her lip as she looked at him.

"Oh, I see." A smile touched the corner of his mouth and he turned away to look at the picture once more.

She couldn't read his expression. At times he was an open book, but now he possessed a poker face that would put any gambler to shame. Just when she desperately wanted to know how he felt, she couldn't read a thing from him. She couldn't deny the chemistry between the two of them. In spending time together she realized how compatible they were—in business and in their interests. She was standing at a crossroad and didn't know which way to turn. Being discovered by Brooke and the press just shed a new light on how stupid they'd been. Now she battled with a new dilemma. Should she continue their affair and face a broken heart when he left in a few months, or break it off now? A little pain now, rather than later.

Maybe if she knew how he felt, it might make the decision easier. She closed her eyes and took a deep breath. "Nate?"

"Yeah." He glanced over at her. "What's wrong?" His face washed over with concern. With a few long strides across the room he was sitting beside her on the couch.

"We need to talk." Jessica saw that flicker of horror in his eyes, which wasn't going to make this easy. She took a large gulp of her wine. "You've avoided the topic all evening. I saw the picture of us in the paper and online. We need to prepare for some PR fallout."

She'd read the article written by Kelly White, Meredith's copywriter. Meredith had been digging around Nate for weeks and she finally had her card to play. *"Like Father, Like Son! Nate Somers With Mystery Woman. Who Is She?"* While there had been no direct names dropped, the article speculated about it being her with Nate. Lucky the photograph didn't capture her from the distant angle. Security around the boat had worked wonders.

She saw his hand tighten its grip on his leg. "Brooke will talk with you if anything further happens in the next few days. We had a couple of calls today from reporters digging around but we've managed to deflect them." He grimaced, looking uncomfortable. "I'm hoping this just disappears. I don't think I'm that much of an interesting subject."

"Will Brooke tell the team?" Jessica asked. "The launch is getting too close; we don't need the media suddenly focusing on us and not the hotel. I like to create media frenzies for my clients, yes—but not when it involves their personal life ... or me." She closed her eyes. She couldn't face being humiliated or her reputation being ruined. She was a fool to think that they could keep their affair secret.

Nate shook his head. "She won't tell anyone."

Being photographed would make Nate more of a target now. There would be more paparazzi and reporters lurking around the hotel and at every corner.

"Things have changed between us," Jessica went on. "You know it has. It's not *just sex* anymore. I really like you ... a lot. But in the light of things, we need to be realistic. The launch is more important than anything else. So, what do you want to do? Do we lie low? Be more careful? Stop—" She didn't like the sound of the last option but was everything worth the risk to be with him for just a few more months?

He took her hand in his. He hung his head low and avoided looking into her eyes. "I can't afford to have any more bad PR at the moment. Especially gossip that mirrors my father's behavior. I'm sure you can understand that."

She felt a crushing pain in her chest. Nate wasn't anything

like his father. He wasn't married and, although she had no way of knowing for certain, she didn't think she was one of many women that Nate was sleeping with around the world.

Silence lingered in the air. His touch felt clammy as he toyed with the fingers of her hand, holding it on his lap. Jessica jumped when his phone rang loudly in his pocket. He grabbed it from his jeans and answered it with annoyance. It was his driver outside ready to take him to the airport.

He turned to her. "Look, I have to go. I'll see you in two weeks."

Jessica's aching heart lurched. "Is that it? Can you honestly say that nothing's changed for you? I think I'm falling for you and I'd like to know how you feel about me. Am I really nothing more than a quick fuck to you? Has Rachael left you so cold that you'll never let anyone in?" Was she so blinded by her own feelings for Nate that she missed vital signs? "Is everything always about business with you?" She wanted to slap herself in the face as she heard her own voice. For so long her life had just been about business, but now things were changing because she had developed feelings for him. That wasn't supposed to be part of their deal. Right now she didn't care if they both made headline international news. She knew right then that she wanted to risk everything to be with him for the next few months.

He grimaced at her comment before standing up and retrieving his jacket and wallet from the table. She stood up and followed him to the door. "You and I are so alike," he said. "Business has to come first. And I have to go and attend to mine. I'll call you from London."

"Right. So that's it?" Frustration was bubbling to the surface. "No more us, is that what you want?"

"Jess, don't." His jaw flexed as he spoke, his eyes full of concern.

"Don't what, Nate? Sorry, I momentarily forgot that this was just an affair. No strings attached, right?"

He sighed. "I have to go." He grabbed her around the waist and pulled her body hard up against his. He pressed his lips tightly to hers and took the breath from her lungs. She tried to push him away, pressing the palms of her hands into his chest. But his arms held on to her so tightly, feeling so strong and protective around her. Her brow furrowed as his lips smothered hers. His kiss so full. Intense. Passionate. She struggled, but all her efforts were futile and her knees grew weak. She opened her mouth and kissed him in return, entwining her hands around his neck. With one final deep luscious kiss, he released her from his embrace. His breath was hot upon her skin. "I'm so sorry, Jess, but this is how it has to be. No strings because business always wins. Always will. I'll see you in a few weeks."

Nate slipped out the door. Jessica stood there stunned, staring at the back of it. Her heart struggled to pump her blood through her constricted veins. *What just happened?* She ran her hand through her hair as she recalled the last few minutes of conversation and replayed it over and over in her head. *'Business comes first, business wins'*. She had told him that she was falling for him and somehow their conversation went off on a different tangent. *Fuck!* Her heart beat painfully as she realized he was gone. Business came first. They had to avoid the gossip. She could only conclude that their affair was over. Work was his priority and always would be. And who was she trying to kid? Because work was her priority as well.

Come on. She tried to pull herself together. This was a good thing. A little pain now instead of a total heartbreak at the end. That was the logic. But why was it so hard to even contemplate moving? Her whole body ached and she felt emotionally drained. Surely this was for the best, because there was no possibility of a happy ever after in the story of Nate and Jessica.

Chapter 13

Nate ran his hand through his tousled hair as the driver sped toward the airport. With Jessica's words spinning around in his head, he felt the early stages of a headache coming on. He closed his eyes and rubbed his fingertips against his temples. Why did she have to go and fall for him? What could he possibly offer her other than a casual affair? He fought off the ache inside his chest as he thought how nice something long-term would be. But his future was the Somers empire. He'd sworn to himself never to get close to anyone again after learning the hard way with Rachael. And he was more than happy with that resolution. Well … content anyway. He shouldn't have let his fling with Jessica get this far. But the look in her eyes when he walked out of her house made his heart falter. He never wanted to hurt her. He never wanted anyone to experience what he went through with Rachael or what he saw his mother go through.

Yet here he was, speeding toward Sydney airport, about to board a plane to go and see the woman who'd turned his heart to ice.

As his fists clenched tight and his nails dug into the palm

of his hand, he had to remember he was no longer that young, naive man from all those years ago. He'd be paying for that for the rest of his life, especially now Rachael used their innocent daughter to tie herself permanently to his wallet. No. There was no way that anyone was going to screw him over again.

But thoughts of Jessica kept on bombarding him. She shot his tainted memories of Rachael out of his mind like a fighter pilot shooting targets from the sky. As streetlights flickered across his face, he closed his eyes and inhaled deeply. The scent of Jessica's perfume lingered on his clothes. The feel of her lips was still imprinted on his mouth. She was so different from anyone else he had ever met before. He wanted to spend evenings at home with her, cooking meals and lazing about on her couch. Take walks along the beach and have dinner together with friends. She had created a sense of longing in him that he'd never comprehended before—ever.

When did things change? It surprised him, but didn't have him running scared when he realized that his frozen heart had certainly started to melt around her.

The vision of Jessica's long legs wrapped around his waist, along with her breathtaking smile, filled his mind. He'd been enraptured by her from the first moment they met. So much for a casual affair! He was in a relationship whether he liked it or not. All those times he didn't understand why he'd concocted some crazy reason to see her and get her into his bed. Now it was all starting to make sense. He'd been falling in love with her. As he brushed his hands over his face, an overpowering sensation grew in his chest. There was no way he could deny his feelings for her anymore.

Had he just screwed everything up between them? He didn't want his affair with her to end. Not like this. Business had been his number one priority for so long he'd forgotten how to care about anyone or consider anything else. Although their remaining time together was limited, he wanted to spend as much of it as possible with her. Plans to win her back were already formulating in his head. He desperately willed the next two weeks to pass quickly so he could return to her. If it cost him his soul, she would be worth every penny.

* * *

Shaking off the tiredness and tension he felt in his shoulders, Nate was looking forward to a few days off with his daughter. A much-deserved break after a week of board meetings and business developments. When Rachael arrived in London with Lucy, Nate was stunned at how much his daughter had grown in the few months since he'd seen her last. She was definitely two or three inches taller. Her beautiful little face now had a dusting of freckles across her nose. Her long, straight black hair, just like her mother's, nearly reached down to her waist. As he picked her up and twirled her around in a big bear hug, he realized how much he missed her.

There was no love lost with Rachael when she left for Edinburgh. Lucy even seemed to come alive the minute her mother stepped out the door.

"Where to first? Grandma's or the park?" Nate asked as he rattled his brain. He had no idea what a seven-year-old girl would like to do for entertainment.

"Grandma's!" his daughter squealed in delight.

After lunch with his mother, a long afternoon in the park and an early dinner, Nate managed to tuck Lucy into bed. He felt exhausted as he sank into the leather chair in his home office and sipped on a steaming hot cup of tea. Oh, he'd missed the strong taste of a good Yorkshire blend! In his haste of making the fresh pot, he'd left the lid off while it brewed. He'd frozen and stared at it lying on the bench. Yet another one of his grandmother's superstitions had played loudly through his mind. *Bad news was on the way!* It wasn't a good sign. The hotel launch was on track. There was no major fallout from his photograph taken with Jessica. His father was lying low. What could possibly be on the horizon for him now?

Whatever was coming his way, he needed to be prepared. Refreshed and re-energized. A few days away to spend some time with Lucy sounded like heaven. As he glanced through the extensive list of emails on his laptop, he was further convinced of the need to get out of London. He picked up his cell phone and dialed Mindy, his assistant while Brooke stayed behind in Sydney.

* * *

As Nate sat down in the seat on board the Somers' private jet, he remembered he'd forgotten to call Jessica and let her know of his whereabouts. *For business purposes, of course!* He chuckled to himself because it felt strange finally admitting that he cared about someone after so long. He was making plans for a reconciliation with her when he returned to Australia, but that was under wraps for now. With a deep breath, he reached for his cell phone and rang her number. One quick call before take-off.

"Hey Jess." It felt so good to hear her voice. "I'm about to board a plane. For a bit of a holiday, I'm taking Lucy to Paris for the week." He glanced over at his daughter, who was sitting quietly next to him in her seat, drawing a picture on her iPad. "We're going to Disneyland, do some sights and some shopping. Then I'll be back in London for a day or two before heading back to Sydney. Brooke is also going to take a week off from this Friday, so for anything work related call William or Martin at the hotel."

"Um, sure." Jessica said. "Will do. You two have a good week."

Hearing her on the phone tugged at his heart. She sounded

so distant, and not just because of the miles that lay between them. He wanted to tell her he was sorry and make up for the words said when he left. But that type of conversation was inappropriate in front of Lucy. Now was not the time. And he would much rather do it in person with the high probability of some great make-up sex. He hung up and closed his eyes. He missed Jessica and was counting down the days until he could be back in her arms.

* * *

Since Nate left for Paris, Jessica had only received the odd work-related email from him and one or two missed phone calls—no messages. The different time zones were a struggle, and she had so much to discuss with him about the launch. Nate was supposed to return in a few days, but suddenly her skin started to crawl with an uneasy sensation. Something didn't feel right. Her intuition was in overdrive and suspicion spread like a nasty disease. Surely it was nothing, she was just being silly.

But her liquid doubts solidified when an email arrived in her inbox early on Friday morning, two days before his return.

To: Jessica Mason
From: Nate Somers
Subject: Delayed
Jess,
Will be delayed in London on business. Fly out on Wednesday. Talk soon.
Nate.

Jessica's heart sank. Even though their affair was over, she was still looking forward to seeing him again. She glanced at her watch and made the quick calculation. It was evening in London, about ten o'clock. She could fit in one quick call to Nate before she headed into her first meeting for the day. She dialed his cell phone and listened to it ring.

No answer.

She gazed out the window. Usually seeing the city gardens come back to life in springtime made her feel re-energized after the long cold winter months. But today the sight of blossom-filled planters and bright green shoots breaking out on all the trees did little to brighten her mood. She needed to shake off this melancholy quickly. If she could kick herself, she would. She gritted her teeth and slapped her hand down on her desk. Enough was enough. No man was worth brooding over. A smile tugged at her lips as she felt her hard-headed determination kick back to life.

The bounce returned to her step as she launched a new fashion magazine in the evening, watched Conner's game on Saturday and attended the Spring Horse Racing Carnival Dinner that night. Sunday she woke up near midday, shocked that she'd managed to sleep in to such an hour. Lazily she stretched out among her crumpled sheets, puffed up her pillow, turned on her side and dozed off again.

It was good to be back in the office on Monday morning. Sitting at her computer with a freshly brewed tea in hand, she truly felt revitalized and ready to tackle the week ahead.

Out of the corner of her eye, her daily media alert email gathering news on Somers Hotel caught her attention. Rather than a listing of items highlighting the opening, this one was overflowing with articles on Nate.

Jessica blinked and had to read it twice. Three times in fact.

The paparazzi had been hot on Nate's tail since he'd arrived in London two weeks ago. There'd been photographs of him laughing and playing in the park with Lucy, out eating dinner with his mother, and several images of Rachael or Nate ducking in and out of what looked like a hotel lobby—she assumed they would have been dropping off and picking up Lucy.

But the headlines were different today. She opened the file and clicked on the first item. There was a photo of Nate dashing into a building, his hand outstretched trying to block the cameras, Rachael running beside him and his arm protectively tucked around her. The news sites read:

"Nate Somers out on the town with ex-wife. Relationship rekindled?"

"Seen at London hospital. Is a baby on the way?"

"Back with his Asian Princess."

"Nate Somers reunited with Rachael Lang."

Jessica stared at the screen. She was gobsmacked as she read article after article and saw photo after photo of Nate with Rachael—in the car, on the street, having a cup of tea, and more—all announcing Nate was back with his ex-wife. Unable to comprehend what she was seeing, Jessica picked up the phone to call him. She didn't care what time it was.

* * *

"Hello. This is Lucy speaking."

"Oh. Hi Lucy, this is Ms Mason calling. Is your dad there, please?"

"He's in bed with Mommy."

What? She coughed as she heard his daughter's innocent voice, and a stab of pain shot through her heart.

Nate is in bed with Rachael! What the hell was going on?

"She's sleeping." Lucy said.

"Okay. That's fine. I'll talk to him later." Jessica trembled uncontrollably as she hung up the phone. Paralyzed, she stared at nothing for a good five minutes as her head reeled from the news. *Goddamnit!*

She yanked the phone into her hand and called him once again. Maybe she was a sucker for punishment. Maybe she just wanted the truth.

"Ha-lo," a woman with broken English said on the end of the line.

"Hello, this is Ms Mason. Is Mr Somers available, please?" Taking a big deep breath didn't help much to calm Jessica's jitters.

"No. Sor–ree."

"May I ask who's speaking, please?"

"I'm the nanny."

Thank goodness it wasn't Rachael. But why is the nanny in London?And why was Lucy up at such a late hour?"I need to speak with Nate on a matter of urgent business, please."

"Mr Nate ... with Ms Rachael. In bedroom. Busy. Do not disturb."

Jessica hung up and anger boiled through her blood. How could she have been so stupid? Nate *was* back with his ex-wife. All his talk about his horrid ex-wife was all bullshit. That bastard! That asshole! He'd lied to her. He'd seemed so genuine and honest. Humiliation raised its ugly head as she stood up and paced the floor behind her desk. How could she have been so vulnerable? So gullible?

She stopped in her tracks and a chill washed over her. A pain clenched tightly around her heart as she clutched her hand to her chest. It was in that moment her heart broke in two. This was worse than when he left because now she knew she'd been betrayed. Her eyes filled with tears and resentment bubbled through her veins.

There was a knock at her office door.

"What?" Jessica snapped.

It was so out of character. Jessica saw Zoe jolt back in surprise. "Um. I have the radio station promotional campaign schedules you requested." She shuffled a folder full of papers onto the desk. "Are you okay?"

Jessica wiped away a tear from her eye and sat back down

in her chair. Drawing on her inner strength she did her best to pull herself together. She was never emotional in the office—ever. "I'm fine. Absolutely fine. Just a lot of work on and feeling a bit stressed."

"You're sure?"

"Yes. Thanks for these. I'll go over them soon."

* * *

Several days passed and Jessica had still not heard a word from Nate. She absorbed herself in her work, rolling out new campaigns, schedules for the launch and overseeing artwork from her team. It was late in the office on Wednesday evening when an email notification from Nate popped up on her computer screen. She toyed with idea of ignoring it, but she couldn't, of course. She clicked on the link.

To: Jessica Mason

From: Nate Somers

Subject: Drama

Sorry haven't called. Lucy was in an accident and broke her leg on Saturday afternoon. She's okay. I'll be staying in London for two more weeks until she can fly. Rachael also staying.

It is crazy over here as I've started a new project as well. I'm about to head into a day of meetings and budget planning.

Talk soon.

Nate

For a split second Jessica was full of concern for his daughter. That quickly disappeared when the daily news alert brought the latest headlines.

"*Rachael moves back in.*"

"*Romance blossoms.*"

"*Happy family reunited.*"

Jessica covered her face with her hands. The horrid facts had finally been hammered into her head as the pictures ground salt into her wounds. On top of this, he'd simply cut off nearly all forms of communication with her. He never answered his cell any more, didn't reply to texts or return calls she made directly to his office. And this had been one of the first emails from him in ages.

Another week disappeared, and slowly but surely Jessica's resilience returned. Each day, she dug a little deeper and tried to lock away her feelings for Nate in the dark dungeons within, and throw away the key. It was so much harder than she thought it would be. Her chest felt hollow, her soul incomplete. But she was tough. She'd get over it. She'd done this before.

Nate was gone. Life would go on.

* * *

Jessica massaged her shoulder and tried to knead out some of the tension, aches and pains she felt from working too many late nights in a row. Four weeks had passed since Nate had left. Not that she was counting. She needed a breather; Gumtrees was the solution. But could she avoid Troy? She didn't want to deal with him with her current state of affairs ... or lack thereof.

With a slight hesitation, she picked up her phone.

"Gumtrees Winery and Retreat, Marie speaking." Jessica realized she'd been holding her breath.

"Hi, it's Jessica Mason. I know it's short notice, but what's the likelihood of a cabin being available this weekend?"

"Let me check." Jessica could hear Marie's fingers clacking away on the computer keyboard. "Yeah, we can squeeze you in. Even in your usual cabin."

"Great. Um ... will Troy be there?" She closed her eyes and said a silent prayer. *Please no. Please no.*

"I'm sorry, no. He'll be in Melbourne at a conference. Do you still want to make the booking?" Marie and Nick had been surprised at finding out about her past with Troy. They all made a good joke about it and concluded that it was a small world.

"Yes, I need a break."

She felt relieved that she could avoid Troy.

* * *

After the long drive up to Gumtrees on Friday evening after work, Jessica checked into her cabin and soothed her aching muscles in a long, hot bath. After lighting the fire, she curled up in her blanket and settled into reading. It wasn't until a knock on the door, early in the morning, startled her awake. She couldn't even remember falling asleep.

"Who is it?" she called out. Rubbing her sleep-filled eyes she saw it was six-thirty in the morning on the digital clock beside the bed.

"It's Troy."

Shit! She raked her hands through her tangled hair, stretched and tried to wake up. Gathering the blanket around her shoulders, Jessica bustled over to open the door. The morning chill hit her, sending a shiver through her her entire body.

"Rough night?" Troy grinned.

"No. I fell asleep on the couch." Jessica felt uneasy. "What are you doing here? I thought you were in Melbourne?"

"Nick really wanted to go and meet up with some new suppliers. He tried to get a last minute ticket, but couldn't. So I gave him mine. He left early this morning to catch a flight."

"How kind of you."

Light shimmered off Troy's blond whiskers as the sun rose behind him in the eastern sky. He was quite a sight standing there in faded blue jeans, oilskin Driza-bone coat, worn-out RM boots and dusty old Akubra hat.

"I'm sorry to wake you. Nick told me you came up last night and I was wondering if you wanted to come for a ride out along the bush trail and up through the hills." Troy gestured toward the stables, nervousness touching his voice.

"Oh, um," Jessica hesitated.

Months had passed since Troy found out about Conner, and phone calls had remained her only contact with him since he'd met their son. It felt so strange trying to rebuild their friendship after he'd been gone for so long.

What the hell. A horse ride can do no harm. "But I haven't had breakfast or anything."

"How about you get dressed? I've got a snack packed and I'll shout you breakfast in the restaurant later. I'll go saddle Stirling for you. See you in about fifteen minutes?"

"Okay."

* * *

Dressed in tight riding pants, jacket and boots, Jessica strolled into the stables. Both horses were ready as Troy finished off strapping a saddlebag to his mount.

"Looks like you need some fresh air," said Troy.

"It's been a rough few weeks. Work's exceptionally busy at the moment."

"Come on. Let's hit the trails."

The two horses, Stirling and Jasper, carried Troy and Jessica through the towering eucalyptus trees, across the stony mountain creek, over the open fields and up into the rolling hills that overlooked the vineyard. Troy pulled his horse to a halt on top of the ridge, overlooking the farm, the Brokenback Mountains and the town in the distance.

"It's beautiful up here, isn't it?" His breath misted in the cold morning air. "Want some tea? I packed a thermos and some muffins that Marie baked for breakfast."

"You came prepared, didn't you?" Jessica reined in next to him. The mention of tea won her over.

They tied up the horses to a nearby gum tree. Troy pointed. "Let's go sit down there on those boulders."

As he slung the saddlebag over his shoulder, he gently took Jessica's hand in his and led the way over the rugged rocks through knee-high tufts of grass. Jessica hesitated at first. She still struggled between hating him and remembering how she felt for him at sixteen. Plus there was Nate. Although Nate had gone, her heart was still healing after their brief affair. Troy's hand around hers set off no fireworks or crazy heat flushes on her skin. Nothing compared to Nate's touch. But what took Jessica by surprise was how Troy's hold felt so familiar after all this time—only weathered and a bit rough around the edges. His fingers laced around hers the same way, he looked at her with the same glow in his eyes. He was her Troy from so long ago.

Mist snaked along the surface of the creek and thick fog hung in pockets like pillows in amongst the grape vines. Rays of sunshine crept up the valley, warming everything in their path as the sun rose further into the sky. Jessica closed her eyes and took in a deep, cleansing breath of fresh country air as they perched themselves on a large rock.

Troy poured her a cup of steaming hot tea into the lid of the thermos and passed it to her. He drank straight from the flask.

"How are you and Conner getting along?" Jessica asked.

"We're taking things slow. I'm going to come down to the city and watch him play rugby. He's also agreed to come out here every now and then to catch up."

Jessica was happy that the two men were making an effort to get along.

They fell into silence looking out at the mountains and farmland. Jessica glanced sideways at Troy and watched him blow softly into the thermos of tea. His lips were still shaped the same way, his round nose unchanged, but the small scar etched into the base of his chin was new.

"Remember we used to ride with my old neighbors up through those hills and out to the old train tracks?" Troy pointed off into the distance to the other side of town.

"Yeah. You always thought you were a better rider than me. We'd argue about it all the time."

"You liked pony club, whereas I liked the rodeos and camp-drafting. I also remember how at school you used to wear your school uniform way too short, and odd-colored ribbons in your hair. And you'd steal beer from your dad's fridge for us to drink."

Jessica let out a laugh. "I'd forgotten about all those little things."

"Do you remember being with me?" Troy rolled the flask back and forth between his hands.

"How can I not? I had Conner, remember?" Jessica stared down at the ground. "You were my first. It's just so long ago. So much has happened since then."

"You were my first, too." He grinned. "Everyone thought we'd be together forever. You wanted to own every business in town and I wanted my farm. Where did it all go wrong, Jess?"

"You left. Remember?"

Troy winced. "Right."

Jessica struggled with the hate and pain she had felt toward him for so many years. But as they talked for hours about old school friends, work, travel, family and Conner, time seemed to disappear. She was suddenly finding it hard not to like him again.

A flock of white cockatoos screeched as they took off from a nearby tree. The deafening noise made Jessica notice that it was now midmorning. Troy looked disappointed that their ride had to come to an end, as he had to return to the office to relieve Marie.

"Thanks for the ride," Jessica said, after they'd returned to the stables and put the horses away.

"Any time."

Troy's gaze lingered on her as he spoke. It made her feel awkward. All this talk had unexpectedly resurfaced old feelings and she didn't know what to make of them. She didn't need any more complications in her life. She broke eye contact and scuffed her boot in the dirt. "Come on. You promised me breakfast."

* * *

Late in the afternoon, Jessica made her way to the stables to feed Stirling and the other horses. She liked to help out when she was visiting, and it took her mind off work.

She tipped a bucket full of grain and chaff into Stirling's bin, and turned to make her way out through the stable door when Troy gave her a fright. He stood holding the door open. She stepped out of the stall and he closed it quietly behind her. Jessica held the grain bucket in her hand tightly. She was apprehensive around him all of a sudden. The talking and reminiscing on this morning's ride filled her head with lost memories of her younger, carefree days.

"Here, let me take that." Troy reached out to grab the bucket from her hand.

She pulled it away. "It's okay. I've got it."

Troy looked at her with his sapphire eyes and her heart leapt into her throat. The air stilled all around her and all she could hear was the sound of her breath rasping in and out of her lungs.

Before she could think another thought, Troy swooped in and kissed her. She froze, not expecting this at all. This was not what she wanted. This was one emotional roller coaster she did not want to ride.

She dropped the bucket with a clang and with both hands

pushed hard against his chest.

Troy took a couple of steps back as her trembling fingers touched her lips. She pushed past him and stormed out of the barn, headed directly for her cabin.

"Jess, wait!" Troy called.

Ignoring his plea, she kept on walking.

Jessica dived into her cabin, slammed the door shut and grabbed a bottle of red. She poured herself a large glass. With trembling hands, she took a couple of quick gulps to clear her head.

Everything she'd been dealing with over the past few weeks finally had her at breaking point. First realizing she was falling for Nate, then seeing him run back to his ex-wife, had left her crushed, and now she had to deal with Troy. She shook uncontrollably as she put the glass to her lips again.

The wine tasted good. She sculled the first glass and quickly poured another.

Hours later Jessica sat curled on the couch, the bottle drained. She closed her eyes as she enjoyed the numbing buzz of drunkenness coursing through her body. Somehow she'd managed to shower and put on her pajamas. In this state she wasn't even going to bother venturing out for dinner. She rarely drank so much, but sitting there mulling over Nate, Troy, Conner, work—everything—the wine had satisfied her appetite.

Jessica was restocking the fire with fresh wood when a soft knock came at her door. She stumbled over to open it up. There, in the dim porch light, stood Troy, looking worse for wear. She suspected he was as drunk as she was, if not more.

"I came to apologize," Troy slurred. "I didn't ... I mean ... My actions were uncalled for. I'm sorry. Everything is crazy about you ... About Conner. I just got lost in the moment. Please accept my apol ... ogy." Troy shivered in the cool night air. He only wore a thin shirt and faded jeans. "Jess, are you drunk?"

"I've had a few," she mumbled.

"I'm sorry. I didn't mean to upset you."

"Don't flatter yourself. There are a lot of reasons why I'm drinking. You just happen to be the main one at the moment."

"Oh."

"Why are *you* drunk?" she asked.

"Seeing you again is driving me crazy. I've been sitting up in the restaurant drinking, and then Marie kicked me out because of the guests. I was wandering around and needed to apologize for my behavior. I promise it won't happen again."

"Apology accepted. Do you want another drink?"

"Sounds good!" He followed her into the cabin and clumsily pushed the door shut behind him.

Jessica stumbled over to the small kitchenette opened a new bottle of wine and made two fresh drinks.

"Cheers!" They clinked glasses.

After they both took a long swill, their eyes met. The cabin air, warm from the fire, pressed against her skin and her heart pounded in her chest. Every cell of her body tingled with apprehension.

"You're so beautiful," Troy whispered. "Even after all these years. Finding you again has given me a new lease on life."

Jessica closed her eyes tightly. The wine made her head feel fuzzy. She couldn't think straight. With her eyes still shut, she nearly jumped out of her skin when Troy stepped forward and took her in his arms. Before she could move, his lips enclosed her mouth.

He smelt of beer and red wine. The distant memory of how he used to kiss her came flooding back as he pressed his body into hers. The shape of his mouth molded perfectly to hers. Feeling like she was freefalling with no end in sight, Jessica parted her lips and returned his kiss. She used to love the way he kissed. He was a great kisser. Her breath rasped as a muddle of thoughts and emotions spun through her head. Nate, Troy. Troy. Nate.

She should not be doing this. She pulled back and stopped still, trying to find her breath. And her common sense.

Nope. There was none of that!

Maybe this was what she needed. *No, it's not. Not so soon after Nate? Was it?* Her mind was spinning like a blender, shredding all rational thought.

Troy waited in silence, swaying slightly as his hands rested upon her hips. Jessica could see his pulse throbbing in the side of his neck. She inhaled sharply and caught her breath as she looked into Troy's eyes. The only thing she could make head or tail of was ... she was drunk.

Really drunk.

All sensibility had gone out the door when Troy walked in.

Troy didn't wait another moment. He drew her in close and kissed her again, wrapping one hand tightly around her waist, the other entangled into her hair. His tongue found hers, tasting her with a new-found hunger.

This time Jessica didn't pull away.

She responded to his touch. Their bodies pressed into each other and her hands clasped around his shoulders. Her hazy mind tried to find reason to stop but Troy felt so good—just like the old times.

"I want to make love to you," Troy whispered in her ear.

"What? Shhh!" Jessica didn't want to think as his warm breath brushed over her skin. She couldn't tell right from wrong. Up from down. She wanted to forget about Nate and didn't know what to think about Troy. Somewhere in her clouded mind this didn't seem like a good idea, considering their past and present. But what the hell. She had so many other consequences to deal with right now, what was one more? "My body isn't the same as it used to be. It's twenty years older. Everything's a little saggy and heading south after having a kid."

"You mean these?" Troy's chuckled as his hand brushed over her breast. "They look as perfect as they always did." She could feel her nipples harden under his touch. The bulge in his pants pressed into her groin as he ran his fingers down over her satin pajama shirt. She felt his fingers fumble for the edge of the fabric before he grabbed it and pulled her top up and over her head.

"I have some cellulite too."

"I don't care."

"I have a caesarean scar."

"I don't care."

"I have—" How could she explain that she was far from sixteen anymore?

"Jess. Shush. Your body is amazing."

His lips locked on to hers again and his hands began to wander.

"Do you have a condom?"

"There'll be some in the bathroom drawers." He winked and disappeared into the bathroom before returning with two blue packets. "Voila."

Jessica giggled and blushed as Troy removed his shirt to reveal his sinewy, muscular arms. As he pulled her body in to his, she tried not to make a mental comparison of his firm, stocky frame to the perfection and height of Nate's as she reached for the buckle of his belt. Nate had gone. She was free to do as she wanted. She reefed the belt from the loops of his jeans and popped open the top button.

Troy smiled at her. "Always knew how to get into my pants, Jess." His erection swelled before her as he dropped his jeans to the floor. "The only difference now is I might actually know what I'm doing."

Jessica shivered with anticipation as they moved and fell on to the bed together.

As she felt his intoxicated breath blow softly on her face, she noticed how his weight lay differently to Nate's. *Stop comparing!* Troy was nowhere near as buff in the stomach as Nate was as he loomed over her, drawing her pajama bottoms away.

He was leaning back, pulling on her elastic waistband. Then, without warning, he lost his balance and rolled off the end of the bed. There was a loud *thunk* as he hit hardwood floor.

"Oh, shit! Are you okay?" Jessica sat bolt upright.

"Fine!" Troy laughed as he made his way back onto the mattress.

The fire cracked and popped in the hearth and Jessica felt a wave of nausea ripple in her belly. An unladylike belch burned her throat as it bubbled to the surface. She put her hand up to stop Troy's advances as she felt the color drain from her face. "Shit! Stop! I can't do this."

Troy's eyes flashed with disappointment.

But it was so much more than the thought of Nate bombarding her mind as she cupped her hand over her mouth and darted for the bathroom. She made it just in time to the toilet before throwing up.

Bracing herself against the wall, she closed her eyes and tried to stop the world from spinning.

Troy called out. "Too much wine, hey?"

"I'm sorry."

With that her knees grew weak and she slid down the wall to sit on the tiled floor. Her eyelids felt so heavy as she struggled to keep them open. She rested her head down upon her arm on top of the toilet bowl. Or was it the tiles of the floor? Then everything went black.

Chapter 14

Jessica stirred from her sleep but refused to open her heavy eyes. She didn't want to move. Couldn't move. The fire must have gone out because the cabin felt cold. She pulled the blankets tightly up under her chin.

Her head felt as if someone had hit her with a sledgehammer and the sickly sweet stench of wine hung in the air. She stiffened as it dawned on her that she wasn't alone. A subtle movement next to her beneath the covers sent a lightning bolt of alarm and sharp pain through the center of her head. Every muscle tensed as images of last night came flooding back to her with a violent rush. The drinking and Troy and *oh God*, did anything else happen?

Please let this be a bad dream. Please make it all go away! This shouldn't have gone this far. But how far did it go? Jessica panicked at the mess she was in and her instinct was to flee. She didn't want to face Troy. Not now. Messing around with someone so soon after Nate was not a smart move, and with Troy of all people.

Jessica slunk out of bed and hurried to put on her clothes. Her mouth felt feral and dry like sandpaper. Every time she swallowed it hurt. Every time she turned around too quickly her head felt fuzzy. She hadn't been drunk in so long, in fact she couldn't recall the last time she'd even had a hangover. Yes, she certainly liked to indulge in a few glasses every now and then with friends, but she never got drunk. Her tummy felt queasy again as she caught sight of the two bottles of empty wine on the kitchenette counter.

Her phone vibrated on the bedside table. With bleary eyes she registered that the caller ID was Nate's. Jessica's head felt like it was about to explode. He hadn't called in nearly two weeks. *Why now?* She cursed and fumbled to switch the phone to silent, letting it ring out and go to voicemail.

She dropped her head back and glared at nothing on the ceiling. How had her world turned upside down in just a few short months? *Men! Who needs 'em!* And there was only one thing to do when she felt all confused. She hurried to pack her bags quickly, then as she was tiptoeing toward the door she heard Troy.

"Morning," he mumbled from the bed. "Going somewhere?"

The flash of his sapphire eyes made her veins flood with regret. "Yes. Home."

"What? Wait. No!" Troy sat up slowly, rubbing his head. "It's Sunday morning at—" He strained his eyes to focus on the bedside clock, "—seven o'clock. Stay for breakfast."

"I shouldn't have come here. This shouldn't have happened," she said as she waved her hand toward Troy.

"What are you talking about? Do you think ... oh?" He grinned. "Jess, calm down. Nothing happened last night. Remember? You were sick and by the time I got you to bed you were bordering on unconscious. I was just going to stay for a while to make sure you were okay, but I must have drifted off as well. But, I must say, being back together is nice."

"Whoa. We're not back together." She stumbled, pulling on her Ugg boots by the door.

"Why not?"

"Because ..." Visions of Nate jumped into her head. Regardless how much she had tried, she was still not over him.

"Why? Oh! Is there someone else?" Troy eyes washed over with hurt.

"Yes ... No ... I mean ... It's complicated." Jessica turned her eyes away.

"Well, he can't mean that much to you after kissing me like you did last night."

"I was drunk and vulnerable and you took advantage of me."

"What? Me?" Troy gasped. "Take advantage of you? You didn't have to ask me in for a drink, or kiss me back, or take my clothes off."

"I know this is ugly. I don't think either of us is in the right frame of mind to call last night justified. Let's forget it ever happened."

"So we had a little too much to drink. But we can make this work. I want to be with you, Jess."

She muffled an exasperated groan. "I gotta go," she said as she clambered around the cabin, gathered her gear, opened the door and rushed out to her car.

Yet again she left for home from Gumtrees in an emotional turmoil. Maybe she should stay away from there for good. On the way back to Sydney, she disgraced herself by having to pull her car up on the side of the road to throw up. Oh, she felt disgusting and ill. Grabbing the tissues from her glove box and water bottle from her bag, she wiped her mouth and had a sip of water before getting back in the car. Five minutes later she had to pull over again. All the time she cursed herself. How could she have kissed Troy? He slept beside her last night in her bed. Why were thoughts of Nate still rattling around inside her brain? Were her feelings for Nate even stronger than she first thought?

There was only one thing to do when the world fell apart around her. Jessica called Max.

Two hours later Max swept into Jessica's house and found her on the couch, tissues littered across her lap, sniffling uncontrollably.

"Honey, what's happened now? Why are you so upset? Are you just having a relapse over Nate?" Max walked into the kitchen and returned with two cups of tea to nestle on the lounge next to her.

"I'm an awful person. How could I do something so horrible to someone so innocent?"

"If we're talking about men, there is no such thing as innocent. Now. Tell me. What's the drama with Nate?"

"Not Nate. Troy."

"Troy? What about him?" She shuffled over closer to Jessica.

"I went out to Gumtrees. We went riding. We talked and talked about the old days. We were reminiscing and he kissed me."

"Oh. That's not so bad. That doesn't make you awful."

"Yes, it does. All I could do was think about Nate. I went back to my cabin and drank myself into a stupor. Troy turned up on my door step drunk as well and ..." Jess couldn't contain her tears.

"And ...? Oh ... *and* you slept with Troy?"

Jessica shook her head and sobbed. "No I didn't. We just kissed and got carried away a little before I was sick," she said, her voice breaking. "I tried so hard not to get emotionally involved with Nate, and when I did, he runs back to his ex-wife. See, I was right. I should never have slept with my client. Then, this weekend seeing Troy was just like old times. And his eyes,"

Jessica implored with a deep raspy voice, "why does Troy have to have the most mesmerizing eyes on the face of the planet? I just lost it. I shouldn't have drunk so much."

Max hugged her tightly. "Don't feel bad. Nate was only short-term anyway. You shouldn't feel guilty about making out with Troy. How do you feel about him now?"

Bewildered was all that came to Jessica's mind. She kept on wondering how different her life would've been if Troy had come back when he said. How would he have reacted to having a child at seventeen? Her parents still would've shipped her off to Melbourne, so would Troy have come with her and helped her pursue her dreams? Or would he have hindered them?

Jessica had always been ambitious, even at seventeen. She was grateful in so many ways to leave the small country town behind her to live in the fast-paced city. With reluctant support from her family she juggled motherhood, study and work for years. Somehow she'd made it through. With her parents reminding her every day of how ashamed they were, it had made her build a tough exterior and given her unrelenting determination. Her hunger for success paid off, and now she had a booming business and a high-flying lifestyle to go along with it.

So many what-if scenarios played through Jessica's mind, but she brushed them aside. There was no point. She had to deal with reality.

"That's just it, Max. Part of me still burns with hate for him leaving. His decision to not come home cost me twenty years. Deep down I've always wanted him to come back. But you know what? Troy reminds me so much of Graeme. Safe, warm, comfortable, a friend." Jessica took a long sip of her tea. "But things are different now. Something changed inside of me when I met Nate. He's the complete opposite of them. Nate's all wild, hot, spontaneous, and it turns me on just looking at him." Jessica saw Max trying not to laugh when she was trying to be all serious. "Troy has always had a piece of my heart, and always will. He's Conner's father, for fuck's sake. But how do I feel about him now?"

Jessica was more confused than ever. Had she been trying to deny growing feelings for him? Was it fate that had brought them back together? Maybe there was something there, deep in her heart for him that could lead to something new.

"Wow! Look at you. Talk about going from a drought to a flood. It's like you're in love with two men."

"Max, this isn't funny. Someone is going to get hurt, or all of us are, and I don't like that one bit. I'm cut up about Nate because he lied to me. That's what hurts the most. Somehow I have to find a way where I can put this mess behind me and work with him and his team for the next few months. My feelings for him were much stronger than I thought. And now Troy is only adding to my confusion. I shouldn't have let things go so far."

"I think it's too late for that, Jess."

* * *

Late in the evening Jessica was tired and ready for bed. She was showered, wrapped up in winter flannel pajamas, and her teeth were freshly brushed. After taking another two aspirin for her splitting headache, she was about to turn the light out when her cell phone rang. Her stomach curled at the sight of the caller ID. It was time to be her professional self again as she reluctantly answered the phone.

"Hi, it's Nate."

Jessica's whole body shuddered. She screwed her eyes shut and bit her lip for a second, trying not to cry. She wanted to hurl a million hurtful words at him but calmly took a breath. "Hello. To what do I owe the honor of a phone call from you?"

"It's been absolutely crazy over here. I've worked every day since returning from Paris. I'm exhausted from too many eighteen hour days. Thank you for your understanding." Nate's British accent sound so much stronger since she'd heard it last. Butterflies took flight in her belly, but she was quick to squash them down.

"Understanding? *Understanding*! What? Do you think I'm all okay with you going back to your ex-wife?" Jessica snapped.

"What?" Nate balked. "What are you talking about? I'm not back with my ex-wife."

A sharp jolt ripped through Jessica's body. "Have you seen the news? You've been all over it. Every day. You haven't returned my calls or emails. Your secretary wouldn't let me talk to you. And one time I rang and talked to your daughter and the nanny, and they both confirmed you were in bed with Rachael."

"In bed with my ex-wife ... are you kidding me?" Nate's voice resonated with fury. "I told you that I had to stay in London because of Lucy's accident and work. The majority of the time I've been locked away in meetings. With Brooke away, I know I've fallen behind on correspondence that needs my attention. But be certain about one thing, I'm definitely not sleeping with Rachael. Or anyone else for that matter."

"But the news ..." Jessica faltered.

"This is bullshit. Never believe in gossip. Lucy broke her leg falling off a climbing tower in the park the day before they were scheduled to fly home. Rachael went berserk. The only time that I ever stepped foot near Rachael or her bedroom was when we came back to the hotel after being at the hospital with Lucy. She'd knocked herself out with a sedative and I carried her onto her bed. That's it."

Jessica sat in strained silence. She covered her face with her hand as the sound of her pulse pounded in her ears. She struggled to find the words as her body rippled with shame.

"How can I believe you?"

"It's called trust, Jess." Nate sounded angry. "Rather than keep Lucy in hospital, I flew the nanny over to help and put everyone up in a suite at the hotel. As for the damn photographers everywhere, they're trying to make a buck out of nothing. I swear to you on my life."

All the pieces of the puzzle fell together. Jessica felt mortified at believing all the gossip. When it came to Nate, her mind just didn't think straight. "Nate ... I don't know what to say. For weeks I've been thinking that you'd gone back to her."

"Not ever going to happen."

"Why didn't you return my calls?"

"When I got the chance, often the hours were all wrong. I'm sorry, but work has been so hectic that hours, sometimes days, slipped by without me realizing it. I've been drawn into so many projects, plans and staff meetings since I've landed here that I've hardly had a break. Any spare moment that I've had, I've gone to see Lucy."

"You have to understand that not hearing from you only added to my confusion. Especially after our fight the night you left. Everything in the news just sounded so real." Jessica paused. "Oh ... Oh shit. Her head spun uncontrollably. "You've been gone for four weeks. I thought we were over. Things have happened."

For a few slow seconds all Jessica heard was Nate's heavy breath in the speaker of the phone.

"What things?"

"I was hurt. There was no explanation." Her hands shook as she tried to hold her phone to her ear.

"What are you saying?"

"You weren't here."

Nate remained silent.

Jessica spoke in a fluster. "I got drunk, and ... and I know it's no excuse. I was trying to get over you."

Nate's voice was barely audible above a soft whisper. "What are you trying to tell me?"

Tears finally fell from the corners of her eyes as guilt weighed down on her chest, making it hard to breath.

Silence.

"Did you sleep with someone?" he asked.

"What? No, it was just a kiss."

"Who? Do I know who it is?"

"Troy."

"Troy? You said there was nothing between you two."

"There isn't." She froze as she jumbled through her messed up emotions.

"It doesn't sound like it. How could you? Don't you think you should have talked to me first about all this stupid gossip with Rachael? I've had to deal with all this ludicrous tabloid news, Lucy's accident, and my ex-wife who I can barely tolerate as a human being anymore. Coming back to you was what has been holding me together."

"Coming back to me? What the hell is that supposed to mean?" Jessica punched her pillow hard. "When I told you I was falling for you, you left me thinking we were through. Business always wins is what you said. You ran away. Just like every other man has done in my life. What was I supposed to think? I'm not used to all this gossip and tabloid hype. You made international headlines over here. I thought it was all true." Exasperated, Jessica took a few deep breaths to try and calm down.

"I'm sorry about the night I left. I really am. But right now, I've got to sort out a public relations nightmare and get back to Sydney to work on the opening and launch. I don't need this crap from you as well."

"Nate, please. This has been a whole misunderstanding and lack of communication. Let's work it out."

"You kissed him. After you said there was nothing between you and Troy. I've never had someone I care about cheat on me before. I don't know how to handle that on top of everything else at the moment."

"Cheat? I didn't cheat." His words bit into Jessica like knives stabbing her heart. This whole mess was making her want to curl up into a tight ball and never see the light of day again.

"Maybe this is for the best, Jess. End this ... whatever this was between us. Let's just focus on the launch and move on. I'm done for now. Goodnight."

* * *

"Mr Somers, your father is on the line for you." Mindy's tired voice across the intercom startled Nate. He'd felt bad at having to call her in to work on a Sunday to help him out, but she didn't seem to mind. And, he couldn't believe he'd done nothing but stare out at the dreary London cityscape for nearly half an hour since his phone call ended with Jessica.

"Thanks, Mindy. Put him through." Nate swiveled around on his office chair to take the call. "Father, what's up?"

"Nathan. I'd like to reschedule the next board meeting to the first week of December, before everyone breaks for Christmas festivities and I head off to Aspen." Nate scowled, wondering which one of his many mistresses he would be taking away on this trip. "I'd also like you to work on a proposal on how to boost the flagging occupancy rates in Europe. They are frightfully low."

"I've already submitted a strategic plan on moving forward with Accor Hotels. They're looking to buy out some of our poor performing locations in Portugal and Greece."

"We'll see. But get marketing onto it. All of Europe is the focus now. So I need you to scale back on the opening in Sydney so we can redirect the funding elsewhere."

"Are you crazy? No way. The board would have to approve that."

"No, they don't. I have final say in all our operations."

"This is my project. You can't do this. The team from Kick Marketing have done so much. It's only two months away."

"I want the funding used in Europe. Effective immediately. Make it happen."

"I ... I won't do that to Jessica."

"Jessica? This isn't about a woman, is it? This is business, son."

Nate tried to control the anger surging through his veins from boiling over. He felt like his skin would blister. His father always did this—called unreasonable shots at unreasonable times with no concern for all those involved. "Sydney is exceeding our expectations. The promotions and pre-launch events have already boosted our bookings above anticipated levels."

"Nathan, scale it back. Have a small gathering with just some key colleagues and guests. Nothing so extravagant. Make it happen."

Yet again his father turned a blind eye to anything he had to offer. Nate got off the phone feeling deflated. While his father was still at the helm of the company, he could call all the shots. Regardless of whether it went against Nate's better judgment.

He'd been looking forward to the launch. It would've been one of the biggest and grandest events that Somers had ever done. Now it wouldn't be the same without Jessica and her team. Nate sighed heavily and felt exhaustion creep into his bones. He could be grateful for one thing, though. His father had just given him an easy way out so he didn't have to see Jessica any more. He brushed his hand over his face and rubbed the tiredness from his eyes.

Some things could be a blessing in disguise.

He spent the following hours running figures, reviewing the remaining promotional schedule, performing recalculations and making plans to pull the launch at his father's request. It took him a dozen attempts to write the email. He reread it a hundred times. He had a strong cup of tea to clear his head. Then, he sat down at his desk, had one last read of the message and hit *Send*. Jessica was about to hate him a whole lot more.

* * *

Jessica was in the middle of paperwork, calculating client billable hours for her projects when her email inbox pinged. She glanced up to see if the message was important. She looked closer when she saw it was from Nate.

To Jessica Mason; Alex Chambers

From: Nate Somers

Due to recent developments and requirements for budget reallocation, Somers Hotels formally gives notice and wishes to terminate all current activities and contracts of business with Kick Marketing and Event Management. Effective immediately. We will internally manage and proceed with a scaled back opening in November. We will pay any penalties and cover associated costs that your company may have incurred up to this date of notice.

Brooke will schedule a meeting to hand over all necessary documentation and sign the Termination Notice.

Nate Somers

President of Global Development and Operations

Somers Hotels and Residential Towers

Jessica read the email several times just to make sure she'd understood it correctly. Her hand flew up to cover her mouth and her body trembled all over. She simply could not keep her emotions contained any longer and burst into tears. She wished the floor would open up and swallow her whole. Nate had sent his message loud and clear—again. He wanted nothing to do with her. Not only had she lost the man she cared for, but a massive client for her company.

Suddenly, a roar came from the hallway.

"Jessica!" Alex yelled as he stormed into her office. "Explain to me how this happened? How did we lose this account? Budget redirection, my ass. Somers Hotels is loaded." Alex was red in the face. "What could've possibly gone wrong? Did the team screw up? Did we not deliver something we promised? How can ... How can you lose a major client so close to a launch?"

"The team did nothing wrong. It was me. I screwed up, okay? Big time," she mumbled through searing tears.

Alex pulled up short. "But I thought everything was going so well. Just last week all the final schedules were done, the entertainment is locked in, everything is all systems go. Why would Nate Somers pull the account now?"

"Because of me," Jessica whispered as she yanked a tissue out of its box.

"You? What could you have possibly done?"

"The one thing you said not to."

Alex looked at her with a blank expression.

"I slept with him."

Alex mouth fell open as he gasped. "You what?"

"You heard me."

Jessica had never broken down like this in front of Alex. Ever. Not even after her divorce from Graeme. But no matter how hard she tried, she just couldn't stop crying. She felt foolish and childish but her world had come crashing down around her like a house of cards.

Alex came to her side and hugged her. "Jess, sweetie. I don't know what's being going on, but we'll work it out. We always do. But for now, go home, and sort yourself out. I'll come over after work. Okay?"

"I'm fine."

"Jess, go. Now."

* * *

Monday morning, Nate packed up his laptop and gathered the last of his belongings for his return flight to Australia. He paused to look out over the sullen city before him. Rain droplets zigzagged down his window like the painful cracks that laced across his heart. He jumped when the phone rang. It was Mindy informing him the car was ready to take him to the airport. He wished it was Jessica wanting an explanation for the termination. He wanted to hear her rant and rave, just to hear her voice again. But the call never came.

He replayed their last conversation over and over in his head. How could she have believed the gossip with Rachael? Was it wrong of him to expect better of her? But then how could he, considering the way he left her. Why did he loathe the idea that she'd kissed another man? He hated to admit it, but deep down Nate burned with jealousy knowing Jessica had been in another man's arms. Especially Troy, given their history together. He'd never known himself to have a possessive streak before.

So much had happened in a matter of a few weeks. Lucy's broken leg, the insanely long hours in meetings, and the gossip with Rachael. It dawned on him that yes, his communication with Jessica had broken down. There'd been too many missed calls. Too many missed messages. Jessica was right. How could she not have drawn the worst of conclusions?

Nate took a moment to remember her long legs wrapped around his waist, her eyes closed as she called out his name as he buried himself within her. For weeks, he'd struggled to function properly without her. His feelings for her were so unexpected. So new. So different to anything else before. *But no.*

No more. It was time to put this mess behind him and move on. Before meeting Jessica he'd been content in his life, so surely this heavy feeling inside his heart would pass in due course. Because his feelings for her didn't matter anymore. He had to keep telling himself that.

He had to refocus because the hotel opened its doors to patrons in two weeks' time and the launch for November now had to be reworked. He had one final handover meeting to get through with Jessica and then his life could return to normal.

Chapter 15

Numb.

It was the only way Jessica could describe how she felt as she worked from home on Tuesday. Preparing all the documentation to hand over to Somers Hotel was exhausting. As she backed up the files onto an external hard drive she was saddened by the fact that she wouldn't see the end of the project. It was the first time in her professional career she felt like a failure, and she had no one else to blame but herself.

The following morning she managed to hold her composure as she entered her office. But the sullen look on her employees' faces nearly made her crumble behind her facade. By now they all knew they'd lost the Somers Hotel account, thanks to an email from Alex. But she was still not looking forward to facing her team and bearing their disappointment. God, she'd let so many people down.

By mid-afternoon, she was finalizing all the artwork and source files for the meeting with Somers when she noticed that the graphic designers had provided the wrong files. With the boys offsite at a meeting, it was going to take a few hours to rectify.

Jessica quickly reached for her phone.

"Brooke, it's Jessica. We have a delay on pulling some files together for you. And I would appreciate more time to calculate all the costings. I won't get everything finished in time for our meeting at five. Can we please reschedule for first thing in the morning?"

"Don't stress, Jess. Nate's been delayed in Singapore and won't be back until later tonight. I was only moments away from calling you. We'll sort everything out tomorrow. What time can you meet?"

"That would be great." Jessica clicked on her calendar. "How's 10.30 am?"

"Excellent. All booked. We'll see you here in the boardroom."

* * *

Alone in the office at nine o'clock, Jessica heard her phone buzz with a message. She was finishing up for the evening and desperately wanted to head for home. She shuffled several papers around on her desk to find her phone lying underneath them all. She looked at the screen.

I would like documentation tonight. Are you in the office? Just landed. Can I drop by and pick them up? Nate.

Jessica's heart ached as she read his text message. How could she face him after everything that had happened?

Consequences. Who would have thought her affair could have led to losing the launch? Just one more meeting and then he would be out of her life forever. *I'm strong. I can do this. I'll just hand him the files in reception and get him out of the office as quick as possible. Done!*

She replied to his text.

YES.

Everything was bundled together ready for Nate. All she needed was this one final document to print. The fifty pages seemed to be taking forever. She was tapping her fingernails against the side of the machine, urging it to speed up when the reception door buzzed. Was that Nate already? He'd arrived at the office a lot quicker than she was prepared for. As she headed down the corridor, she ran her hands through her hair, straightened her skirt and her posture, hoping to look presentable at this late hour of the evening.

After opening the door, the very sight of Nate took her breath away. He looked fresh, even after a long flight. She remembered how soft his hair felt, how his lips tasted, and how it felt to be wrapped in his arms. But now, just looking at him sent arrows through her heart. He was no longer hers. Not that he ever was.

"Hey," she greeted him, unable to look him in the eye.

He slowly stepped inside the foyer. "Evening." The word sounded as if it caught in his throat.

"Look, it's been a really long day," said Jessica. "Let's get this over with so we can both get home."

She turned to lead him down the hall. The main building was dark. Only a few dim spotlights lit the way toward her office. But they hadn't made it halfway down the passage before Nate grabbed her by the hand, spun her round and pinned her up against the wall, kissing her hard on the lips.

"Jess." The sound of him whispering her name sent an explosion of desire coursing through her body. Pressing his groin into hers, he kissed wildly down her neck and slid his fingers through her hair.

"What are you doing?" His actions weren't making any sense. She pushed against his shoulders even though her body was aching to belong to him again.

He lifted his head to look at her. "I'm so sorry. I've been trying to convince myself that we were through and to walk away from you. But the moment I saw you, I knew it just wasn't possible. I'm crazy about you. I never meant to hurt you. I beg of you to forgive me."

Breath escaped her as she heard his words. His eyes fixed on hers; she saw his pain and sorrow reflected her own emotions. His lips found hers again as he pushed her harder back against the wall, forcing her breasts to arch into his chest.

She yanked his tie free from around his throat and ripped opened his shirt as his hands hooked up her skirt and tore off her panties. Tears streamed down her cheeks as he released his belt, opened his trousers and thrust into her fevered wetness.

He drove into her again and again—up against the wall. Passion and desire took over, wiping away all hurt, pain and stupidity. Nate wailed as he exploded inside of her. She held on to his shoulders as he shuddered against her, savoring the feel, the smell and the touch of his body next to hers.

Panting, they sank to the floor in a pile of entwined limbs. Exhausted. Gasping for air.

"Nate, I thought ..."

He took her head between his hands and kissed her lips tenderly. "I don't know where to begin. I'm sorry for everything that's happened or didn't happen. Everything got all screwed up. I know this is crazy considering we only have a few months together, but I want to spend it with you. If you'll have me. Out of all this mess there is only one thing I know for certain. And that is I'm ... in love with you."

Jessica couldn't breathe as she drowned in the depths of his eyes. His words wrapped around her heart, filling her with a warmth that she had never experienced in her life. She rested her head on his shoulder. "I've been losing my mind over the way I feel for you. Because I love you, too."

"I don't know how you can after what I said."

"I can honestly say I have never felt like this about anyone else in my life."

"Me either." Nate's smile made her heart melt. "But what about Troy? Do you have feelings for him?"

"I do care for him. But I don't love him. It's been hard dealing with him back in my life, but you have to believe me, nothing's ever going to happen there."

"I do. And you're going to have to believe me that nothing happened with Rachael. You're it, Jess."

In that spilt second she knew Nate had her heart and everything that had been clouding her mind became crystal clear. She knew she wasn't in love with Troy. Too much water had gone under the bridge and their worlds and ambitions were too far apart. She had fond memories of her times with Troy. He was her first love—but a past love. Nate was her present love, now and for at least a little bit further into the future.

Nate's fingertips brushed away her tears and he pressed his lips against hers. "You also have to know that it was my father who interfered, as always, and wanted to scale back the launch. I couldn't bear the thought of you thinking the cancellation was personal."

Jessica nodded, listening.

"So here's the thing," he continued, "I did a lot of thinking on the flight, and I ended up missing my connection because I was rallying support from the board. I want to proceed with the opening. As planned. No changes."

"Are you defying your father's wishes?"

"Yes."

Jessica smiled as she pressed her lips to his.

"So, do you think we can get up off the floor and tear up those termination agreements?" said Nate.

"Absolutely." Elation filled her as he stood and offered her hand to help her to her feet.

"After that, how about heading back to your place for the

night?" he suggested.

"I'll lead the way."

* * *

"Are you free this Sunday?" Jessica asked Nate while they were packing up their things after their meeting the following week. The rest of the staff had returned to their desks, she was alone with him in her boardroom. Her stress levels were once again manageable with the launch now back on track.

"You know that's the day before we open to guests, but I can make some time free," said Nate. "What did you have in mind?" He moved around the table to stand in front of her, sliding his hands around her waist.

Jessica stepped away and waved a finger at him. "Not in the office." She couldn't help but feel her cheeks flush.

Nate playfully pouted. "I thought you didn't want to sneak around anymore?"

"Yes, but we agreed to keep things low-key." A select few people like Zoe, Brooke and Alex now knew about their relationship, and that was more than enough in the workplace. Outside of work, Jessica didn't really see any problem. "It's my birthday and I'm having a few friends and Conner over for a barbecue. I'd like you to join me as my date."

"A date?" He ignored her futile attempts to push him away as he moved his hands around onto her bottom. "So we've snuck around for ages doing unimaginable things to each other in private, and now you want me to come out and meet your friends?" Nate's eyed sparkled with cheekiness.

"Well, half of them already know we're seeing each other. I know it's a big step being seen together, but it's only within the confines of my home." She shrugged. "Besides, I want to show you off a little. Come on, it will be fun."

"So you just want to use me and parade me around in

front of your pals." As he whispered in her ear she flinched as goosebumps shot down her neck.

"I didn't think it'd be a problem for you."

"No. None whatsoever. I look forward to escaping from the hotel for a few hours." Nate leaned in and kissed her on her mouth before she had time to think.

* * *

Early October saw the grass in Jessica's small garden lush and green again. Roses and gardenias lining the fence filled the air with their fragrance. In the distance the harbor waters glistened in the sunshine. As Jessica set the outdoor table, she realized she hadn't celebrated her birthday in years. Usually it was just dinner somewhere with Conner. So this gathering of family and friends was a real treat. A simple backyard barbecue sounded so much better to her than some outlandish cocktail reception like she was always throwing for her clients.

Nervous about her friends meeting Nate, Jessica wiped her sweaty hands on her jeans as she went to answer the door. Maxine and her husband, Patrick, and Alex with his partner, Dylan, were the first to arrive. Jessica's eyes widened with surprise as Alex had brought a case of her favorite wine, and Max presented her with an incredible-looking chocolate torte birthday cake.

"Where do you find the time to make a cake like this?" Jessica asked Max, as she placed it down on the kitchen bench, sneaking a taste of the delicious icing.

"I am a superwoman and don't you forget it," said Max. "Pat was working on a case last night and the kids were having sleepovers at friends. I had a bit of time on my hands." She shrugged her shoulders as if it was all too easy.

Conner and Becky rocked up, along with two other couples—friends of Jessica's from Conner's school days.

Then the doorbell rang, sending off a flutter in Jessica's stomach—this would be the first time in years that she'd introduced her friends to a new partner. Mild panic set in.

She opened the door. Nate stood there with flowers, champagne and gift in hand.

"Happy birthday," he greeted her with a lingering kiss on her lips.

She closed her eyes and inhaled the fine, spicy scent of his cologne before she turned her attention to the beautiful bouquet of pink roses he held in his arms for her. "Thank you. These are gorgeous. Come with me. I'll get a vase."

The flowers filled the kitchen with their sweet perfume as she placed them on the counter and dug out a vase from the cupboard.

"Here, you have to open this, too!" He held out a black Chanel gift bag on the end of his finger and jiggled it in front of her.

His blue-gray eyes took her breath away as she accepted the gift from him.

"Open it," he said quietly.

She beamed up at him. "Now? Okay." Inside the bag was a rectangular case covered in black velvet. She flipped it open to reveal a simple gold bracelet with the famous Chanel logo as the clasp. "Nate, it's beautiful." She grinned from ear to ear. "Here, can you help me put it on, please?"

Nate's fingers fumbled with the clasp as he clipped the bracelet around her slender wrist. When he'd finished he kissed her palm.

She detected he was maybe a little anxious about meeting her friends as well. "So, did you buy this or did Brooke?" she smirked.

"I did, thank you very much. And yes, it is beautiful, just like you." Nate kissed her lips softly.

"And what's this?" Jessica held up an access card with the Somers Hotel logo on it.

"Tomorrow we're opening our doors for the very first time and I would be honored if you stayed with me for the night. In the presidential suite."

Jessica's could feel her smile broaden as she nodded. "That sounds amazing. I'd love to join you."

After Nate popped a bottle of champagne and poured her a glass, Jessica took his hand in hers and led him outside to the garden.

"Everyone, this is Nate Somers. Nate ... you know Alex. This is his partner, Dylan. You've met Max, her husband Patrick, Lilly and Nolan, Kane and Michelle. And this is my son, Conner, and his girlfriend, Becky. That's everyone!"

"Nice to meet you all." Nate effortlessly remembered everyone's names. It was a gift that Jessica did not possess, in spite of all her years of experience networking at events.

As Nate turned to talk to the men, Jessica caught sight of Max miming, "Oh my God. He's so hot!" Jessica's cheeks blushed red with embarrassment but she had to acknowledge Max was right.

Alex and Dylan cooked up the gourmet meats on the barbecue and then they all sat around trestle tables on the paved terrace.

"So, Nate, how is the launch coming along? Has Jessica pulled together one hell of a show for you?" Patrick asked.

"Absolutely. It's going to make the opening of Atlantis Palm Hotel in Dubai look amateurish in comparison. Isn't that right, Jess?"

"I don't know about that," she replied, "but we'll certainly give them a run for their money. If nothing else, we'll outdo them on the list of celebrities attending. We're having fireworks, laser shows, the fountains all synced to music, gift bags of goodies, and loads of entertainment across the entire weekend. Nate's just got to make sure that over the next few weeks everything is operational, his staff excel in their service, and then we'll let social and traditional media do the rest."

"Do we get an invite, Nate?" Conner jumped in. "I want to rub it into my friends because they never believe me when I say my mom does all these fancy events. I promise not to post any photos on Facebook or Instagram of your drunk guests."

"Conner!" Jessica gasped.

Nate laughed. "The evening functions are restricted, but how about you come to the barbecue on Sunday, if you like?"

"What barbecue?"

"It's the wrap up on Sunday afternoon. There'll be plenty of celebrities around for you to rub shoulders with then."

"You don't have to do that, Nate. Conner is just joking around." Jessica glared at him.

"He's more than welcome."

"Cool!" Conner's face lit with excitement at the prospect.

* * *

After cake and more champagne, everyone stood about the garden in conversation, stretching their legs after eating too much lunch. Nate was by Jessica's side when she noticed Alex's watchful eye. He raised his eyebrow as Nate placed his hand comfortably on her back as they stood talking with her friends. Jessica knew Alex loved her like a sister, and watched over her protectively. It was natural after working together and knowing each other for so long. After everything that had happened with Nate, Jessica was comforted by the fact that she had such good friends. She prayed that she wouldn't have to call on him, or Max, to put her back together again when Nate left.

Chapter 16

"Where can we go for the weekend? Away from the hotel, work and any possibility of interruptions," Nate whispered into Jessica's ear as they walked back into the foyer of the hotel after meeting with the stage and lighting crews.

"A whole two days away? But we have a rehearsal with some of the performers." Jessica couldn't even contemplate such a thing just four weeks away from the launch.

"I have every confidence in Martin and Lin to oversee everything. Don't you agree?"

"Yes ... but ..."

The look on his face was adamant. As the items on her To Do list flashed through her mind, her body ached with tiredness and begged her to take this very small window of opportunity and have a break. There were plenty of other rehearsal times in the next few weeks for her to fine tune anything before the big event.

"Okay. We could go to my holiday house—well, Alex and I own it. It's at Byron Bay, up on the northern coast."

Jessica hadn't been there in nearly two years. Had it really been that long since she'd had a holiday? Her weekend getaways at Gumtrees seemed less likely to be an option now Troy was there. So a minibreak in Byron sounded like a perfect plan before the chaotically busy weeks leading up to the launch began.

"How do we get there? Car? Plane?" Nate asked.

"It's too far to drive for a weekend. I'll get Zoe to sort out flights."

* * *

The chartered plane touched down on the small airstrip in what looked like the middle of nowhere. Nate certainly didn't miss air travel, especially in small planes. As he collected their luggage, Jessica picked up the keys to their hire car.

"It's only a thirty-minute drive to the house from here," she told him, walking out of the tiny terminal.

Nate was more than happy to let her drive; he hadn't driven a car in months. As they passed rolling hills, and green pastures and clusters of evergreen trees, the fresh breeze blew against his face and having a healing effect on his overworked body and mind.

Jessica took the exit off the highway into Byron Bay. The hippy township full of colorful tourist shops and cafes was certainly an eye opener. Nate felt like he was on a different planet. He hadn't been anywhere like this in years; Hawaii would be the closest comparison. The car wound along the narrow road, over the palm-covered hilltop and into Watego Beach. Jessica pointed toward her house nestled somewhere down on the hillside below. But his gaze was quickly drawn up to the crest of the headland to take in the majestic sight of the towering, white lighthouse standing guard over the turquoise waters of the bay.

Nate fell in love with Byron Bay then and there.

Jessica pulled the car into the garage and Nate was amazed by the opulence of this little pocket of housing, nothing like the town they'd just driven through. He was expecting a rundown beach shack with only the bare necessities. While this was certainly more what he was accustomed too, as long as he had time with Jessica he didn't care either way.

He hopped out of the car and followed her inside, gazing around the massive, earthy-toned house with its large windows covered in bronze plantation shutters. Decked out in Balinese furniture, it felt like they were in another country, not just a few hours up the coast.

"Alex and I bought this place about four years ago," Jessica said as she led him into the living area. "We rent it out or give it to clients for holidays. It's a great write-off for tax purposes. Alex comes here with Dylan quite often, and I used to come here with Conner."

"It's magnificent. Beats the hell out of city hotels for a few days."

"There are four bedrooms upstairs, but we'll use the master bedroom down the hall to the left. Bathroom and games room are to the right." She pointed absentmindedly as she walked around the living area opening up the shutters, unveiling the breathtaking view over the beach.

Nate dumped their bags on the floor near the kitchen and continued to watch Jessica. The way her hips moved. He couldn't wait to peel that top of hers off and see her beautiful skin quiver beneath his touch. This was something he could get used to; being with her every day. He'd never felt so comfortable and in sync with someone in his life. He rubbed the back of his neck with his hand as reality hit him hard like a brick. Their expiration date was getting closer, and it would be time to move on.

Her voice pulled him back to the present.

"Zoe called ahead, so the housekeeper has stocked the fridge with a heap of food and drinks. We shouldn't have to go into town at all," Jessica said as she peered into the fridge. "How about a drink? Gin and tonic?"

"Sounds good!"

* * *

Jessica was digging in the kitchen cupboard for glasses, while Nate opened the bottle of tonic water. It released a refreshing fizz into the air.

Her lips parted and desire exploded within her like a firework. How could he make opening a bottle look so damn sexy? Their eyes met. Her chest tightened and her breath deepened as he held her gaze. The air rippled with heat.

Oh yes, this was going to be an interesting weekend away.

She managed to draw her concentration back to making the drinks. She filled the glasses with ice and poured the gin, then the tonic. She handed Nate his drink, and clinked their glasses together before taking a long thirst-quenching mouthful. As she licked her lips to savor the taste, Nate stepped closer and slid his arm around her waist. His lips met hers. The sour taste of lime, the slippery taste of gin and his cool lips on hers sent shivers down her spine.

Jessica had waited long enough. She'd persevered with impeccable restraint through city traffic, plane travel and the drive here, now she had him alone.

"Follow me." She took Nate by the hand and led him to the bedroom. The inviting king-sized bed, dressed in a new brown satin quilt and pillows, graced the center of the room. Jessica took Nate's glass from his hand and placed it with hers on the bedside table.

His smile captivated her as she slowly pushed him to sit

down on the side of the bed. She started to unbutton her blouse, and then shimmied her hips around as she slid her jeans off onto the floor. His eyes darkened with desire as she stood before him in her white lacy underwear. It was empowering. She loved the way he made her feel, like she was the only woman on earth.

She heard a rumble deep within his throat as he uttered her name. He reached out, put his warm hands around her waist and pulled her in toward him. He placed the softest of kisses on her belly. Reaching around his broad shoulders, Jessica pulled his T-shirt over his head to reveal his toned torso. His strong arms, ripped with muscles, flexed as they moved up above his head. Playfully shoving him back on the bed, she removed his jeans and trunks and his glorious nakedness lay before her.

"Okay, you're too big for me to throw around—so up on the pillows, please."

Nate smiled and obediently shuffled to the center of the bed and lay amongst the soft pillows. His eyes sparkled in the dim afternoon light that filtered in through the shutters.

Jessica reached for her glass, took a swig and captured one of the ice cubes in her mouth. She straddled Nate in the center of the bed, kissed his fiery lips and then, clenching the ice cube between her teeth, slid it down over his neck and onto his chest, making her way to his nipples. A trail of water was left behind as she circled the cube around one nipple then the other. His chest muscles tensed and his nipples hardened as she licked and kissed away the droplets of water.

Taking another sip of her drink and yet another cube, Jessica continued south from where she left off. Down across the muscular plane of his stomach, over across the smooth skin of his hip and down to his groin. His erection lay long and firm before her. He flinched sharply as she ran the icy cube up along the length of his shaft and circled it around the head.

She felt his thighs tense with every stroke.

She did it again. Slower. He squirmed underneath her touch.

The cube melted and Jessica continued the same action, this time with her tongue. Licking away the droplets of water and taking him fully in her mouth.

"Jess. Enough." The strain in his voice evident. "While I do love you blowing me off—it's time for your torture instead." He sat up on the bed taking Jessica in his arms, and kissed her. "But you are wearing way too much clothing," he whispered. He released the clasp of her bra and slid it away to reveal her aroused breasts. Then laying her down on the bed, he whisked away her panties and threw them on the floor.

Nate took the same long, quenching drink from his glass and took an ice cube between his teeth. He slid the cube across her shoulder, down onto her breasts—torturing her already hardened nipples. His hand rubbed down her body and over her thigh. His touch made her skin singe with fire as he nudged his weight in between her legs. Her want for him rose to dangerous levels as he wriggled lower. His icy kisses left a trail of cool water in their wake as he headed between her legs. Jessica's toes curled and her eyes widened at the startling cold sensation when he nuzzled the cube on to her sensitive clitoris. Fire and ice sent jolts through her body. The pleasurable heat and the painful cold was nothing short of mind-blowing.

She grabbed handfuls of her pillow and squeezed it tightly.

The cube melted quickly, only to be replaced by his expert tongue. First he licked her slowly. Playfully. Taunting her; making her want more. She closed her eyes as his kisses and hot breath tantalized her skin. She gasped as he slipped his warm tongue inside her and sent her to the very edge.

Heat flooded through her as she pulsed her hips in time with the delectable flicks of his tongue. Her fingers clawed at the sheets as her thighs began to quiver. Every muscle in her body tensed, begging for release.

The orgasm shot through her body like a bullet from a gun. She exploded, convulsing in euphoria. Nate didn't relent until she could bear it no more.

"Enough," she gasped as she laced her hand into his hair and drew him away. Nate had satisfaction written all over his face as he moved to hover over her body, before plunging himself inside her.

* * *

The afternoon was nearing an end. The sun sank slowly behind the hills to the west while a pod of whales stopped off to play in the warm waters of the bay before migrating south. Lazing outside on deck chairs, laptops resting on their legs, Nate and Jessica checked their emails as they sipped glasses of crisp chardonnay and watched the world drift by.

"You want to know something funny?" Jessica asked Nate as she paused from replying to one of her messages. "My ex-husband would have a hissy fit seeing me here like this— replying to work emails on a weekend."

Nate grinned. "My ex would want to be out on the town at some fancy restaurant."

"What are you working on?"

"Europe. Looking at ways to improve occupancy. Since I'm going ahead with the launch, I have to find some cuts elsewhere."

"I like the idea you mentioned of Accor buying out some of your hotels," said Jessica. "If that doesn't come off, why don't you consider converting them to budget-style three star hotels? Three-star instead of five. Not many people can afford to spend five hundred dollars-plus a night when times are tough. Strip down the services to a minimum. Spend a bit on rebranding and promotion. You could have those three hotels ready for the northern hemisphere's summer next year.

"I love it." Nate's face lit with excitement. "That may be a very viable option if Accor doesn't come through. Providing you do the promotions and brand management."

"Ha. Funny joke. I can't do that from here. Nice try, though."

Jessica loved being able to discuss work with Nate. The thought of more international business thrilled her to pieces, but she and Alex just didn't have the resources at the moment.

One thing was festering in the back of her mind—the inevitable end of her and Nate. In four weeks the launch would be over and he would be leaving Australia two weeks after that. God only knew if and when he would return. Jessica closed her laptop and put it on the side table. Picking up her drink, she enjoyed a sip as she collected her thoughts. She already knew the outcome but it needed to be discussed.

"Nate, what do you want to do when you leave ... about us?" She twisted the wine glass stem between her fingertips.

"You want to talk about this now?" He stared out to the ocean, his eyes the same color as the rolling waves.

"I just can't see it working, can you?" Jessica could think of creative campaigns, ingenious promotions, had an endless supply of innovative ideas for her clients, but she couldn't think of one viable solution that would allow them to continue their relationship.

"I've told you. I travel constantly. One month here and there. London, Singapore, Los Angeles, New York—it's endless."

The odd rendezvous around the world when their paths managed to cross just wasn't an option. The *let's just be friends* scenario made her cringe.

"Despite the way I feel for you, it's an impossible situation," Nate went on. "I don't want you jumping to wrong conclusions every time I'm photographed with some other female, or panicking when I can't return your phone call immediately. And I don't want to wonder where you are and what you're doing without me." He paused. "I'm set to become chairman in the next year or two. I can't give that up—it's my family's business. We've talked about this before."

"I know. I'm just not looking forward to having to say goodbye to you."

Nate closed his laptop and turned to face Jessica. "Me either. Leaving you is going to be hard for me, too. But don't you think a clean break is best?"

The ache in her heart was heavy but she nodded in agreement. This was going to be harder than she thought.

"What?" Nate gave her a wry look. "No screaming and kicking and begging me to stay?"

Jessica resorted to her only defense. The one she could always depend on and hide her emotions behind. "I have my business to think about. There's a lot more at stake here than just our hearts."

"I don't want to hurt you when I go. We both went into this knowing the end result. Can we please just enjoy our remaining time together? No dark clouds looming overhead." He took her hand in his and kissed her palm. "I swear to you to make it my mission over the next few weeks to give you enough orgasms to last you a lifetime."

Jessica gasped in shock.

Nate's eyes were full of mischief. "Are you up for one before dinner?"

* * *

The weather was perfect for the weekend at Byron Bay. Jessica tried to ignore the heaviness in her heart as they climbed the steep headland to the lighthouse, watched dolphins frolic in the waters below, and walked hand in hand along the white sandy beach.

They made love again after dinner by candlelight on the comfy couches. Jessica's heart beat in time with Nate's as she curled in his arms, her chest against his. She was bewildered by how this man had turned her life upside down in just five months. He opened her heart when she didn't think she needed anyone in her life. The very thought of Nate leaving on a plane in a few weeks tore at her soul.

But no other outcome seemed viable. She wasn't going to leave her company, and he was tied to the Somers empire.

Jessica had to brace herself for the end.

Chapter 17

Jessica typed away at her computer, lost in writing a press release for the opening that was only two weeks away, when Zoe knocked on her office door.

"Yes?" Jessica looked up from her work.

"There's a cowboy in reception for you. He's so hot!" She fanned her hand in front of her face. "He says his name is Troy and he doesn't have an appointment. Is this Troy from Gumtrees? Conner's dad?"

"What's he doing here?" Jessica murmured. She thought she'd made it clear during their phone calls that they could only be friends. Had he traveled all this way into the city to see her? She rolled her eyes and sighed. What could he possibly want?

Jessica walked out to the reception area to find Troy leaning against the reception desk. Arms folded. Ankles crossed. Dressed in jeans and dark shirt, Troy was definitely a good-looking man, just not anywhere near as breathtaking as Nate. No sparks flew as Jessica greeted him. But his face lit up at the sight of her, which made her proceed with caution.

"Hi, Jess. I was just wanting to make sure you're still alive," he said as he kissed her on the cheek.

"You know I am. We only talked the other day on the phone. So what brings you here?"

"Is there somewhere we can talk?" he said. "How about I buy you a cup of tea?"

"Sure." Jessica motioned Troy to the elevator doors.

"You look out of place in the city," she said as they ordered takeaway cups of tea from the cafe downstairs.

Troy leaned back against the counter and looked awkward as he crossed his ankles while they waited for their drinks. "I only come into the city when it's absolutely necessary."

She smiled at him as she grabbed their drinks and headed out the door. Traffic noise and the commotion of people bustling along the street surrounded them as they meandered down the streets to Belmore Park.

"So what did you want to talk to me about?" Jessica asked as she pointed to a graffiti-covered bench under a tree. When he nodded, she settled on the seat and took a long sip of her drink.

"I had to see you again. It's been too long." Troy put his already empty cup on the ground and turned to face her. "Phone calls are just not enough anymore. I wanted to do this in person. Location and timing may not be in my favor, but I don't want to delay things any longer. I wasn't sure at first, but I know now that I've fallen in love with you all over again."

"What?" Jessica jerked in shock at his words, splashing tea all over her pink shirt.

Troy was quick to react, ready to blot at the stain with his napkin, only to stop just inches from her breast.

"Being with you again has been the best thing that's happened to me in a long time. I want to know if you feel the same."

"Whoa, Troy. No!" She grabbed the napkin from his hand and dabbed at the mark on her shirt. She had to hold her thoughts together. She closed her eyes so she wouldn't get distracted by those sapphire eyes of his, and took a few seconds to carefully piece the words together. "I told you on the phone, Nate and I are back together."

She opened one eye to peek at his face. His cheek muscle flexed and his Adam's apple slid hard in his neck as he swallowed.

"But he's leaving, and I'm not. You did love me once, and I can tell you do have feelings for me. You can't deny it. Why won't you let me love you the way you should be loved? Like I should have done all those years ago. Please, just give me a chance."

"Are you out of your mind? You had your chance and you left for someone else, remember?" Her tone was cutting. "You don't owe me anything and I don't regret for one second having Conner. I'm sorry the people in your life kept information about him away from you. But I had to get over you. And I did. So much has happened in twenty years. I'm not that high school girl anymore."

"But I'm here now and not going anywhere."

"Troy, did you not hear me? I'm in love with someone else. I don't want to hurt you, well, any more than I already have."

"Please, just think about it." Troy reached for her hand and held it tightly in his.

Jessica forced herself not to jerk her hand away. "We've just got our friendship back after all these years. I want that to continue. I can't tell you how sorry I am about that night at Gumtrees." Slowly she pulled her hand free. *Funny!* She thought to herself. If Nate had touched her like this she wouldn't be able to let ago. The chemistry between her and the two men was just so different.

"Since we kissed I haven't been able to stop thinking about

you and want to be with you."

"Kiss? I was ridiculously drunk off my nut and so were you. Look, I won't come out to Gumtrees anymore if it upsets you." Her heart ached as Troy laid his on his sleeve. The timing of Troy coming back into her life was all wrong. Things might have worked out differently if Nate wasn't in the picture.

Troy furrowed his brow. "You love the country. This city life is not for you."

She gasped in shock. Her life and her work meant everything to her. She lived and breathed her business every day. It was part of her soul. The very blood that ran through her veins. She wasn't about to change that. Not for Nate, not for Troy, or any other man for that matter.

"And that's the deal-breaker." Jessica slapped her hand on her thigh. "You just stated what I always had as a deep suspicion. You really don't know me, because this is me. This is who I am. The city, the travel, the action. I've worked damn hard for my agency and it's what I truly love to do. I'm not relying on or bending to any man's wants or needs. I've never forgotten my roots—but I will never go back. I had to grow up very quickly after having Conner. Now with him grown, a successful company, my freedom, I feel like I'm living life for the first time in years."

Deep down she knew Troy was another Graeme. Neither could understand or tolerate her drive for success. Nate, on the other hand, couldn't get enough of her ideas and her ambition. That was what she loved about him. But when he left, she was determined to move forward, not backwards. In many ways, she was looking forward to the day she'd be by herself again, especially when it would take nothing short of a miracle to find a man who could fill Nate's shoes.

"I was so stupid for leaving you." Troy's shoulders slouched as he exhaled heavily.

"Well, you did," Jessica said plainly. "This has been one crazy chapter in my life, with you coming back into it, and me meeting Nate. I don't know what's in store for me after he's gone, and I'm really sorry if you thought there could be more between us, but there isn't."

"I'll be here for you, Jess," said Troy. "I'm not going to stop hoping that there's a chance for us. When does he leave?"

"Two weeks after the launch." A heavy sadness hung in her heart. "Troy, please don't wait for me. I want us to be friends. I can't offer you anything more than that."

"It's enough for now, Jess."

* * *

Lounging on her couch at home, Nate lay with his head resting in Jessica's lap. She ran her fingers through his soft hair and traced the outline of his face with her fingertips. It was a rare relaxing moment on a Saturday afternoon before they both had to head off to separate work functions in the evening.

"Tomorrow Conner has his first cricket match of the season. Would you be interested in coming? It'll involve hours of sitting in the sun, drinking and chatting. Oh, and you can watch the game as well."

"I do love cricket, but it usually involves corporate boxes and airconditioning." Nate's eyes remained closed. She could almost hear him purring as her soft strokes combed through his hair.

"This is no Ashes Test, but it's still entertaining." Jessica paused. "Before you decide, you should also know that Troy and Graeme will be there."

She felt Nate's body stiffen. It took a moment for him to start breathing normally again. "I'd love to come, you know that. But I could use the time to finish off some things at the hotel before the launch next week."

So could she. But she had to take the opportunity when she didn't have a work function on to go and see her son play sport and catch up with friends.

"Promise me, not too much drinking, and keep your hands off both of your exes," Nate said playfully. "Don't you find that weird to be hanging out with both of your ex-lovers? I couldn't think of anything more unpleasant." His brow furrowed as if he was contemplating being in that very situation.

"Yes, three of my lovers in the one place could get a little uncomfortable. I just might have to sleep with all of you again to see which one is the best." Jessica raised her eyebrow and grinned.

"What?" Nate started tickling her in the ribs. They wrestled around, until he pinned her down on the couch with all of his bodyweight. She was laughing so hard her rib cage hurt.

"Okay, stop. I promise. No one but you. How could there ever be anyone else but you?"

His lips found hers. Her legs wrapped around his waist and she drew him in closer to her. She'd never felt so in love in her life.

Nate looked down at her. "This is so nice here in your home, watching old movies on television ... spending time with you. It's a life I've never had nor wanted before. It's going to make getting on that plane in a couple of weeks very hard."

"Well, you'll have to find a way to stay."

Jessica knew they were just not meant to be together long-term. She had to enjoy the last remaining weeks with Nate before he left. But deep down she didn't want to say goodbye.

* * *

The Sunday cricket game arrived, and the local university grounds teemed with bodies clad in white cricket longs when Jessica pulled in to the carpark. Surrounding the field were scattered families and friends set up on blankets and foldout chairs, all ready to waste the afternoon away in the sun, watch the game and devour vast quantities of food and drink.

Conner looked handsome dressed in his whites. Jessica was no doubt biased, as any mother would be. His stunning blue eyes, just like his father's, sparkled in the daylight.

"Have a good game," she said, as he gave her a hug then joined his teammates to take to the field.

Jessica spread out her picnic blanket among other parents, friends, and team members. Graeme arrived with his girlfriend, Chelsea, shortly after the game commenced. Jessica tried not to gag as the two of them showed off with overtly public displays of affection. They were worse than a hormonal teenage couple making out at the movies. She ignored their antics as she cracked open a bottle of chilled wine and chatted away to one of the moms next to her.

As the alcohol flowed, gossip and conversation proved to be much more interesting than the game. An hour had passed before Jessica saw Troy strolling around the grounds, looking for her and Conner. He smiled when he caught sight of her and walked over. She greeted him pleasantly and offered him a spot on the blanket beside her.

He sat down and stretched out his jean-clad legs. "Good to see you, as always."

She shuffled over slightly to put a little more distance between them and turned her attention to the field. "Conner is over there in the slips."

"Thanks. They all look the same to me from this distance. I might need glasses soon. This getting old thing really sucks." He took off his sunglasses and rubbed his eyes. "You're looking good."

Jessica blushed as she shied away from his compliment. "Want a beer?" She opened the lid to Conner's cooler and took out a bottle.

"Sure!" said Troy.

Jessica was surprised at how the time drifted by so easily with Troy. She remembered why she loved him all those years ago. He had such an inner peace and calm that she'd rarely ever experienced in her crazy whirlwind life. It was a constant rush. Go, go, go. But then, she wouldn't have it any other way.

* * *

After the game Troy walked with Jessica back to her car. She smiled as she caught him looking at her from underneath his Akubra hat.

"It's been a great afternoon," he said. "It's a shame Conner's team lost."

She turned and leaned against the car. "Yeah, I don't think anyone in his team will be picked to represent the country any time soon."

"No, I don't think so." Troy paused and looked deep into her eyes. She saw him reach out his hand toward her, but he obviously changed his mind and slipped it into his pocket instead. "I'm going to a viticulturists' conference in two weeks' time in New Zealand."

"Oh, that's nice."

"I'd like you to come with me and have a holiday," Troy went on. "You'll need it after your launch next weekend. Spend some time with me. Just as friends—no strings attached."

Jessica gasped at his proposal. He had such nerve. "I told you—"

"I know what you said about Nate. But he's not here with you. I am."

Jessica shook her head as she felt anger start to bubble to the surface. What did she have to do to set the record straight? "I can't and I won't, Troy."

"Just as friends. I mean it. No funny business. You mean too much to me to stuff that up again. Just think about it. I'll call you, okay? I leave on Thursday week."

Before another word left her month, Troy leaned in and gave her a soft kiss on the cheek, then turned and walked away.

It took a moment for her to be able to breathe again.

Her eyes followed him across the carpark. His boots scuffed at the gravel. She cocked her eyebrow as she watched him. Yeah, his backside did look awesome in jeans. She certainly wasn't blind and smiled as she enjoyed the view. Troy was persistent if nothing else. He was just too nice. And nice boys lost out.

Jessica knew exactly who had hold of her heart. She opened the door of her car, jumped in and drove to Nate's hotel.

Chapter 18

The hotel's moorings on Darling Harbour were crowded with sleek luxury cruisers. Radars swirled on the tops of cabins and the sun reflected brightly off their silver rails. Jessica took one last glance over the harbor before she made her way into the hotel. She tried to control the butterflies swarming in her stomach as she entered through the glass doors into the foyer. It was only a few short hours before the start of the festivities. This was one of the biggest events she'd ever done. It was now time to show it to the world.

Pulling her small suitcase and suit bag, she stopped in the lobby, closed her eyes and inhaled deeply, taking it all in. The space was magnificent, all decked out with bright decorations, ready for the grand opening. A massive three-story-high glass atrium overlooked the harbor, allowing the sun to shine right across the beautiful sandstone floor. The polished wooden staircase leading up to the mezzanine floor and a central fountain were the final elegant touches. Well-dressed patrons already crowded the bar and lounge areas, and the reception desk bustled with people.

Stepping into gear, Jessica headed for Nate's apartment in the Residential Tower. She swiped the access card he'd given her through the slot and pushed the heavy door open. She hung her clothes in the closet and placed her toiletry bag in the bathroom. As she glanced over Nate's toothbrush, colognes and shaving items, she sighed. She was only privy to this—to him—for two more weeks. It would be sad to see him go. She shook off the heavy feeling because there was no time now to wallow. She walked into the bedroom and sat down on his bed to glance over her agenda one last time. She knew it by heart, back to front and upside down. But her nerves had jumped up a few notches and were getting the better of her.

Friday: press junket and the grand opening: a five course meal for eight hundred guests to be served in the ballroom; crowd entertainers and troops from Cirque du Soleil topped off the festivities. Saturday: the opening of the retail corridor with fashion showcases and parades; a Black Hawk helicopter spectacle over the harbor; cocktail reception, followed by a lavish dinner and several international artists performing live; fireworks and laser lightshow, and the opening up of the nightclub. Finally, Sunday: a gourmet barbecue, abseiling display down the side of the building and poolside entertainment.

Jessica closed her eyes and said a silent prayer that all would go smoothly.

Eager to get the show underway, she took the lift down and crossed over into the hotel. She found Lin running final sound checks with the team in the grand ballroom. Rigging and lighting technicians were clattering about and making final adjustments for the night's entertainment. Stage crew were setting up and the hotel staff were dressing the tables. The room was a mass of bodies scuttling in every direction, all with set jobs to do. Jessica strode over to Lin, pulled out the chair next to her and jumped straight into work. She glanced down at her watch.

One hour to kick off.

Poor Lin looked like she was about to throw up, but Jessica reassured her everything was ready to go.

"So are you okay, Lin? I have to go now and coordinate the media and press junket that's about to start over in the meeting rooms."

"Sure. I think. I'll catch up with you later this evening. Just keep your two-way headset on so I can contact you if I have any questions." Lin had beads of sweat on her brow, but Jessica had every faith in her to pull the entertainment together. As she stood to leave, she gave Lin a reassuring touch on the shoulder.

"We're going to knock 'em dead tonight," Jessica said, and made her way out the door.

* * *

From a registration desk in a foyer between two meeting rooms, Jessica ushered the journalists to their interviews with Nate and Martin, the general manager. Both men faced interviewer after interviewer in fifteen-minute slots. As Jessica jostled between the two rooms, she noted that after the first four interviews, all the questions sounded the same and the responses were all too familiar. Constantly keeping an eye on the clock, she had to ensure they kept to the tight schedule.

At four o'clock she ticked off the last of the press interviews and packed away the spare media packs into a box behind the table. Her eyes lit up when Nate walked out from the boardroom, buttoning his jacket as he made his way over to her.

"Well, it looks like you've survived the media onslaught."

Jessica was grateful to cross this item off the agenda. But as she thought about all the things she had to do, adrenaline still rushed through her veins. Nerves, excitement, stress all pummeled her at once.

"Time to schmooze," said Nate as he tugged at his shirt sleeves and smiled at her. "You look nervous. Don't be. Everything will be great. I have every faith in you."

His words didn't do much to lower her stress levels but his smile was encouraging.

She was startled by her headset buzzing loudly in her ear. "Hey Lin—what's up?"

"First drama. Fran's sick. She's come down with bad gastro and vomiting. What should I do? Who should take over her place? Ryan or Gabby?" Her voice was full of panic.

Jessica rubbed her eyebrows and took a quick moment to think. "Ryan went through everything in dress rehearsal, so use him. Gabby needs to stay on video."

"Okay. Great. Thanks." Lin sounded relieved.

Jessica looked at Nate with dismay in her eyes. "First drama. Nothing serious though. One of our main sound technician has come down sick, so our back-up, Ryan, has been put into place. I better go make sure that's he's okay with everything."

"Will I get to spend any time with you this evening?" He tugged playfully at the collar of her shirt.

"Maybe after the main show. But on a night like tonight, you of all people must know business must come first."

She saw disappointment in Nate's eyes, but his nod assured her that he fully understood. She had worked so hard to pull this event together; she would do whatever it took to avoid any mishaps.

"I better get going. It's nearly showtime." She kissed him on the cheek and headed to the ballroom. She gathered her team together and gave one last pep talk. "Okay everyone. This is what we have been rehearsing for weeks. Let's have a great show and heaps of fun." Everyone cheered and clapped before they all disappeared into their positions about the room and readied themselves to turn the night into a magical affair.

Jessica took her seat next to Lin and the lighting technician at the control panel desk at the rear of the darkened room. Bright blue and green LED lights shimmered across their faces as they placed their headsets on and tested their volume controls. Jessica watched guests dressed in immaculate gowns and suits, enter and fill the tables quickly—all were oblivious to what was going on behind the scenes. Her headphones muffled their conversations and the music that resonated across the room as people settled at their allocated seats. She licked her lips and swallowed, her throat was feeling dry. She was envious of those guests having their glasses filled with champagne or wine by the waiters that circled the tables. She'd love a drink, even if it were only to settle her nerves.

All the commotion and seconds ticking away to the start of the entertainment had Jessica's heart racing like a speeding train. She'd done events hundreds of times before, but had never been this nervous. Was it because there was so much at stake—her business reputation, exposure to the world, and being in the spotlight to attract new clientele? Or maybe she was just flustered because it came down to the fact that she'd never been in love with the client before. That was a pretty compelling reason. She looked up and saw people overhead creeping silently along in the rigging getting into final position. She glanced at the clock on the panel before her. Two minutes to go.

"Final sound check." Jessica talked to her team quietly through her headset.

"Check." Lin replied.

"Final lighting check."

"Check."

"Let's go on … three … two … one."

The grand ballroom disappeared into darkness. The crowd

slowly but surely settled into silence. With a flick of a switch on the control panel by the lighting technician, several bright spotlights shone up onto the ceiling.

"Cue music," Jessica said into her mouthpiece.

Lin pressed several buttons on the backlit panel.

The haunting, almost eerie violin music resonated across the room, entrancing all the guests as their gaze turned skywards. Silken ribbons in vibrant colors of red, blue and green fell from the ceiling as the Cirque du Soleil aerial performers emerged from the colorful tassels. In the bright circles of light, three slender dancers in gossamer costumes slid with athletic grace down the sashes; sequins and sparkles shining off their delicate wings. Silence washed over the crowd.

"All systems are go." Jessica confirmed softly to her team. Slowly she let out a deep breath as the dancers began their routine. She looked at her watch. *How many times had she done that today?* Two more minutes of aerials, then the music would hit disco mode, the stage would be flooded with more performers, and the party would be well under way.

Three days to get through and it would all be over.

* * *

A wave of relief washed over Jessica as the star-studded night of entertainment went off without a hitch. All the guests continued to party on until the wee hours. It was three o'clock in the morning when security ushered the last guests out of the ballroom. Jessica's night couldn't end until she knew that the room was cleared and ready for the stage crew to commence relay. They had to start setting up for the bands playing on Saturday night.

After a long hot shower, Jessica collapsed into bed at four o'clock. Her feet ached. So did her shoulders. And her mind was racing with her To Do list for the next day's events. She reached out and felt the smooth sheet of the empty bed next to her. Nate was still out partying somewhere. But his smell lingered on the pillows and the bedding. She turned off the light. Thoughts of being wrapped around his naked body filled her mind. But the weight of exhaustion took over and she drifted off into a deep sleep.

The buzz of her phone alarm going off on the bedside table woke Jessica at six-thirty. She struggled to open her eyes and found Nate sprawled out next to her. She hadn't even heard him come in. He reeked of champagne and was still dressed in his suit pants and shirt.

Someone had a good night!

Jessica snuck out of bed, dressed, and headed down to the retail shops area to prepare for the day's events. With cup of tea in hand, she walked outside to the pool area. Clear plastic runways had been set up, zigzagging across the lap pools for the models to catwalk down. She weaved her way around the chairs placed along the poolside and found Lin at the sound booth.

"Did you manage to get some sleep, Lin?"

"A few hours. Thank God for Red Bull." She took a long swig from her can of energy drink.

"Still no sign of Fran?" Jessica straightened her sunglasses on her face.

"No. Ryan's here though."

"Excellent. You're both doing a fantastic job, so let's get this day underway, shall we?"

The afternoon was full of dilemmas. Two models didn't turn up. A tripod broke, resulting in expensive camera equipment falling in the pool. The helicopters were delayed, which put them behind schedule. Jessica was glad to see the end of the daylight hours as she headed for the ballroom.

It looked like a totally different venue compared with the

previous evening. The nets, trampolines and harness riggings were now replaced with video screens, massive speakers and band equipment. Sound checks were underway as Jessica and Lin greeted the pop star artists and their entourages arriving to perform for the party.

"You better go and get ready for the big meet and greet tonight." Lin waved Jessica off. "Don't worry about a thing. I've got it all under control." The nervous look in Lin's eyes made Jessica hesitate, but she had to let go and hand the reins over. Even if it was only for just a little while.

"I won't have the two-way on, so buzz my phone if you need me and you know where I'm sitting. You'll be fine. Good luck."

"Thanks," Lin called after her.

Jessica hurried through the crowd that was gathering in the foyer for cocktails. Through the sea of colorful dresses and black dinner suits, she caught a glimpse of Nate dressed in his tuxedo. He looked enraptured with all that was going on around him. His eyes found hers. Everyone else seemed to disappear from her view as she felt that all too familiar pull toward him. She smiled and enjoyed the fine view for a few seconds before darting for the elevators.

After a quick, rejuvenating shower and a blow-dry of her hair, Jessica dressed in fresh lingerie and rushed out of the bathroom to put on the dress that she'd left hanging on the cupboard door. She hadn't noticed the red paper shopping bag hung over a coat hanger when she dashed past before.

On the bag was a post-it note written in Nate's handwriting. *Thought this might go with your dress. XO Nate.*

Jessica smiled as she reached into the bag; her hand enclosed around a velvety box and pulled it out. Her heart pounded in her chest as her fingers ran over the embossed Cartier logo.

With hands shaking like a leaf, Jessica opened the case. She gasped. Inside, brilliant against the black satin, lay a necklace.

White gold and diamonds! The entire length was encrusted with stones. Her fingers trembled as she slowly and carefully took the necklace out and clasped it around her neck. She glanced at herself in the mirror and ran her fingers over the jewels sitting at the base of her throat.

Holy shit! They're magnificent.

With no more time to ogle her present, Jessica slipped on her dress, did a quick reapplication of makeup, strapped on her sparkling stilettos and headed down to join the party.

Nate's eyes lit up as Jessica approached him through the crowd. She felt as if others were looking at her as well, but ignored their gazes. Was it the diamonds? Was it her dress? The combination of both? She felt glamorous and radiant, like a Hollywood star ready to walk the red carpet at a movie premiere. The elderly gentleman Nate was talking to looked startled when Nate put up his hand to stop him talking and made his way over to her. His hand slid around her waist and he kissed her on the cheek.

"I thought we were being discreet." Jessica blushed.

"I don't care anymore. You're breathtaking. And you're mine," Nate whispered in her ear.

"The necklace is beautiful. Thank you." She touched her hand to her neckline and felt the diamonds beneath her fingertips.

"You outshine it by far," said Nate.

"I've never worn so many diamonds in my life."

His lips pressed to her ear. "I can't wait to see you in nothing other than that necklace."

"That's a promise." She felt her cheeks color.

"Here—I have some people I'd like you to meet."

Nate introduced Jessica to financiers, senior executives of Somers Hotels, celebrities who were renowned patrons of their hotels, and then, his father.

"Mr Somers. It's nice to finally meet you." Jessica shook his hand firmly. Henry Somers pulled himself up straight and looked at her with sharp, blue eyes. His gray hair was cut short and showed signs of thinning on top. He looked refined and handsome in his stiff tuxedo as he glanced up and down her figure.

"Ah, Ms Mason." He took in a long breath. "So you're the reason my son defied me and went ahead with this outlandish party."

An uncomfortable sensation coursed through Jessica's body. From the look of his flushed cheeks and the sway in his stance, he'd already had a few too many drinks.

"Well, I, for one, am glad he did." Jessica smiled as she glanced at Nate. "I hope by the end of the weekend you'll see what an amazing event we've managed to create to showcase your hotel to the world. Nate's a great businessman, and it's been a pleasure working with him."

Henry Somers smirked at her. "Yes, I can tell it has been *pleasure* if nothing else. Maybe I should've been the one to come and oversee the opening instead of Nate, hey? I wouldn't mind working with a pretty woman like you either."

Jessica mouth dropped open in shock.

Nate's eyes widened and his face reddened with anger. "I beg your pardon. I will not have you talk like that in front of Jessica. It's rude and uncalled for. How dare you?"

There was no way on this earth that Jessica was going to be humiliated any further by this arrogant bastard.

"Excuse me, gentlemen. I have things to attend to." She made a quick exit for the ballroom. As she walked away her blood boiled. The nerve of Henry Somers to talk to her like that. *Men! Who needs 'em.*

* * *

The dinner proceeded with spectacular food and wine. Scallops, salmon, wagyu beef and delectable desserts filled everyone to the brim. Jessica thought last night had been a big night in regards to alcohol consumption—this one was even bigger. Endless champagne was consumed—corks popped, glasses clinked, toasts were made. When the first band took to the stage, everyone hit the dance floor to gyrate away to the pulsating beat. Another weight lifted from Jessica's shoulders. *One more day to get through*, she thought as she glanced over the agenda for tomorrow.

"Ms Mason."

She turned to see Henry Somers approaching. She straightened her shoulders, ready for another onslaught. He stopped in front of her. She noticed he looked even more intoxicated than before.

He inhaled deeply. "In spite of the fact that Nate disregarded my decision, I'd like to thank you for such a wonderful opening. You've exceeded all expectations, in more ways than one."

His suggestive tone made her skin crawl as his gaze sailed up and down her body and rested upon her cleavage.

Jessica grew self-conscious and hugged her clipboard to her chest. "I'm glad you've enjoyed the event so far, Mr Somers. From what people are saying, and the positive reservation numbers that Nate has told me about, things are looking extremely positive. I wish your hotel every success."

"Maybe we should get together for a drink while I'm here and discuss ... *business.*" He stepped towards her and ran his finger down her arm.

Jessica stepped back in shock, repulsed by his actions. From out of nowhere, Nate appeared, grabbed his father by the scruff of his jacket and pulled him away.

"What the hell are you doing?" Nate glared at his father in disgust. "Leave her alone. Stop embarrassing yourself and tarnishing our company's name in front of all these people. I don't need another PR nightmare. I'm sick and tired of having to clean up the mess that you create with your inappropriate behavior. Now, get yourself together and do everyone a favor and go to bed. Please."

Jessica stood there shaking as she regained her equilibrium. Everything happened so fast.

Henry slurred. "Just wanting to thank this lovely lady. I meant no harm." He held his hands up in surrender, then he turned to face her. "Please accept my apologies. It was inappropriate. Forgive me."

But the smirk on his face left Jessica feeling assured that the apology was far from genuine.

"Let's get you to your room." Nate turned his father around by the shoulders and headed him for the door. As he helped Henry along to avoid stumbling over, Nate looked back over his shoulder towards her. "I'll be back in ten minutes."

She nodded. "Okay. See you soon."

Relief washed over her as Henry exited the room without any commotion. Her heart ached for Nate, because now she understood even more about his struggles and strained relationship with his father.

She wished she could take all of Nate's worries away, he seemed so happy when he was with her. But their time together was almost up. They'd have to burst their bubble and get back to reality. No more affair. No more Nate.

The sound of the band drew her attention back towards the stage. The crowd jumped around on the dance floor in time to the beat.

Time to get back to work!

* * *

The last band had taken the stage and was belting out tunes

that boomed loudly from the speakers. If the talk Jessica had heard throughout the night was true, everyone was raving about the hotel, its exceptional service and the entertainment.

After giving Lin a quick break at one o'clock, Jessica found Nate leaning wearily against a table talking to William. Nate looked at her from underneath his dark eyelashes as she approached. Her heart still fluttered when he looked at her that way. That look of possession. Of love. Of desire and need. He smiled as he took her hand and kissed it.

"You had enough for the night?" he asked.

"It's only two in the morning. I'm doing okay considering the lack of sleep."

"Would you do me the honor and have a dance with me?"

"I'd love to. One dance. Maybe two if you're lucky. Then I'll have to get back to work."

"Deal."

Nate led Jessica out onto the dance floor, wrapped his arms around her waist and twirled her underneath the disco lights. She couldn't help but be swept off her feet.

"Your dad okay?"

"I threw him into bed where I hope he'll stay. I'm sorry about his behavior." Nate shook his head, looking ashamed. "He can be such an ass sometimes."

Jessica touched his face with her hand, feeling the shaven hairs beneath her fingertips. "It's fine. But before he tried to hit on me he did say he liked the launch."

"He said that?" Nate's face looked doubtful. "He liked the launch?"

"Yes he did. And I just want you to know that I'm beyond impressed with all your work and what we've managed to pull together." Jessica slipped her arms around his neck.

Nate chuckled. "Thank you." He spun her around on the dance floor, drew her in close and brushed his lips against hers.

"I couldn't have done this without you. Even the impossible seems possible when you're around."

She could feel his heart beating next to hers beneath the fine fabric of his shirt. She wanted to be even closer to him—if only that was possible. She rested her head upon his shoulder enjoying the feel of him next to her. She closed her eyes and breathed him in.

Would *this* be their last dance together before he left?

* * *

Sunday morning Jessica woke early feeling less than average. She was tired and lacked decent sleep. With much effort she nudged Nate awake. They both dressed and headed down into the hotel for the final day of events.

Conner and Becky arrived near lunchtime, taking advantage of Nate's offer to attend the Sunday barbecue. Jessica shook her head and chuckled to herself as she saw them in the crowd with starstruck looks on their faces and snapped photos on their smart phones.

At last the afternoon wrapped up and the launch was complete. Jessica was relieved to finally be packing the headsets away, when Conner walked over to her.

"Hey, Mom. How'd it all go?" He swigged on his cold beer.

"I think very well. Nate seems to be happy."

"So do you. I saw you with him at lunch today. I haven't seen you smile like that in a long time."

Jessica wound up the charger cords and placed them in the equipment case. "Well, it doesn't matter. He leaves soon."

"Are you okay about that?" Conner asked.

"You know I'm a tough cookie. I'll be fine." She closed the lid of the case and clipped it shut. She didn't want to think about the end—it was coming too close, too quickly.

"You sure?" Conner's face was full of concern for a moment.

But then he went on, obviously forgetting his worry. "Well, Mom, I've got something more important for you to think about now. Since you put on one hell of a show here, what can you pull together for my twenty-first birthday party next year?"

Chapter 19

Jessica was glad to see the light of Monday morning shine through her window. She'd given her team the day off to sleep and recover, but she was too eager to get into the office and view all the online news reports about the opening. After a quick shower and breakfast, she drove into work and was behind her desk, sifting through newsfeeds and video highlights from around the world. Nothing but positive reviews brought a smile to her face. Somehow she'd managed to pull it off—a world-class event in a ridiculously short timeframe. Upcoming Christmas functions and advertising campaigns would be a piece of cake after what she'd been through over the past several months.

A letter on top on Jessica's in-tray caught her attention. She grabbed it and quickly read over it. Through all the crazy workload of organizing the launch, she'd forgotten that Kick had been nominated for an International Advertising Award. Yet another achievement for her company, as the IAAs were equal to the Oscars in the advertising world. She was quietly chuffed that she'd also been selected to present an award on the night.

Jessica flicked through the pages of the letter. Zoe had attached flights, accommodation, and details of the rehearsals—all to be held in Los Angeles at the end of the week.

Her calendar flashed through her mind. Nate left in two weeks, and there was no other major function until mid-December. The very thought of more events, long days and late nights made her aware of her fatigue. Regardless, she would attend the IAAs. A few days chilling out in LA would do her a world of good. Maybe Nate would go with her as her *'plus one'*?

Jessica's belly grumbled loudly. It was time for a cuppa and a snack. She grabbed her mug from her desk and headed for the kitchen. Alex stood at the coffee bar frothing milk for his cappuccino.

"What are you doing here, Jess?" he asked. "Everyone else on your team has the day off—why not you?"

"Too much to do," Jessica sighed as she grabbed the tea tin.

"You're married to this place like I am, sweetie."

"Yes, I am indeed." She nudged his arm. "Hey, the IAAs are on in LA at the end of this week. I leave on Wednesday, and I'll be back Monday morning."

"I know. Zoe emailed me a copy of your itinerary. We need to catch up on so many things now the launch is over so I've scheduled some time with you for next Tuesday after your return. Is that all okay with you?"

Jessica was about to respond when she felt a bit strange. The sound of the machine gurgling made her ears ring. The seductive aroma of coffee usually filled her with comfort, but this morning things were different.

Very different.

Her stomach flipped and curled itself into tight knots. Her throat went dry. All she wanted to do was ... throw up.

Jessica cupped her hand over her mouth and fled past Alex, across the hallway and into the toilets just in time.

"Goddamn it!" Jessica coughed and spluttered. "I'm never sick like this!" Beads of sweat broke out on her brow and she felt lightheaded. She convulsed and vomited again.

Alex came in through the doors. He grabbed her hair back off her face and rubbed her back. "Jess? Sweetie, what's wrong? What brought this on? Did you drink too much last night after the launch?"

"No, I went straight home. I was too exhausted. I hardly touched a drop all weekend."

"You got a bug or something?"

"Fran was sick. Maybe I've caught something off her." She pulled off a run of toilet paper and wiped her mouth clean.

"Throwing up like this in the morning is no fun." Alex shook his head with a grimace. "I've done it way too many times."

Jessica froze as the words left Alex's mouth. *Throwing up in the morning. Nausea at the smell of coffee.* She quickly did some calculations in her head. Counting days, weeks and the month. "Oh shit!"

"What, Sweetie?" Alex looked oblivious as she flushed the toilet and walked to the basin to wash her hands and mouth.

"Oh Alex! What have I done?" Panic flooded every cell of her body. She stared at his reflection in the mirror. "I ... I think I might be pregnant."

Alex gasped. Then a look of sheer excitement swept across his face. "Really? A baby?"

* * *

Jessica sat in the sterile waiting room at her doctor's practice. Her mind was in overdrive. She'd only missed her scheduled contraceptive injection by a week. Surely there was more of a grace period with these injections than a few days. *Oh please, God. No!* As always, work had absorbed her so much, she'd simply lost track of time.

What am I going to do?

A million thoughts ricocheted around her head. She already had Conner. She'd been there, done that! Sure, she had wanted more children when she was younger, but it just didn't happen. She couldn't possibly consider a child at this time in her life.

Could she?

Thirty minutes later Jessica walked out of the doctor's office and shut the door behind her. She leaned back against the smooth surface of the hard white door and tried to absorb the coolness into her heated skin. She shut her eyes tightly to stop the tears from escaping.

Pregnant! Two blue lines on a stick confirmed it all.

Jessica sucked in a deep hard breath. Putting one foot in front of the other in a trance-like state, she made it back to her car. She got in and sat staring out the windscreen at nothing for a good fifteen minutes.

Slowly sensation returned to her hands, fingers and toes. She became aware of air moving in and out of her lungs, and the beating of her heart in her chest.

First things first. She had to tell the father.

* * *

Jessica hesitated before she swiped her access card to enter Nate's apartment, and made her way down the short hallway.

"Hi. Did you forget something? I didn't expect to see you until tonight," Nate said as he stood at the dining table staring down at a newspaper, barely raising his eyes to greet her. "Want to grab some lunch?"

Taking a deep breath, Jessica's whole body trembled from head to foot. She wrung her hands together as she tried to piece the words together.

"Nate, we need to talk."

"'Bout what?" He glanced up. There was no way Jessica

could hide how upset she was. She felt the color drain away from her face. Nate rushed to her side in two long strides and slid his arm around her waist. "What's wrong? Come and sit." He led her over to the couch and sat down beside her. "What's wrong?"

Jessica shook her head slowly and stared at nothing in particular on the coffee table. "Everything was going so well. Why did this have to happen now?" Her hands sweated and shook uncontrollably as she rested them on her lap.

"I don't understand. What are you talking about?" Nate's expression was full of concern.

Her eyes focused on his and she blurted. "I'm pregnant."

His mouth fell open. He jumped to his feet and raked his hands through his thick brown hair, leaving tousled tracks. "What? You said you were on birth control."

"I did. I was. I mean, I am. When we went to Byron last month, I delayed my injection by just a few days. And well ..." she winced.

Nate pulled his shoulders back straight, his jaw flexed with tension. The look on his face was hard and cold as ice.

"Is this some kind of sick joke?" He started to pace back and forth across the floor. "I don't want any more children. I have one and I'm a terrible father to her. You've got Conner. Surely you don't want more kids at this age. You're like me, work is our life. You're ... you're ... going to terminate it, aren't you?"

Wow. Abortion. She hadn't thought that far ahead. She'd been operating in a void since finding out she was carrying his child.

"I haven't had time to think this through yet. But what ... what if I decide to keep it?" Jessica shut her eyes and waited in silence for his response. All she could hear was the rasping sharpness of his breath. When she looked up again he was just standing there. Would he still leave? Abandon her, just like she thought Troy did all those years ago? She knew his answer even before he spoke a word.

Nate turned his back on her.

"I know getting rid of it is the easy option," said Jessica. "We have to sort this out because you're only here for two more weeks—"

"Jess." Nate turned to face her again. He swallowed hard and the muscles in his jawline twitched. "News came through on our latest refurbishment this morning. I leave for London on Thursday."

Although she was sitting down, Jessica felt as if the floor gave way beneath her and she was plummeting into the unknown.

"What?" She wasn't ready to say goodbye to him. Not now. Not yet. She tried to steady her breath. "You're leaving? In three days? I was going to see if you wanted to come with me to the IAA's in LA for a few days."

"I was going to tell you tonight. But now this. You being pregnant changes everything."

"You make it sound like I'm diseased or something." She fought with all her might to control her flaring emotions. "It's a baby, not something contagious."

Nate clenched and released his fists several times, before he turned away from her again to face the window that overlooked the harbor. The air between them was usually hot and heavy, now it was cold as ice. Ready to shatter like a crystal vase falling on to the floor.

"You know what I want you to do. I don't want another situation like Rachael in my life."

Jessica nearly choked. "Rachael? I'm nothing like her. I don't want or need your money, if that's all you care about. I'm perfectly capable of supporting myself financially. I would never guilt trip you into being part of our child's life if you didn't want to be. This was an accident, not some malicious plan to trap you."

"My life is based out of London and yours is here. You know the responsibilities of being chairman lie ahead of me. Keeping this baby is just not an option for us."

Jessica crossed her arms over her chest. "Keeping it is an option, but not one you have to be part of."

Nate glared at her. "Let's be realistic so we can get on with our lives."

Jessica nodded slowly as his words sunk in. Wiping her clammy palms across her thighs she stood up. "I'm going to go now." She was no clearer on what to do about being pregnant. It was not a decision that could be easily made. At least she knew exactly where Nate stood on the matter, and somehow she had to work out where she did.

Picking up the pieces of her heart, Jessica headed for the door. With the baby hanging between them, there was no point in delaying the inevitable any longer. It was time to say goodbye. She'd make this decision on her own and like everything else of late, live with the consequences. "Don't bother about dinner tonight. Don't bother about tomorrow either. Saying goodbye to you now will be hard enough. I love you, Nate—but that just isn't enough."

Nate dashed over to her and took her face in his hands. His pressed his lips hard up against hers. Every fiber of her being wanted to stay. As his hold on to her tightened, tears fell from her eyes. He had kissed her like this once before … the last time he left. But this time she knew it was for good.

"Don't leave, Jess. Not like this. We still have time."

She pulled away gasping for air. He reached up and wiped the tears from her cheek. His eyes were dark with emotion; she had to look away.

"Goodbye, Nate."

Somehow her hand found the door handle and opened it.

Her legs managed to carry her down the hallway and into the elevator. She found her way into her car and started the engine. As tears streamed down her cheeks, she tried to resist, but had to glance in the rearview mirror as she drove out of Somers Hotel for the very last time.

* * *

It was mid-afternoon by the time Jessica dragged her weary feet back into her office. As she pulled into the carpark underneath her building, she saw Troy's Landcruiser parked in the visitor's bay.

Just when she thought the day couldn't get any worse.

Troy smiled broadly from where he stood at the reception counter as she walked out of the elevator. But the smile dropped when he caught sight of the look on her face. "Jess?" He rushed toward her and put his arm around her waist. "What's wrong?"

"What are you doing here?" She tried to brush him away and keep the exasperated tone out of her voice.

"I wanted to see if we can catch up before I head off home. I've just been at a meeting about some renovations we're going to do at Gumtrees."

"What, one last feeble effort in trying to persuade me to be yours?"

"There's always hope." He smiled warmly.

"I haven't eaten all day. I'm not sure if I can stomach too much, but let's go to the cafe downstairs." She turned back toward the elevator and headed down with Troy.

They slid into a booth at the side of the restaurant. As they perused the menu, Troy kept on glancing at her. Worry filled his eyes. The waitress momentarily interrupted and took their orders. After she turned to go, Jessica leaned back into the soft leather seat, trying to make sense of the day.

"You've been crying," said Troy. "Is it not all bells and

whistles with Nate?"

"Okay, this has to stop or I won't see you. Do you understand? We're not in high school anymore." Tears welled in her eyes again.

"Sorry. I wanted to find out how your big launch went on the weekend."

Jessica blinked hard. A distraction was what she needed. Talking about the hotel was ideal. "The launch went great. Did you see it on the news? We had a few hitches along the way, but other than that it was spectacular."

"So why the tears?" He leaned forward and rested his arms on the table. "What's lover boy done?"

"Nothing." She squirmed uncomfortably in her seat.

"Jess?"

He wasn't going to let up. "Not that it's any of your business, but I just found out I'm pregnant. I told Nate. Of course, he doesn't want a bar of it. He's returning to London on Thursday. That's it."

"He's going to leave? What are you going to do?"

"I just don't know yet whether I'm going to keep the baby or have an abortion." This time it was her choice to make, not her strict Catholic parents giving her no rights.

"Are you serious?" Troy gasped. "I'd do anything to have a family."

Jessica stared at her hands as she twisted them in her lap. "I could have two children with three different fathers. Does that make sense?" She shook her head and tried to laugh. It was the best she could do. The only other option was to cry.

"Lots of families have kids with different fathers these days. It's becoming the norm."

"I'm far from normal though, aren't I?" Jessica shook her head bleakly.

"Well, I'm not going anywhere. I'll be here for you as a friend or in whatever capacity you want me. You know I love you."

The waitress defused the moment when she placed their orders in front of them. Jessica dipped her spoon into the bowl of hot soup and took a bite of the freshly baked crusty bread roll. She didn't know how to handle Troy's confession of being in love with her when her heart lay elsewhere. Hadn't she hurt him enough already?

"I fly out to New Zealand on Thursday," Troy went on. "You could do with a break. I'll be true to my word—come with me as a friend for a holiday."

A vision of what could be flashed before her. A happy home life raising a child together. Sitting together on rocking chairs on their veranda looking out over the countryside. All peace and serenity. She wanted to scream as she thought about it. It was like something out of her nightmares.

"I can't, Troy. I just can't."

* * *

Nate's concentration had evaded him ever since Jessica left an hour ago. Anger had the better of him at the time, but at least she knew how he felt about the baby and what she needed to do. Jessica knew he loved her, but the end had finally come. His shoulders slumped toward the ground and every footstep took too much effort. Why did an end to a relationship have to hurt so much? He unconsciously wandered over to the kitchen and made himself a pot of tea. He sculled the hot liquid down and placed the cup on the bench before him. His heart jolted as he looked at the dregs laid out in the perfect shape of an anchor, signifying the end to a personal affair. *Ha!* Even the damn tea leaves knew.

He wished at that moment that his superstitions could have given him warning about her falling pregnant. But no. There'd been no two teaspoons on saucers. Jessica hadn't poured tea from the same pot as another woman. There'd been no shapes of eggs in his drink remains. Or had he missed them? Somewhere? Surely not. Why did he get hints about everything else, but this news managed to evade his cup? He sniffled loudly and blinked his eyes to ward off the tears that he felt forming. There was to be no baby. No more Jessica. Back to work. Sydney was done.

* * *

On the terrace at her house later that evening, Jessica watched with envy as Alex drank down a cool bourbon and coke while she could only indulge in soda water and lime. She managed to keep her voice from failing as she told Alex about her confrontation with Nate.

"I already hate being pregnant and not being able to drink," Jessica grumbled as she ran the tip of her finger around the rim of the glass.

"Dylan and I would love to have a kid. We'll be the daddies!" Alex raised his glass to her, unable to hide his excitement over her pregnancy.

"Troy wants me to have it. You want me to have it. Everyone except the one person I need to want it. How am I going to make this decision, Alex? What if I do have this baby? How will we cope at work?"

Alex took a deep breath as he leaned across the table and covered her hand with his.

"Sweetie, we've been through thick and thin together. We'll get through this. Every curveball life has thrown at us we've survived and come out on top. I know you have a tough choice to make. Take the next few days off and enjoy LA … and bring back that award."

"I'll do my best."

"We'll talk about everything on Tuesday." She saw Alex hesitate. She knew him too well—something was on his mind.

"What is it that you're so eager to discuss? Don't hold out on me. Out with it."

Alex rolled his eyes and smiled. "You're too perceptive. EyeOn rang. They're super keen to talk to us again. After the success of the launch, we could raise our price tag. A lot."

"You want to sell Kick just to make more money?" She felt as if a knife was driving into her heart. "We won't exist if we're bought out. Staff will lose their jobs and you and I will have to start all over again. I'm not prepared to do that at this stage of my life, Alex. Pregnant or not! Do you really want out?" She thought she knew her partner, but had he really had enough?

"Oh lord, no. With you being pregnant, I thought you might want to consider their offer."

"Never." Jessica shook her head.

"You know I want bigger. I want more. I see dollar signs flashing before my eyes," Alex beamed.

"We'll make it happen ourselves. Like we always have. This opening has put us on the international stage. Let's enjoy the ride and see where it takes us." She reached out and touched Alex's hand to reassure him she was totally committed.

"You just want to tell Meredith to fuck off." He winked at her.

"You know me so well." She smiled cheekily at him. "Can I be the one to make the phone call?"

Alex laughed hard and nodded in agreement. "And what are you doing about Nate?"

"Nate who?"

"Come on, baby girl."

"What else can I do? He wants me to get rid of the baby. If I keep it, he wants no part of it." She shrugged, but the truth hurt her deep inside. "He's leaving on Thursday for London. I knew this was only temporary, so I'm not going to be delusional about it."

"You're crazy in love with him, aren't you?"

"It doesn't matter, Alex. It's over."

Chapter 20

The Sydney International Terminal was busy with passengers making their way through customs and buying duty-free goods. Nate noticed many faces looked daunted with pre-flight jitters as he made his way, trundling his cabin bag at his heels, towards the first-class lounge. He didn't share the travelers' concerns because he had flown so often and so many times around the world that an airplane cabin felt like his home away from home.

"Excuse me, Nate Somers?"

Nate halted, unable to recall ever meeting the man standing in front of him who blocked his path. "Yes?"

"I'm Troy Smith. Jessica Mason's friend."

He sucked in a sharp breath. "Conner's father, right?" Yes, after meeting Conner at Jessica's, he could see the resemblance.

"Um, Yes." Troy looked surprised that he made the connection. "It's about Jess and the baby."

"I beg your pardon?" How did he know she was pregnant? She'd told him already?

"How can you leave her knowing she's pregnant with your

child?"

"That's none of your business." His jaw clenched as he glared at Troy.

"I care for her a lot. If I know Jessica, she won't abort. That would make it an easy option for you, wouldn't it? How can you leave your own flesh and blood? I never would've left her all those years ago if I'd known she was pregnant with our son. I missed out on twenty years of Conner's life because of that. Don't do the same thing to her. Don't abandon her like this. I'll be there for her, but it's not the same. She doesn't love me like she loves you."

Troy's words speared Nate right into the center of his heart. It took every ounce of his strength to stand strong. Inhaling deeply he dropped his eyes to the floor and barely managed to nod. "Jessica knows where I stand. We've discussed the matter. Thank you for your concern. Have a good flight, Mr Smith." He turned away and headed off in the direction of the airline lounge.

* * *

Nate dropped down into one of the leather couches in the Qantas Club and ran his hands across his face. Sleep had escaped him for days as Jessica filled every one of his waking thoughts. The way she looked at him when he walked in the room. The way she smelled after making love. How he missed the sound of her voice that entranced him during their in-depth conversations. He'd never believed in soul mates and called anyone a fool if they tried to convince him otherwise. Now he had to eat his words because he'd felt connected to Jessica in every way possible.

But she's pregnant! Something he never wanted to face again.

His phone chimed in his jacket pocket; he took it out and

read the screen. He opened an email from Brooke. It was an article from the Sydney Morning Herald, front page news. There was another rave review, but it was the photo that caught his attention. It was of him standing with his arm wrapped around Jessica at the gala dinner. Her eyes sparkled in the flash of the camera, just like the diamonds that hung around her neck. The ones he gave her to wear with her dress. The ones he'd given her so she'd remember him. He stared at the image for ages, then funnily, he noted her arm resting casually across her belly.

His baby was in there.

But there was just no way he could face another situation like Rachael.

He opened the photo gallery on his phone and scrolled through the few holiday snaps he had taken at Disneyland in Paris. The smile that lit up Lucy's eyes as Mickey Mouse cuddled her touched his heart. He loved his daughter and wished he could spend more time with her, but thanks to Rachael that was never going to be possible.

His own relationship with his father brought a bad taste to his mouth. For so many years Nate had drowned himself in his work to make his father proud and prove his ability to run the business. For all his achievements, he'd never received any recognition, reward or respect from the man who stood at the helm of the Somers Hotel enterprise. The only form of fatherly love he ever got was the occasional handshake if the two crossed each other's paths somewhere in the world.

Nate gritted his teeth. He'd sworn a long time ago to himself that he never wanted to be like his father. Not to his daughter, not to anyone. Yet here he was, heading down that exact pathway.

Well, that had to change.

So what was he doing sitting here? He'd finally found a woman who loved him and inspired him every day. And he loved her. But there was just no way …

He didn't want to make the same mistakes he'd already made in his life again. His gut clenched as if he'd been kneed when he thought about how Jessica must have felt when he said he wanted to leave and have nothing to do with the baby. Letting her walk away had been the hardest thing he'd ever had to do.

He exhaled deeply as he wiped his tired, stinging eyes. All he had managed to achieve was hurting her beyond repair. That was the one thing he'd wanted to avoid and he'd failed dismally.

Was it too late to make amends? What could he do?

Somehow he had to make it right. How?

He closed his eyes. His chest ached too much these days; even breathing seemed difficult without Jessica. Then, out of nowhere, it struck him. A plan appeared clearly in his mind.

It would work … Yes … It had to work.

It was a thin thread of hope and had a small chance of success, but definitely worth the risk to find out. Why hadn't this come to him before? Regardless of the travel, his work or their crazy, mixed-up, busy lives—Nate wanted to be with Jessica. He had to get her back at all costs.

Nate glanced down at his watch. Jessica would be in Los Angeles by now. He stood up, straightened his jacket and walked over to the enquiry desk. He smiled his best charming smile at the girl sitting at the computer. "Excuse me. Something urgent has come up. I need to change my flight."

* * *

The bathroom was clouded with mist and steam fogged up the full-length mirror. Heat enveloped Jessica and soothed every aching muscle in her body as she slipped deeper into the bubble bath. The flight had been long, jet lag had kicked in, and exhaustion from the past few weeks had caught up with her. A little soak in the hot tub before tonight's awards seemed like a great plan.

Even after two headache tablets, nothing relieved the tension that seemed to have taken up permanent residence in the center of her forehead. With her head tilted back resting on a folded towel and her body submerged in scented bubbles and hot water, Jessica started to drift off and relax for the first time in what seemed like months.

Why did the bath gel have to be scented with citrus? It reminded her of Nate.

But he was gone. It was time to get on with her life. She stretched her neck from side to side. The launch had moved Kick onto the world stage, surely new clients would come on board. More than anything Jessica wanted to start expanding globally. Could she and Alex pull it off? Her head rattled with ideas, plans started to take form. Where else could they open an office? Logically, Singapore and New Zealand seemed like the best options. They were close to home and they already had clients in those locations in their portfolio.

Yet again the buzz of business opportunities excited her. She'd love to spend a few months overseas setting up an office. The thought was exhilarating—new culture ... lifestyle ... sightseeing ...

But what about the baby?

She let out a deep sigh. With a gentle hand, she rubbed her tummy and squeezed her eyes shut. Silence and calm filled her head. Peace. Quiet. So rare. Her body felt radiant. She smiled remembering how Conner had brought so much happiness and fulfillment into her life. With her biological clock ticking, an opportunity like this might never present itself again. This time she knew what to expect. She was prepared. More mature. More determined and ready for this change in her life.

With or without Nate ... yes, without Nate ... Jessica decided she was going to have this baby.

* * *

Dressed in a long dark-red evening gown, Jessica applied a coat of oriental red lipstick to her lips and assessed her appearance in the mirror. She adjusted the cowl neckline of her dress so it hung correctly at the peaks of her shoulders. Her fingers felt along the strand of diamonds that hung around her neck. Her Cartier necklace, yet another reminder of Nate. She shook her head. She should have ducked out to the shops this afternoon and brought some different jewelry to wear, but the past two days in Los Angeles had been busy with preparations and rehearsals for tonight.

Her hand slid down, smoothing her dress, and rested on her tummy. *Thank God I'm not showing yet, otherwise I'd never get into this dress.* After slipping on her towering gold strappy stilettos, she grabbed her evening bag and headed for the door.

She caught the elevator down to the ballroom of the Beverly Hilton, closing her eyes in a silent prayer. *I need a pick-me-up. A win would be ideal!* She stepped out of the open doors into a sea of people mingling in the large reception area. Tuxedos and evening gowns swirled around her in all directions. Music chimed softly above the muffled sounds of conversation.

In the center of the floor she was confronted with a towering ice sculpture of what she assumed were meant to be two angels. Beyond it lay the extravagant bar. As Jessica meandered among the guests, waiters dressed in stiff black attire moved through the crowd, carrying trays of drinks and hors d'oeuvres. She desperately wanted to reach for the champagne but opted for iced water instead, and started making polite conversation with a group from Saatchi and Saatchi. It would be nice one day to be as big and as global as her competitors. One day. But that was a long way off. She was distracted when her phone buzzed loudly from within her clutch. She excused herself from the group, put down her drink on a nearby table, clipped open the latch on her bag and read the screen on her phone. The message was from Nate.

How's the IAAS?

Jessica's heart faltered in her chest. Why was he texting her? What happened to a clean break? No contact should pass between them if she was to get over him. And why were the IAAs the first thing he asked about? She fumbled with the phone as she contemplated what to do. Should she reply? Before she had time to do anything, it beeped again.

Sorry haven't called. Long haul flight. Phone doesn't work at 40,000ft.

So that's his excuse? Pathetic! She pulled herself up short. Maybe he was trying to take the high road and be pleasant by putting their rough ending aside. *Men!* They could forget things in an instant. Maybe she should do the same.

She hit reply.

You should see the hideous ice sculpture here. Too 80s! Never see one of these at my functions.

She bit her lip, trying not to giggle as she pressed send. His reply came quickly.

I don't know. I kind of like it.

She was confused, but before Jessica could think straight, another message appeared.

What will you bid on at the silent auction?

How did Nate know there was a silent auction? Maybe he saw the details on the web or something. She was a little baffled by all these messages but played along with the game. She typed her message.

Maybe Tahiti beachside resort. I need a vacation.

Nate replied:

Who's the blond? He's trying very hard to get your attention.

What the ...? Jessica hit her call button. "Where are you? Are you here?" Anger, hurt and fear made her voice sound shrill in her own ears. What was he doing? Did he want to make sure that there was absolutely nothing left of her heart? He was supposed to be on his way to London.

"Find me." Nate hung up.

Her eyes swept over the crowd. She picked up her dress to keep her hem out from under her high heels, as she darted around guests, bar tables and waitstaff. All the men in dinner suits looked the same, until she caught sight of one who stood out like the shining moon against the dark of night. He was like a homing beacon.

Nate!

The world stopped spinning on its axis as her eyes met his. She pushed her way through the throng of people, ignoring those who tried to grab her for a chat. She stopped three feet in front of him.

"What are you doing here?" The pain in her heart was too strong to be totally swept away by how dashing he looked dressed in a tuxedo. Her defense mechanisms were up.

"I was invited, if I remember." He looked disappointed that she didn't throw herself into his arms.

"I think, with the events over the past few days, that you were uninvited." Oh boy, was she ready to vent some of her anger at him.

"Stop." He put his hands up to defuse the situation. "I know you're angry and hurt. You have every right. But something has come up. We need to talk. Can we go out on to the terrace? Please?"

"Just say it to me here, Nate."

He glared at her, making her feel like a stubborn child. Nothing he could say was going to make a difference. He stood defiantly, as if he wasn't going to take no for an answer. She sighed, and reluctantly strutted out of the room and into the open air.

* * *

Nate stood with Jessica looking down over the pool area. Swirls of color danced on the water's surface from the videos projected on the side wall of the hotel. But Nate's attention was solely focused on the vision before him. The lights shone softly across Jessica's features. Her hair look like spun gold as it danced in the evening breeze. Her skin was radiant, and he hoped he could put a smile back on her face.

"Nate, I can't do this. My heart can't take it anymore. Just you being here hurts too much." The look in Jessica's eyes cut him to the very core. He never wanted to see her like this again.

"I didn't fly halfway around the world in the wrong direction just to see you, then leave. I think I've come up with a solution, if you'll just hear me out."

"What? What are you saying?" She shook her head and turned away from him. "We've investigated all avenues, there's nothing we can do. So please, leave me alone. Just go."

"This came to me while waiting for the plane. I don't know why we didn't think of it before. Maybe losing you and running into your old boyfriend, Troy, made me see everything in a new light."

"You saw Troy?" she gasped and turned to face him again.

"Yes. Now please, will you just hear me out?" He would resort to begging if he had too.

Though pain was still evident on her face, Nate felt relieved when she nodded. He stepped closer, narrowing the distance between them. The ache to hold her grew unbearable.

"I love you." He stepped towards her and caressed her cheek. "More than anything. I want to be with you ... and raise our child together."

"You ... you want to have our baby?" Her eyes searched his face, unconvinced his words were honorable.

"Yes. I know it's no excuse, but the lack of sleep and stress over the launch weekend were clouding my head when you told me that you were pregnant. I handled the whole situation terribly. I didn't think things through. Now I have, I know I made the biggest mistake in my life letting you walk away. Please forgive me. I'll do anything to make this right."

Jessica's eyes were wide with shock and her mouth hung slightly open. He saw she was about to protest and he raised his finger to silence her.

"Hear me out, okay? I think I have a proposition that may just work." Her eyes flared with worry but he continued. "You want to expand. Right?"

Jessica furrowed her brow.

Why did she still have to look so goddamn sexy? It made it so hard to concentrate.

"Remember we talked about our European hotels? Well, it clicked. I need them rebranded and promoted. So, what do you say about opening an office in London? I'll help you by giving you some office space in our building while you find your own feet. I'll give you the Somers Europe hotels account and a few friends owe me a couple of favors, I'll easily convince them to use your agency as well. So you'll have an office, clients ... and me ... if you want."

She gasped. "I can't just up and leave my business to be with you in London. Are you crazy?"

"Absolutely. Just think for a moment. I know it's a lot to take on board and there'll be a lot to sort out," Nate went on. "This is what you've always wanted. I'm not asking you to leave your business—I'd never do that. We're both tied to our companies and we're both pigheaded and unwilling to sacrifice everything. So is this a compromise that could work? We could spend half of our time in London where I can work on business development alongside the board, then the other half back in Sydney, or wherever in the world you want to call home. But the main point here is that I want you, our baby and a life together. What do you say?"

Was that fire burning in her eyes? Oh shit, he'd blown it. Jessica's hand trembled even more and her eyes filled with tears. *Damn it!* He'd approached this all the wrong way.

Nate felt drained. How could he convince her that this would work? "I love you Jess, please say yes!" He stroked her tears away with his fingertips and caressed her cheek. "We can do this."

Her eyes, swarming with tears, wrenched at his heart. *Oh God! Was this it? She was going to turn him down? No! He wouldn't let her. He'd do everything in his power to win her heart back.*

"Baby, please tell me what you're thinking. You're killing me here."

She closed her eyes and her lips trembled. "Tell me what you said again, so I know I'm not dreaming."

Hope filled his heart as he raked his brain trying to quickly recall his jumbled words.

"First—I love you. Second—I want to be with you and have our baby. And then, do you think you could live between London and Sydney with me?"

She laughed through her veil of tears. "You want to have our baby?"

Nate nodded, sucking in a hard breath trying to keep his own charged emotions at bay. He entwined his fingers with hers.

"I was going to call you." Her lips trembled as she spoke. "Or email you. Or somehow tell you that I couldn't abort our baby. I couldn't get rid of the little part I had left of you."

"Believe me, I'm glad you didn't."

"And you want to live between two countries?" Her eyes shone with tears. "Alex will take so much convincing. I've always wanted to expand, but I was thinking about different locations—not London. The UK? I'll hate the weather."

"Jess, stop for a moment. Neither one of us thought about this as an option. I suppose we were too focused on the launch. I just want to be with you with no deadlines or end dates in sight. Just a due date in nine months' time."

He drew her hand up to his mouth and kissed the back of her hand, thankful she didn't pull away. "You'll love London. The shopping, the theatre, the lights. There's so much to do. Our hotel and offices are in the heart of the financial district. We're right next to the Gherkin—that egg-shaped building on St Mary Axe. And I do actually own a house in London, so there'd be no living in a hotel."

His excitement was starting to light fire within his chest, but it immediately fizzled out when Jessica shook her head. "I've got so much work on over Christmas. We have to look at this realistically."

"I know it's a big decision and you'll have to discuss it with Alex. I'll come back to Sydney with you and attend the board meeting by video conference. I can delay the new renovations for a little while longer until January. Let's spend Christmas and New Year's Eve together, then if we can get everything in order you could come over with me and start working on campaigns for Europe."

"I can't move countries in a month."

He pondered the idea for a moment. Would it be possible? Pack, sort out work commitments, staff rearrangements, visas, Alex. He knew she couldn't just up and leave her business partner in the lurch. Then there was her son, Conner. *Goddamnit!* There was so much to consider. But, if there was anyone who could do it, it would be Jessica.

"You, the woman who just pulled off a massive hotel opening in six months. You, whose business needs this. What else do I have to say or do to convince you that this is right? Do you want me to get down on my knees and beg?"

He started to bend down on one knee when she hooked her hand under his arm to stop him. He stood back up and wrapped his arms around her waist.

He could see doubts and questions rattle though her mind. But this was a way for them to be together. She'd still have her business and finally expand. He could keep the Somers empire growing. They'd travel the world, have their baby and be a family. A real family. They'd both be crazy to let a chance like this at happiness slip by.

As she wiped the wetness off her cheeks, she looked at him. "You know you're crazy, right? Coming all this way, halfway across the world."

He nodded holding his breath, waiting for her response.

"But I love you so much," she whispered. "And I do like your proposition."

Nate curled his fingers around her neck and drew her lips to his. His heart thundered within his chest as she finally melted into his body and kissed him.

No more heartache, no more pain, no more end in sight. She was his now and forever more and had given him a new lease on life. One they'd share together and raise their child in a home full of love. Nate took her face gently in his hands and looked down at her beautiful smile and sparkling eyes.

"Love you, too. You're my life. My love. My everything."

Epilogue

The sun shimmered on the surface of the clear turquoise waters in front of the bungalow, where Jessica lay on a deck chair reading a book. Nate had magically won the tickets to Tahiti at the silent auction back at the awards night in Los Angeles. After months of hard work, they finally had time to take a much-needed holiday, a few weeks' rest before heading back to Australia.

In addition to a few contacts of Nate's, Jessica had managed to score several stable accounts, hire a small team and set up Kick's first international office in London. Alex had been over to visit twice to handle all the rigmarole of paperwork, accounts and company incorporations. She was more than glad to pass that process over to him.

Wearily she rubbed her hand over her protruding belly. Her feet ached, her breasts were swollen like melons and her nipples stung when she went in the salt water, so she was content to lounge around like a beached whale.

She looked out into the ocean and saw Nate snorkeling

across the coral reef in front of their hut, duck diving under the surface and floating about. The muscles on his arms flexed as he swam toward her. His buffed body looked magnificent. She thought she was bad before, but being pregnant made her randy as hell. As he climbed up the ladder out of the water, he flicked his head back. Droplets of water fanned out behind him and danced above him in the shape of a halo.

Mmm, my angel all right.

He grabbed a towel off the railing and rubbed himself down. He walked over to her and sat down on the edge of the chair next to her legs. "Here, I found this."

Nate placed an oyster shell on her big belly.

"Oysters? Do we really need an aphrodisiac, Nate?"

"Definitely not. But open it." He smiled.

Jessica was about to tell him not to be stupid and say that she'd need a knife when she saw the shell was already cracked. She opened it up and gasped. Inside lay a ring sparkling with a massive princess-cut diamond, at least a few carats. It was the most beautiful ring she'd ever seen.

"Please don't tell me you've been swimming around with this stuck down your pants somewhere?" she said, waving her finger toward his groin.

"No," he chuckled. "I left it down on the steps, wrapped up in my shirt." Nate dropped to his knees and took her hand in his. "Jess, you have turned my life around and now it would mean nothing without you in it. You complement me in every way and I can't wait to share our life together and raise our child. I love you and want you to be my wife. Will you marry me?"

Jessica looked at the ring, then at Nate, then back at the ring. Her belly lurched with a massive kick from the baby inside. Was it protesting or screaming in delight? Her hand cradled the place where she'd just been kicked. Nate leaned down and kissed the very spot.

"We're two of a kind, you and I," he said. "Meant to be together. You're my world, my universe, my life. Marry me and make me the happiest man alive."

Images flashed before her eyes—their first meeting, their first time together, the night they made slow love after the industry event, Byron, their dance at the launch. Jessica had never been in love like this in her life. Her heart and soul were complete with Nate.

She looked up into eyes that reflected the color of the ocean. Her heart pounded like waves crashing against the shoreline. "Yes. Yes, Nate ... I will marry you. I love you so much." She leaned over and kissed his lips. "I should sleep with my clients more often!"

NEXT IN SERIES

Dangerous Acquisitions – Strictly Business Book 2

A new start. A short-term project. That's all it was meant to be.

Available in ebook and print at:

https://www.books2read.com/DangerousAcquisitions

OTHER BOOKS BY TANIA JOYCE

visit: taniajoyce.com

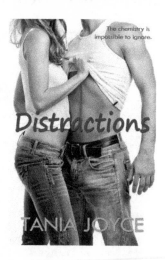

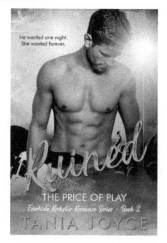

THANK YOU

Thank you for reading
Tempting Propositions – Strictly Business Book 1.
It would be appreciated if you could take a moment and leave
a quick review on Amazon.

http://amazon.com/author/taniajoyce

TANIA JOYCE AUTHOR NEWSLETTER

For staying in touch with new releases, news and events, sign
up to Tania Joyce's newsletter.

Subscribe at:

http://taniajoyce.com/newsletter/subscribe

FOLLOW TANIA JOYCE

You can follow and find Tania Joyce on the following social
media platforms.

Web: http://taniajoyce.com

Facebook: https://www.facebook.com/taniajoycebooks

Twitter: https://twitter.com/taniajoycebooks

Pinterest: https://www.pinterest.com/taniajoycebooks/

Goodreads: https://www.goodreads.com/taniajoyce

Instagram: https://www.instagram.com/taniajoycebooks/

Book Discussion Group: https://www.facebook.com/groups/taniajoyce/

BookBub: https://www.bookbub.com/authors/tania-joyce

Amazon: https://amazon.com/author/taniajoyce

ACKNOWLEDGMENTS

For all the dedication, motivation and time it takes to write a book, there are many who have encouraged me, tolerated me and kept me motivated along the way.

In no particular order, I'd like to thank:

Katrina Hill, my best friend and guinea pig. The first one to ever read my stories and your feedback is always invaluable.

Yon Beyond Writing Group - you motivate and inspire me every day. What a team we make!

NightWriters Writing Group - thank you for your feedback and support over the past few years.

To my cousin, Christopher Roberts, who gave me in-depth and informative facts about hotel operations and what goes on behind the scenes.

To Haylee Nash and the team from Momentum Books and Pan MacMillan for believing in me and my story.

To my husband and my family. Words cannot describe how much I thank you for supporting and giving me the opportunity to pursue this dream of mine.

Love to you all.
XOXOXO
Tania Joyce

CPSIA information can be obtained
at www.ICGtesting.com
Printed in the USA
LVHW111331180720
661048LV00002B/388

9 780994 577481